Also by Kris Tualla:

Loving the Norseman
Loving the Knight
In the Norseman's House

A Nordic Knight in Henry's Court
A Nordic Knight of the Golden Fleece
A Nordic Knight and His Spanish Wife

A Discreet Gentleman of Discovery
A Discreet Gentleman of Matrimony
A Discreet Gentleman of Consequence
A Discreet Gentleman of Intrigue
A Discreet Gentleman of Mystery

Leaving Norway
Finding Sovereignty
Kirsten's Journal

A Woman of Choice
A Prince of Norway
A Matter of Principle

An Unexpected Viking
A Restored Viking
A Modern Viking

*****

A Primer for Beginning Authors
Becoming an Authorpreneur

A Modern VIKING

Kris Tualla

A Modern Viking is a work of fiction. Names, characters, places and incidents are products of the author's imagination or are used fictitiously and are not to be construed as real. Any resemblance to actual events, locales, organizations, or persons, living or dead, is entirely coincidental.

Published in the United States of America.

ISBN-13: 978-1517770273
ISBN-10: 1517770270

This book is dedicated to
everyone who loves the Hansens
as much as I do,
and who believes in
heroes who don't wear kilts.

Chapter One

Saturday
January 9

Sveyn Hansen inhabited his body for the first time in nine hundred and fifty years and it hurt like hell. His first breath set his lungs on fire. The fabric of his clothing sandpapered his skin. Blood gushed from the gash in his side.

Shouting and chaos swirled around him and threatened to drown him.

"Hey! Where'd this guy come from?"

"I don't know, but he's been stabbed and he's bleeding pretty badly."

"Is she stable?"

She?

Hollis.

She did it.

"She's getting there. Call for another unit for her and take this guy in now."

The pressure on his gut felt like an anvil. A clear cup was

strapped over his mouth and nose. Sveyn tried to push it away, afraid he would suffocate.

"Easy, buddy." The man's voice was calm and near his head. "Just breathe."

Sveyn gasped. Whatever was in the cup was cool and soothing to his burning chest. He focused on breathing in, then breathing out. Willing his body to remember what to do.

"What's your name?"

Sveyn forced air through vocal chords too-long dormant and managed to create a rough but audible sound.

"Sveyn." *Breathe.* "Hansen."

"Sveyn—do you know who stabbed you?"

How could he answer that? "He's…" *Breathe.* "Dead."

"Where?" The voice sounded startled.

Sveyn closed his eyes. He couldn't explain it so there was no point in wasting what energy he had.

He could feel his heart beating. The rhythm was crazily erratic at first, and even though it still surged painfully against his ribs, the pace was settling down.

"He's shocky. Let's get a move on."

Hands gripped him like vises and Sveyn knew he must be bruised by their excruciating strength. He was lifted and set down again. Then the platform he was laid on popped upward. He moaned with every touch, every jolt, and every movement that caused his shirt or pants to shift.

This was not what I expected.

Sveyn turned his head to look for Hollis. She was still on the ground where he last saw her. And though she was awake and talking to the men in dark blue uniforms, her eyes were fixed on him.

Ӂ

He's alive. Sveyn is alive.

Hollis's chest felt like it was hit by a hammer—which it had been. A medieval stone hammer, thrown by a Renaissance Faire trainee. A hammer into whose path she stumbled when she was crying hysterically and arguing with Sveyn.

Arguing about Matt.

"What's your name, miss?" a paramedic asked as a grunting and groaning Sveyn was loaded into the ambulance.

Thank you, God.

She drew a breath to push her words past the oxygen mask but ended up coughing weakly, her chest in agony. She moved her hand and rested it over her heart.

"You're in pain because you were hit in the chest and your heart stopped. We used the defibrillator to start it again." A kind smile hovered over her face. "Both of those things do hurt, I'm afraid."

She moaned her agreement and moved her hand to her head.

"Does your head hurt?" The paramedic pulled a tiny flashlight from a pocket under the embroidered words *Paul Saxon, EMT*. "Look at the light for me."

Hollis focused on the penlight while the medic flashed it in both of her eyes. "You do have a concussion. Not surprising with the flat fall you took."

Tears started to leak from the edges of her eyes.

"Don't cry, miss. You're going to be fine in a few days." Paul smiled again. "Can you tell us your name?"

She tried to inhale enough to answer, but couldn't.

"Hollis McKenna."

Hollis's gaze moved past the paramedics to where her asshole of a once again ex-boyfriend was answering for her. "Her name is Hollis McKenna and she works at the Arizona History and Cultural Center."

"Are you with her?"

Not in any way imaginable.

"Yes."

Hollis groaned. More tears flowed.

Paul turned his attention back to Hollis. "What about the man who was stabbed? Do you know him?"

Hollis nodded weakly.

"Do you know who stabbed him?"

"No," she croaked.

Matt leaned over her, his expression stern. "You knew him? How?"

Hollis refused to answer Matt or even look at him. She wanted to wipe the tears from her cheeks but didn't feel like she had the strength. The faint whine of an approaching ambulance edged into her consciousness.

She grabbed Paramedic Paul's arm. "Am I going to the same hospital that man did?"

"Yes," he assured her. "We always transport to the closest facility."

Hollis tried to relax and concentrate on something other than the pain in her head and chest and the tears that wouldn't stop coming.

Sveyn.

Obviously he had returned to his body in exactly the same condition as it was when he left it, blood-gushing wound and all. Except in the eleventh century a broadsword wound through the gut would be fatal.

In the twenty-first century, however, he would be immediately taken into surgery and the damage repaired. The Viking was going to be in pain, but he was going to be alive.

The ambulance siren grew closer.

"Hollis!"

She glared at Matt. The man had no idea what sort of pain she was in, in spite of her snuffling sobs.

"How did you know that man?" he demanded.

Hollis would have laughed if it didn't hurt so much. "You're such an idiot."

Matt recoiled. "What?"

"That was Sveyn, asshole." She sniffed. "Now go away."

ӜК

Sveyn shouted when the needle went into his hand.

"Sorry. But we have to get you rehydrated from the loss of

blood." The man sitting beside him in the van hung up a clear bag of liquid with a tube leading to the needle, and then started squeezing a bulb as a band tightened around Sveyn's other arm.

Sveyn grunted against the painful pressure. At least he was somewhat familiar with these procedures from his manifestation to the soldier during the war with Germany. But they didn't have so many lights and screens and beeping noises back then.

"The police will want to talk to you about the stabbing," the medic said calmly, though Sveyn thought his arm was being cut from his body by the tightening band.

Just before he reached over to pull it off, the man released something and the pressure eased. "Ninety over fifty-five. We're getting there."

Breathe, he reminded himself. *In. And out.*

The medic looked at him. "We've radioed ahead. You'll go straight into surgery. They'll stop the bleeding and get you put back together. Once you're out of that, the cops'll make their visit."

What about Hollis?

"The woman…" he managed.

"What's that?" The man leaned closed.

"The woman…"

He shook his head. "Are you asking about the woman whose heart stopped?"

"Yes," Sveyn grunted.

"Were you together?"

"Yes."

"Did you see what happened to her?"

"Yes."

He nodded. "She'll be brought to Gateway Medical Center as well. You were just a higher priority."

Good.

Sveyn tried to relax although every single thing in his new existence hurt him. One step at a time.

First I must survive the surgery.

Ӂ

Once she was transported to the hospital's emergency room, Hollis's information was taken down and she was shuttled off to x-ray. Her sternum was cracked by the hammer's impact, but the fact that she fell backwards to the ground absorbed a good deal of the force.

Of course, that was also how she sustained the concussion.

Matt had followed the ambulance and brought Hollis her purse, much to the admitting department's relief. Copies of her healthcare card were made and Hollis signed the necessary releases.

She told Matt to call Stevie and then go home. At least, she thought she did. By the time she was assigned to a room hours later, her memory was getting fuzzy.

"Did they bring that man who was stabbed to this hospital?" she asked her nurse.

Nurse Marla, as she was identified on the whiteboard mounted on Hollis's hospital room's wall, stopped writing notes there and turned to look at Hollis. "What's his name?"

"Sveyn Hansen."

"I'll check." Marla went back to writing the time on the board. "I'll bring you an ice pack for your chest. And we'll be in every hour to make sure you can be awakened. Concussions are sneaky bastards."

The nurse walked back to Hollis's bedside to check the leads on her heart monitor. "I'm going to turn the sound down, but don't worry—if your heartrate changes significantly the alarm will go off at the nurses' station."

"Thanks, Marla."

Hollis felt like her body was made of lead. At least the anti-inflammatory pain meds had dulled her earlier agony.

Stevie poked her head into the room. "Can I come in?"

Marla stepped forward. "Ten minutes. No more."

Stevie saluted the nurse. "Yes, ma'am."

"I'll check on that other patient for you," Marla promised

and slipped out of the room.

Stevie walked to Hollis's bedside. "Oh my God, Hollis. What happened?"

Hollis scowled. "I got hit in the chest with a hammer."

Stevie rolled her eyes. "I know that. But Matt said you were acting completely crazy—shouting at nothing and running around literally like a headless chicken."

Hollis tried to imagine what her argument with Sveyn must have looked like; that description was frighteningly accurate.

"You ran right into the guy's training area." Stevie shook her head. "What were you doing?"

Hollis felt the damned tears start again. "Benton offered me a permanent position at the museum, so I asked Matt if he would move to Phoenix, or should I move back to Milwaukee, and he said he just wanted things back to how they were."

She paused to draw a slow and painful breath before she continued. "So I told him to get lost, and then Sveyn was there, and he was right about Matt, and I was crying so hard, and he wouldn't let me get past him…"

Hollis tried not to cry too hard now because it hurt her chest in spite of the medication, but she was failing miserably.

"Oh, sweetie." Stevie hoisted herself onto the hospital bed next to Hollis and rubbed her shoulder. She glanced around the room. "Is Sveyn here now?"

"No—that's the thing." Hollis hiccoughed. *Ouch.*

"Oh, no!" Stevie looked horrified. "Is he *gone* gone? Did he manifest forward?"

Hollis shook her head and immediately regretted it. She reached up and rubbed her aching forehead. "I almost died. I went to that place with the light…"

The petite blonde's cheeks paled under widened eyes. "You did?"

Hollis wiped her tears, though it was a futile effort. "Sveyn was there. He said I had to come back and bring him with me."

"Hollis!" Stevie swiveled to her knees on the mattress and faced Hollis straight on. "*Did* you?"

"Yes." Hollis reached for a tissue and Stevie pulled the box onto the bed. "But he came back in the same condition as he left."

"Hold on!" Stevie sat back on her heels and lifted her hands so they framed her face. "Sveyn. Came. *Back?*"

"Uh huh." Hollis blew her nose.

Ouch. That hurt, too.

"Where? Where is he?"

Nurse Marla walked into the room as if waiting for that cue and handed Hollis the ice pack. "I found your friend. Sveyn Hansen was brought in by paramedics and went straight into emergency surgery. He's still in recovery."

"Recovery?" Hollis felt a rush of relief. "So he's going to be okay?"

Marla gave her a sad smile. "I can't tell you any more than that, I'm afraid."

"Thank you, though." Hollis wiped her eyes.

Marla looked disapprovingly at Stevie, still kneeling on the bed. "Five more minutes."

Stevie nodded as she slid off the bed. "I'm watching the clock."

Marla made her exit and Stevie faced Hollis again. "Oh, my freaking goodness! Surgery?"

"He was run through by a broadsword," Hollis repeated Sveyn's own explanation.

"So that's what you meant by the same condition." Stevie wagged her head. "This whole thing's absolutely crazy!"

"Yeah." There really wasn't any other term for it.

Stevie's eyes jumped to Hollis's. "Who knows?"

"You." Hollis shrugged. "And Sveyn, of course."

Her friend's brow lowered. "How will you explain him?"

Hollis shook her head—slowly this time. "I have no idea."

"He's got no identity, right?"

Oh, crap.

"No driver's license, no birth certificate," Stevie continued. "No job—no health insurance."

Crapola crapsalot.

Hollis stared at her friend and cursed the concussion that was making her thoughts so muddy. "What do we do?"

Stevie pointed at her. "If you weren't so bashed up, you'd realize the perfect ruse."

Hollis wiped her nose with a soggy tissue. "Just tell me."

Stevie grinned. "We'll say he's a Gypsy."

Chapter Two

The last thing Sveyn remembered was being in a bed with bars on the sides and being rolled into a bright room filled with men and women dressed from head to toe in light blue. They wore caps and their faces were covered with masks.

Surgery?

I know this word.

He steeled himself for the pain, wondering if his body would reach its limit and die. Finally.

Hollis.

Please, God. Let me live.

Then his body dissolved.

Now his eyes were closed, but he was not asleep. Had he manifested forward? No, that wasn't possible any longer. People were conversing. Machines were still softly beeping.

A soft roar startled him and something squeezed his legs from ankle to hip. His eyes flew open with his grunt.

"There you are." A smiling woman wearing a pale green version of the light blue uniforms leaned over him. "I'm Nurse

Sally. Are you awake?"

Though he still smelled the cool, soothing gas, Sveyn realized the clear cup wasn't over his mouth, so he attempted to use his voice. "Yes."

Rough and dry, but the word was understandable.

"Excellent. Your surgery went very well and you are in recovery." Sally looked at his monitors, then back at him. "The doctor will come in and explain the surgery in a little while and then we'll get you to your room."

The surgery was finished? He felt nothing. He remembered nothing. Was this a miracle?

Sveyn reached for his legs and met some sort of cushioned brace.

"Those are for compression, to keep the blood flowing in your legs so you don't develop a clot. That can happen after surgery." The nurse flashed an empathetic smile. "It's only the first twenty-four hours, then we'll take them off."

He touched his face next, feeling the tube that looped under his nose.

"Oxygen. You lost a lot of blood." Sally explained it like he should understand the connection.

Sveyn nodded weakly and tried to release the tension in his body. He recalled what he knew about hospitals in this century. He had spent the night with Hollis in her hospital room after her abduction, and followed her through all the medical interviews and examinations.

What he saw since arriving here in the ambulance—the same word as during the German war, though the two vehicles looked nothing alike—was similar enough to Hollis's experience that he felt like he wasn't in an entirely different world.

Except he had not been interviewed yet.

And when he was, he needed help. Quite a lot of it.

"Hollis McKenna?" he croaked.

Sally leaned over him. "What was that?"

"Hollis McKenna."

Sally frowned. "Is Hollis McKenna your next of kin?"

Sveyn opted for the easy answer. "Yes. She is here?"

"Are you asking if Hollis McKenna is in this hospital?"

"Yes."

"Was she injured as well?"

"Yes."

Sally squeezed his hand—the one that did *not* have a tube trailing from it. "Let me see what I can find out."

Sveyn closed his eyes, exhausted. He realized that though he still felt his heart beating, he no longer had to think about breathing. That was a relief. And with whatever magic the surgeon worked, his wound wasn't paining him at the moment.

If only his skin would adjust to the constant pressure of the blankets. His leathers and linen shirt had been destroyed, cut away from his body when he reached the hospital. Being naked provided him some brief relief, until he was covered in a cotton tunic and sheets.

His hand ached where the needle entered it.

The machine compressed his legs again, bringing tears to his eyes. Twenty four hours of this was going to test his mettle more than most of his Viking hardships.

"Sveyn Hansen?"

He opened his eyes. "Yes."

"I'm Doctor Randall and I performed your surgery."

Sveyn could only think to say, "Thank you."

"You were a lucky man. The blade went through your liver, which is why you bled so much, and exited through your latissimus dorsa, your back muscle."

Sveyn blinked, trying to commit those words to memory so he could ask about them later.

"We had to remove your gallbladder," Dr. Randall continued. "Before you leave the hospital we'll explain how that impacts your diet. Do you have any questions?"

Sveyn wanted to laugh.

More than you can answer, I am afraid.

He just shook his head.

Dr. Randall frowned. "I've asked Doctor James Lance, our head hematologist, to speak to you tomorrow. Your bloodwork showed some anomalies that he'll want to discuss with you."

Sveyn nodded. He understood enough of that sentence to realize that his eleventh-century blood was somehow different from twenty-first century blood.

Why was obvious. In what way was the question.

"Good. I anticipate a full recovery with no other issues."

"Thank you."

Randall's brow flickered oddly, then he turned and left Sveyn's privacy-tented bedside.

Nurse Sally came in as soon as the surgeon left. "I found your Hollis McKenna. She's in room three-oh-five. I can't tell you more than that, except it's a regular floor."

Sveyn heaved a relieved sigh. With real air.

"When you are moved onto the surgical recovery floor, would you like me to let her know what room you're in?"

Sveyn nodded, concentrating on not crying out as the damned machine squeezed his legs. Again.

ӜК

Nurse Marla came into Hollis's room about an hour after Stevie left. "I have good news. Your Mr. Hansen has just been moved to a room on the surgical recovery floor."

Hollis would have whooped her joy if she wasn't in so much pain. Her head pounded and it hurt to breathe.

Marla noticed and approached her bedside. "Pain level?"

"Eight," Hollis admitted. She hated to be a wuss, but…

"I'll refresh your ice pack and I can give you acetaminophen," the nurse offered. "But no more anti-inflammatory meds for another hour and a half."

"I'll take it."

When Nurse Marla returned with the ice, a cup of water, and the little white caplets, Hollis asked, "Can I see him?"

She waited for Hollis to down the drugs before answering. "Let me check with the doctor about temporarily disconnecting your heart monitor. If he says yes, I'll get an orderly to wheel you to his room for ten minutes. But that's it."

Hollis forced a smile. "Thank you."

Fifteen minutes seemed to take fifty, but the mild pain medication and ice were starting to help. Hollis pinched her cheeks for color and agonizingly pushed herself up straighter in her bed. When Nurse Marla returned, Hollis's smile was more genuine.

"Okay," Marla began. "Doctor says that since your heart rate is steady and has been since you were admitted, I can disconnect you for a short time."

"Ten minutes is all I ask," Hollis said. "And it means the world to me."

Marla nodded. "All right. I'll call the orderly."

Ӝ

Sveyn lay in his hospital bed with cool oxygen flowing into his nose, clear liquid flowing into his veins, and counting the seconds in his head until his legs would be released from this round of compression hell. He was finally alone for the first time since Hollis brought him back into his body.

Until Hollis nearly died and joined him in his undefined not-dead, not-alive, caught-in-between state, Sveyn never considered that the answer to his situation was not to die at last, but to live again.

He never considered that was even possible, but when she appeared beside him all that had gone before made sudden sense: why he manifested to a woman for the first time, why he was beginning to smell and taste, to be heard and glimpsed.

It was his destiny to fall in love with her, and her destiny to save him. The only glitch in this situation was that Sveyn had not revealed everything about his manifestations to Hollis.

After this was finished, he would need to. He owed her that.

When we are both recovered.

Someone knocked on his opened door.

"Sveyn?"

Hollis?

He turned his head—the only part of him that he could currently move—and watched the love of his life be pushed into his room in a wheelchair.

"Hollis…" he breathed. "Thank God you are here."

Hollis turned to the man pushing her chair. "Will you give us privacy?"

He nodded. "I'll be back in ten."

"Thanks."

Hollis faced Sveyn again. "Are you in a lot of pain?"

He managed a crooked smile. "Not from the surgery. There is some magic there."

"Sveyn, can you understand me?"

"Yes." His smile faded. "Why do you ask me?"

"Raise your right hand."

Sveyn complied with the odd request. "Why?"

Hollis tried to move her chair forward but winced and abandoned the attempt.

"What is wrong, Hollis?"

She looked like she might cry. "My chest hurts too much to roll the chair closer."

"No, why did you ask me to raise my right hand?"

Hollis glanced toward the door, then pinned Sveyn with a concerned gaze. "Do you know that you're not speaking English?"

Sveyn recoiled inwardly; outwardly he was immobilized by tubes and contraptions. "What?"

"You aren't speaking English."

"I thought I was."

"You are speaking a language I never heard. Maybe it's your old Norse?"

Sveyn frowned. His heart beat harder in his chest. "Is this English?"

"Concentrate. Like when you moved through things."

Hollis stared at Sveyn, clearly hoping her suggestion would work.

What if he couldn't speak English anymore?

But I understand everyone around me.

So if he concentrated, he should be able to respond in that language.

"Is this English?" he asked slowly.

Her shoulders sagged in relief. "Yes."

"I must think hard," he managed. "This will not be easy."

"Not at first," she agreed. "But at least we know you can do it."

Yes. I can. And I will.

"I love you, Hollis."

Hollis's sudden smile was all the medication he needed. "And I love you, Viking. Welcome back to earth."

Sunday
January 10

When Hollis was awakened at six o'clock the next morning she didn't even try to go back to sleep. Nurse Marla had handed her off to Nurse Beth last night, and the cheerful Filipina made her hourly appearances as required.

Her chest actually hurt more this morning than it had yesterday.

"Your pectoral muscles are stiff from the shock and contraction of the defibrillator," Nurse Beth explained. "And the crack in your sternum is now a bone bruise."

"What can help?" Hollis asked.

"Anti-inflammatories. And I can give you another ice pack. Twenty-four hours after the injury, you can start using heat."

That would have to be enough for now. "Do you know how long I'll be in here?"

Nurse Beth gave her an apologetic moue. "I don't. You'll have to ask the doctor when he makes his rounds."

"When will that be?"

"Hard to say. Sorry." Beth turned to the white board and noted the ice pack request. "Marla will be your nurse again today. Maybe she can find out when he'll be on this floor."

"Thank you." Hollis slumped down in her bed and tried to

find a comfortable position.

She didn't have time to talk to Sveyn about the gypsy ruse last night before she was banished from his room and wheeled back to her own. But he came out of surgery speaking not-English, so obviously he hadn't answered any hospital questions yet.

I'll need to be his emergency contact.

How could she accomplish that?

"He has to designate you," Marla answered when Hollis asked. "Will he do that?"

Hollis frowned a little. "I think so. I'm the only person who knows him."

Marla looked at her strangely. "How is that possible?"

Crapazoids.

Now was the time to begin laying the groundwork and see if the planned ruse had legs. "He's a refugee. From the gypsy culture."

"Really?" The nurse's expression didn't change. "Is that a thing?"

"Yes." *Let's go with that.* "He came to my museum looking for a job, but he doesn't have any documentation."

Marla's expression eased. "Right. They live completely off the grid."

This was good. "So I was going to help him get, I don't know, *real*."

"I see." The nurse shrugged. "Well, good luck with that. I have no idea where you'll begin."

Hollis smiled politely.

Neither do I.

Chapter Three

In the middle of the morning, when Hollis was at the height of her impatience to see the doctor and get back to Sveyn's side, Matt showed up at her door.

"What do you want?" she asked.

"I wanted to see how you're doing."

"You drove all the way out here for that?"

Matt's cheeks pinkened. "I actually stayed in a hotel down the road."

Damn. The man could be a very good boyfriend when he tried, but that was the problem. He was a complete and utter failure in the commit-and-stay-married arena.

"Why, Matt?" Hollis pressed, allowing her impatience to spill onto him. "You and I are finished. Forever this time, in case I wasn't clear enough before."

She could practically see the cogs turning in his manipulative little mind. "I wasn't at my best, yesterday. I admit it. I'm hoping you'll cut me some slack, considering."

Hollis stared at him. "Considering, what?"

He shrugged one shoulder. "Considering your breakdown."

Hollis's eyes narrowed. "What breakdown, exactly?"

Matt stepped closer to her bed and lowered his voice. "You were acting totally crazy, Hollis. You were waving your arms, and shouting, and crying, and running back and forth like—I don't even know what."

Hollis sighed. She had already told Matt about Sveyn; now was the moment of truth. "That's because Sveyn was blocking my way and arguing with me."

Matt straightened, the former pink in his cheeks draining away. "What? He really was there?"

"Yes." Hollis tried to fold her arms over her chest but was stopped by the pain and the heart monitor leads. She laid her hands in her lap instead. "I was giving him his *I told you so* opportunity."

"What does that mean?"

Hollis sighed another necessarily shallow sigh. "It means that Sveyn told me several times that men don't change. He said you aren't any different now than you were two years ago, and that you would break my heart again."

Matt sank into the only chair in the room. "I broke your heart?"

If Hollis could get out of her bed, she'd punch him again, and much harder this time. "You are *such* an idiot, Matt!"

His mouth gaped soundlessly.

Hollis stabbed a finger in his direction. "The only reason I even considered letting you try to win me back, as you so deceptively put it, was because I thought you wanted to marry me!"

Matt's brow plunged. "In time—"

"You had *ten years,* asshole." Hollis snorted. "You're dead to me now. I'm moving on."

"Moving on to what?" he taunted. "Some ghost? Yeah, that's a great life decision."

A slow smile spread over Hollis's face. Oh, this was a sweet, sweet moment. One she never anticipated, but was welcomed nonetheless.

Savor it.

She relaxed against her raised mattress. “Did you see the man who was stabbed yesterday?”

His lips twisted. “Of course.”

“The one dressed all in leather with fur boots?” She paused as Matt’s mouth fell open again.

I should tell him that’s not a good look for him.

“The very tall man dressed like a Viking? Run through the gut by a broadsword?”

“So when you said Sveyn…” Matt’s chest heaved. “Hollis, be serious. That’s not possible.”

“Except that, obviously, it is.”

“So that’s why you’re breaking up with me?”

Hollis glared at Matt, incredulous. “I know I have a concussion, and bits of yesterday are still fuzzy, but I remember that I hit you and told you to go away before that man appeared.”

Matt folded his arms.

Sure he could; he wasn’t hit with a hammer.

“Did you, Hollis?”

Hollis spread her arms as far as she could without causing herself searing pain. “Did you see him on that field with me? When I was having that breakdown that you said I was having?”

Matt was obviously trying to lie. “I don’t know.”

“Of course you didn’t.” Hollis dropped her arms on her blankets and sneered at him. “Just get out.”

“Okay!” He threw his hands up in surrender. “I didn’t see him until after the paramedics zapped you. But that’s because I was concentrating on you.”

“And so were they. Until he appeared out of nowhere.” Hollis definitely guessed on that part, but it seemed logical.

Matt was quiet. Admitting he was wrong was always hard for him and he usually beat her down with objections before backing off.

“Yeah.” The word was hardly more than a soft grunt.

Hollis had to poke him. “What?”

“Yes,” he hissed. “He did appear out of nowhere.”

Hollis decided not to give Matt any details about how the

Viking was able to do that. He didn't deserve them.

"And now Sveyn's here, Matt. Upstairs. On the surgical recovery floor."

Matt wagged his head. "I can't believe it."

"Go visit him."

"Not that—well, yes that. Obviously *that*." Matt ran a hand over his perfectly trimmed hair. "But I mean you choosing some weird dude, that wasn't even real, over me."

"You made that choice for me, Matt, when you refused to make a commitment. When are you going to get that through your Neanderthal skull?"

He made a disgusted face. "Oh, come on."

"Sveyn *was* real, only now he's *really* real."

Yes, that sounded like a five-year-old. *Tough*. "And he's the man I love."

"Love?" Matt chuckled. "Good luck with that."

"Thank you." Hollis flashed a super-sweet smile. "That's very nice of you."

"I didn't—"

"I know.

Matt sat back in the chair and stared at her. "What now?"

"Now you go back to your wife and beg her forgiveness."

Matt's gaze fell to the floor. "What if I don't want to?"

"Then move to Tibet and become a monk," Hollis huffed.

His gaze jumped back to hers. "I'm serious."

"So am I."

Matt was the one looking heartbroken now. "So we're really finished?"

Hollis was amazed how easily the next words flowed from her mouth. "We were finished once before, and now, as I said, we are finished forever."

"Hollis—"

"Matt," she said as gently as her anger would let her. "You failed the test. Go home."

A quick knock on the door preceded the appearance of a man with a stethoscope looped around his neck and a metal flip chart in his hand.

"Hollis McKenna? I'm Doctor Sajid Khan." He looked up, clearly surprised to see Matt. "Oh. Hello."

"He's leaving, Dr. Khan." Hollis gave Matt an impatient look. "Aren't you."

Matt rose to his feet and strode out of her life without another word.

Ӝ

Lunch was comprised of several containers of liquids. Just like breakfast.

Sveyn had been instructed several times that if he wanted or needed anything to press the red button on the end of a cord clipped to his bed. He pressed it now.

A nurse walked into the room and turned off the alarm. "What do you need Sveyn?"

He waved a hand over his tray while he concentrated on English. "I am hungry."

She smiled apologetically. "Have you passed gas yet?"

The look of shock and disbelief that must have reflected Sveyn's stunned reaction to that question made her laugh. She clapped an apologetic hand over her mouth.

"Gas?" He struggled to get the words out in his newly permanent language. "Does this mean flatulence?"

The nurse uncovered her mouth but she was still smiling. "Yes. After abdominal surgery, the patient—that's you—can't have solid food until we know that their body is functioning correctly. And that's how we know."

Sveyn nodded solemnly, considering this startling information. "I understand."

What must be done, must be done.

He shifted his weight away from the nurse and squeezed. In spite of the discomfort from his surgery, a little rumble escaped his buttocks.

He settled back in place. "Now I eat?"

ӝ

The nurse was crying, she laughed so hard. Sveyn didn't care, as long as he received food that actually required chewing. While he waited for a new tray to be delivered, another nurse came in and released him from the compression contraption.

"I thank God," he said. "You are angel."

The sheets and backless tunic still irritated his skin, so he lay still as much as possible. He held the television's remote in his hand and flipped through channels, sorry to see that the offerings were limited.

An official-looking woman walked through his open door without knocking. "Sveyn Hansen?"

He only moved his eyes. "Yes."

She pulled the room's single chair next to the bed. "I'm missing your information." She opened a notebook. "I need to ask you some questions."

Sveyn lifted one hand. "Before you ask, I need Hollis McKenna."

The woman looked up from her papers. "I'm sorry. Who is that?"

"Hollis McKenna. Room three-oh-five."

ӝ

Hollis received Dr. Khan's go-ahead to check out of the hospital the next day as long as she continued to blow in the little plastic air-measuring thingy between now and then. The doctor explained that he wanted to make sure she didn't develop pneumonia from the shallow breathing which her injury prompted.

"You do not want to start coughing, Ms. McKenna. Trust me on this," he said in his delightful East Indian accent. "If you think deep breaths are uncomfortable now, then coughing will be a very unhappy surprise."

I can imagine.

"Thank you."

He scribbled notes in his chart. "I want you to see your primary care physician as soon as possible. Have him contact the hospital and we will send him your chart."

Hollis looked at the heart monitor, blinking silently and measuring her steady pulse. "I'm going to be okay. Right?"

"Right as rain." He glanced out the window at the desert. "Or perhaps I should say, right as the hope of rain."

Hollis grinned her appreciation of the jest. "Thank you, Dr. Khan."

Nurse Marla hurried in. "I'm glad I caught you, Doctor. We just received a call that Ms. McKenna's presence is required on the fourth floor."

Sveyn's floor.

"What's happened?" Hollis asked.

The nurse continued to address the doctor. "The man who was brought in at the same time as she was has asked for her to be present while he talks to the admitting staff."

"That's right," Hollis forestalled Dr. Khan's questions. "He has a special circumstance, and I'm like his… sponsor."

"Sponsor?" he asked.

"He's a refugee. From the gypsies." At the doctor's blank stare, Hollis continued. "I'm hiring him to work at the Arizona History and Cultural Museum."

Now I have to make that *happen.*

"So I have his pertinent information."

Dr. Khan watched her heart monitor for a minute, then nodded. "Go ahead and unhook her, Nurse. But I want her back in this bed and reconnected to the monitor within thirty minutes."

Ӝ

When Hollis was rolled into Sveyn's room, the atmosphere was tense. The Viking's mattress was raised at the head, and he sat silently waiting. Only his eyes moved.

"Hollis McKenna?" the admin gal asked.

"Yes."

"Finally." She flipped her notebook open. "Now, Mr. Hansen, what is your date of birth?"

"February twelfth."

"Year?"

Sveyn had done his math and named the year that made him thirty-four. Almost thirty-five.

"Where were you born?"

His gaze shot to Hollis and screamed for her help.

"Sveyn's mother was a gypsy, so he was born somewhere in the desert," she said, adding the best possibility, "But it was in Maricopa County."

The woman gave Hollis an irritated look. "And why doesn't he tell me this himself?"

Hollis gave the woman an understanding smile. "May I tell you what I know?"

"Please."

Hollis drew as deep a breath as she could without coughing.

That's for you, Dr. Khan.

"Sveyn appeared at the museum where I work and asked for a job."

The Viking in question was listening intently.

Good.

"That's when I discovered that he has no driver's license, birth certificate, or state ID because, as you know, gypsies live off the grid."

"And no insurance, of course," the woman growled, making a note on her paper.

"Sveyn is leaving the gypsy lifestyle with the intention of becoming a legal and productive member of modern society."

The woman glanced at Sveyn.

He gave her a solemn nod.

Hollis kept talking so the woman couldn't ask any questions. "That's why he was attacked and stabbed. Some radical gypsies think like street gangs do—trying to leave the lifestyle is tantamount to treason."

"Huh." The woman seemed to be softening. "So what happens now?"

"We have to get him documented." Hollis tipped her head and enlisted the woman's help. "Is there a social worker in the hospital who can help him with that?"

"I'll check. But—"

"Because as soon as he is recognized as a citizen," Hollis interrupted, "I can hire him as a fulltime museum staff member and he can start paying the hospital back."

Chapter Four

Hollis was infuriatingly exhausted when she got back to her room. She liked to think it was because she was awakened every hour last night and not because her heart had stopped and she nearly died yesterday.

She considered the blinking monitor beside her bed.

Maybe I should stay another day.

Sveyn wasn't going anywhere for a while. Plus this hospital was a good twenty miles from her condo and she wasn't allowed to drive until she saw her own doctor.

As much as she wanted to, Hollis wasn't able to stay behind and talk to Sveyn after the admin gal left because she ran out of time. She couldn't face Nurse Marla, who had been so kind to her, if she deliberately disobeyed Dr. Khan's orders.

She looked at the old-fashioned phone sitting on the stand beside her bed.

If I call his room, will he answer?

Hollis lifted the receiver and dialed Sveyn's room.

The phone rang six times before a deep masculine voice said, "Hello?"

"Sveyn, it's Hollis."

"Ah, good. I want to talk with you." His voice was rough and his words halting, but the Viking was speaking English, and through real live vocal chords. "Your story was very good. That woman believed you."

"It's the story we both must tell, all the time, to everyone," Hollis stated. "Do you understand that?"

"Yes."

"Good. And when we get better and they send us home, you'll come live with me."

Sveyn was quiet.

Hollis's heart lurched, causing a momentary disruption of the steadily blinking lights. "What's wrong?"

"I do not want to ask you this question when I cannot see you."

"Ask me what?"

Sveyn made an airy, irritated sound. "I cannot see you. So I will not ask you."

"Oh." *Duh.* "Are you all right? Are you upset about something?"

"I am not upset. I am in pain. I will stay in bed until tomorrow, when I will walk in a circle."

Hollis tamped down her apprehension as best she could. "Okay…"

"We have much to talk about, Hollis McKenna," he said gently. "And now we have time. I am not leaving you. Not ever."

Ӝ

Two men in uniform with badges and guns entered Sveyn's hospital room.

"Fifteen minutes, guys," a petite African-American nurse warned. "Then I'm kicking you out. Got it?"

"Yes, ma'am," the younger of the two answered. "We shouldn't be long."

The older man approached the bed. "Sveyn Hansen?"

"Yes." He vaguely remembered the paramedic telling him

that police officers would be coming to speak with him. Thanks to Hollis, he now had a tale to tell them. "You are police?"

"Sheriff's Deputies, actually. The attack took place on unincorporated county land. That's our jurisdiction."

Sveyn nodded and pretended he understood what they were talking about.

"I'm Deputy Smith and this is Deputy Wisenhauer." He held out a business card and Sveyn accepted it. "We have a few questions about the man who attacked you at the Renaissance Faire."

"Yes."

"Did you know him?"

"No."

Deputy Smith frowned. "No? Then why do you think he attacked you?"

"I am leaving gypsy life." Sveyn remembered what else Hollis said. "This makes people angry. Like street gangs."

"So you're saying you were stabbed with a massive, what? Machete? Because you are leaving the gypsy community?" Smith looked at Wisenhauer for back up. "Have you ever heard of such a thing?"

The younger deputy cleared his throat. "Yes, I actually have, sir."

Smith's eyebrows shot upward. "Really?"

Sveyn was as surprised as Smith. "You have?"

"Yes. There is an enclave up in the Superstition Mountains that has a reputation for being radical." He tapped his chin with his pen's clicker. "The Romano Clan, I believe."

"Searching for the Lost Dutchman's mine, no doubt." Smith's voice dripped with sarcasm. He turned back to Sveyn. "In that case, this appears to be a rather fruitless conversation. But if we send over our artist, will you give a description so he can make a drawing?"

"I will help any way I can," Sveyn promised.

And I'll describe the miscreant who did run me through—in ten-seventy.

"I guess we're done here." Smith held out his hand. "Thank

you for your cooperation, Mr. Hansen."

"Thank you for protecting the people."

"Uh, yeah." Deputy Smith turned crisply. "Let's go Wisenhauer."

As Sveyn watched the deputies leave, relief flooded his veins. He closed his eyes, relishing the relaxing sensation.

As much as every inch of his body hurt, to be able to feel pain again was more refreshing than he could ever have imagined. Because it meant that he was alive.

Ӝ

Sveyn's peace was sadly short-lived. This seemed to be the normal state for both this hospital and the one Hollis stayed in after her abduction. He decided to ask her later how the sick and injured were expected to recuperate when they were never allowed to rest.

"Good day, Mr. Hansen. I'm Doctor James Lance, hematologist."

When Sveyn didn't respond, the doctor explained, "I'm a blood specialist."

"Yes. I was told you would come." Sveyn wondered what sort of obstacle he was up against now—and how he would defeat it.

Dr. Lance sat in the chair beside the bed. "I ran some tests on your blood and I have a few questions."

Sveyn nodded.

"What immunizations have you received?"

Sveyn felt his cheeks warming with his embarrassment. "I do not know this word."

Dr. Lance looked surprised. "It's where you are injected with a small amount of a virus with a needle."

Sveyn was shocked. "Why?"

"So your body builds up an immunity against that disease."

Sveyn understood the concept and decided to give an answer based on Hollis's story. He prayed that it made sense. "My mother was gypsy. I never had these."

"None?" the doctor clarified. "Not ever?"

"No." Sveyn tried to sound certain.

"Then why..." Lance looked at his chart again, then back at Sveyn. "Why do you have smallpox antibodies?"

Sveyn hesitated, wondering if the question was some sort of trick. But even if it was, he could not lie.

"Because I had smallpox when I was a boy?"

"You had smallpox, what, twenty-five years ago?"

Sveyn had to accept that accounting; he had no other choice. "Yes."

Dr. Lance shook his head. "In Maricopa County? That's not possible."

He frowned. "Why?"

"Because there have been no reported cases of smallpox in the United States since nineteen-forty-nine."

Clearly it was time to invent more of his story. Hollis only mentioned his gypsy mother, so, "My mother spent time looking for my father. We traveled for a very long time."

"How old were you?"

"Five. Six." He intentionally looked confused. "I am not certain."

"Might you have crossed the US border?" the doctor suggested.

"Yes. It might be Mexico. Or farther south?" Sveyn decided to enhance the story to make it more believable. "I remember mountains. And it was hot."

Dr. Lance stared at him. "What was it like, having smallpox?"

This part, Sveyn did not need to fabricate. "I was miserable. My body was covered with it. My younger brother died from it."

Finally I can say I will see you in heaven, Urgaard.

Sveyn almost smiled before he stopped himself. It would be better to divert the doctor. "What other odd things did you see in my blood?"

Dr. Lance startled; obviously his thoughts had wandered further down the smallpox path. "I suppose there might have been straggling random cases in the jungles that were never reported."

Sveyn said nothing. What could he say? He was never stuck with a needle and yet he had the anti-things in his blood.

"Were there other odd things in my blood?" he prompted.

"Uh, yes." Dr. Lance looked at his chart again. "You have an unusually high number of regenerative cells."

Sveyn wondered if he would have to ask, or if the doctor would launch his explanation on his own.

Thankfully the doctor did so on his own. "These types of cells are normally found in babies, because they grow so rapidly in their first year."

Sveyn frowned. "Is this bad?"

"No! Not at all." The doctor chuckled. "It'll keep you from aging too rapidly, I suppose."

That was more of a relief that Dr. James Lance could ever imagine, though until that moment Sveyn assumed that since he was once more in his body, he would age at the normal rate for a man nearly thirty-five years of age.

The idea that he might have come back as a weak and withered old man, dropping dead in a blink, had never crossed his mind.

Because—he never knew he could come back at all.

"So I will live a long time?" he asked.

Dr. Lance closed his flip chart. "You'll have a better chance if you don't get stabbed again."

The doctor stood. "That said, I recommend a full round of immunizations, starting in about six weeks. No sense in you contracting another nearly-eradicated disease."

Sveyn nodded. He'd ask Hollis about this.

"Get some rest." Dr. James Lance turned and left the room.

Sveyn snorted.

I am trying.

Ӝ

Something woke Hollis from her dozing nap. She opened her eyes. Miranda stood at the foot of her bed.

"Are you up for company?" the nearly six-foot-tall brunette asked. Her smile was apologetic but hopeful.

Hollis looked at the clock on the wall behind her boss. "For you? Yes." Hollis pushed herself up straighter, wincing at the resulting pain in her cracked sternum. "Besides, dinner's coming soon and you can distract me from wondering how bad the food will be."

Miranda sank into the single chair. "I was so worried when I heard you were hurt. So was Mr. Benton."

Hollis flashed a wry smile. The museum's director wasn't known for his touchy-feely style; economics made his heart go pitter-patter. "I'm surprised he hasn't found a way to spin this for media attention."

Miranda gave her a stricken look.

"Oh no." Hollis slumped. "Don't tell me."

"I'm so sorry." Miranda reached for Hollis's hand and gave it a squeeze. "That's part of why I'm here now—to watch the evening news with you and see what he's come up with."

"I should have known." Hollis made a face. There was nothing to be done about this turn of events except just get through it.

It was time for a change of subject. "Did he tell you about my job offer?"

Now Miranda slumped. "No. Where are you going?"

Hollis coughed a weak laugh. "Nowhere. Especially not now."

Miranda frowned. "What're you talking about?"

Hollis smiled a truly happy smile. "I'm afraid you're stuck with me, Boss Lady. I'll be permanent staff starting March first."

Miranda let out a loud whoop, then clapped her hand over her mouth. But her eyes were smiling.

"Sorry," she whispered after dropping her hand. "Forgot I was in a hospital."

Hollis chuckled. "I was able to negotiate a pretty sweet deal. I'll still have to do the ghost hunter stuff, but I'll have flexible hours. I'll come in at noon if I have to stay until eight. That sort of thing."

Miranda looked impressed. "He agreed to that? He must really want you. But will you be able to get everything done that way?"

"I will with Tom's help." Hollis grinned. "Benton's moving him up from intern to full-time staff. He'll be my assistant."

Miranda clasped her hands together. "Oh, I'm so glad! I really like him."

"So do I," Hollis agreed. "But more importantly, he really knows his stuff when it comes to European history. He's perfect for the position."

Hollis's dinner tray was carried in; she smelled some kind of white meat. "Thank you," she said to the aide.

Miranda stood. "Is there anything I can do?"

Hollis pulled the lid from her plate. Her nose was correct. The white meat was sliced turkey with mashed potatoes and gravy. Looked like a Swanson frozen meal, down to the peas.

She handed Miranda the lid. "Can you set this aside? There's not really room on here."

She did. "Can I turn on the television?"

"Yeah—the remote's clipped to the bed." Hollis said as she liberally salted and peppered the bland meal.

Miranda flipped through channels until she reached channel twelve. "Benton's loyal if nothing else. He always goes to these guys first."

Miranda turned her chair to face the TV and Hollis dug into her dinner. Neither woman spoke as story after story passed with no mention of Hollis, the Renaissance Faire, or the accident.

"Maybe it wasn't newsworthy," Hollis said as the newscast went to yet another commercial break. "One can always hope."

"Benton will be pissed if that's true." Miranda looked at Hollis from the corner of her eye. "Maybe I'll stay home tomorrow."

The image of the perky blonde newscaster reappeared. "And now we have an update on yesterday's freak accident and stabbing at the Renaissance Faire…"

Chapter Five

Hollis groaned, her eyes pinned to the screen as a photo of her at the Kensington Wing's opening appeared in the corner.

At least it's a good one.

"The woman hit by the stray hammer on Saturday was our own Hollis McKenna from the Arizona History and Cultural Center."

While the reporter kept talking, the image switched to a random interview clip of her from the cable-based ghostbuster show that was filmed at the museum in December.

"You may have seen her appearance last Wednesday night on the season premiere of *Ghost Myths, Inc*. where this image—" The clip showed the glowing, green, non-descript Sveyn who showed up on the crew's infrared depth camera. "—was caught."

Miranda straightened in her chair. "Wait a minute…"

"The stabbing victim with Ms. McKenna at the Faire has been identified as thirty-four-year-old Sveyn Hansen—"

A photo of Sveyn taken on somebody's phone sometime between his reappearance and his exit by ambulance now filled the box over the reporter's shoulder.

"—who was allegedly stabbed in retaliation for recently abandoning his gypsy community."

Miranda turned slowly to face Hollis as the blonde newscaster signed off and wished everyone a great Monday tomorrow.

"What?" Hollis asked, even though she had a fairly good idea.

Miranda put up one finger as if she had several questions. "Why were you at the Faire with that ex-gypsy?"

Hollis turned off the television and faced her friend. Giving a consistent explanation was key.

"He came to the museum on Friday asking for a job, but he didn't have any documentation." She shrugged with one shoulder but it still tugged painfully at her injured sternum. "You know: no driver's license, birth certificate, or social security number."

Miranda gave her a skeptical frown. "So you adopted him like a puppy?"

"No, of course not." *Keep it simple.* "I ran into him at the Faire, right after my argument with Matt."

Miranda's eyebrows rose. "What did you argue with Matt about?"

Though Hollis was furious at the man and had no doubt that she made the right decision, Matt's deep betrayal yesterday still stung. "When I told him about my new contract, I asked if he would move to Phoenix, or if I should decline it and move back to Milwaukee."

Miranda knew enough of Hollis's story that understanding washed over her expression. "And he said neither one."

The silent blinking beeps on Hollis's heart monitor stepped up their rhythm. "Yep."

"Oh, Hollis."

"I was angry and hurt and crying hysterically when I ran into Sveyn." Hollis continued with the same explanation she gave the Sheriff's Deputies when they asked. "I was so upset, in fact, that I didn't see Sveyn get stabbed."

Miranda considered her through narrowed eyes. "Did you notice how much Sveyn looks like that ghost image?"

There it is.

It probably wasn't going to be the last time she would be asked this, especially when he became a solid part of her world.

What do I say?

"I did. It was weird."

That's safe.

Miranda looked like she couldn't believe she was asking the next question. "Is Sveyn your guardian angel?"

Hollis thought out loud; that seemed the most logical and believable way to answer the expected query. "Angels can't bleed, can they? Or be operated on?"

Miranda looked disappointed and relieved at the same time. "No, I don't suppose so."

Good.

This train is rolling.

"And this guy was definitely not angelic in any way while the paramedics loaded him into the ambulance," Hollis continued. "I was sort of out of it, but it sounded like he was swearing worse than any sailor."

She smiled inwardly at her own reference.

Captain of her heart.

Miranda shifted in her seat as she shifted her point. "Do you think the angel appeared in Sveyn's likeness so you would want to help him when he asked for a job?"

Ooh.

Good tie-in.

Hollis puckered her brow. "I hadn't thought about it, Miranda, but you could be right."

"Two lives saved," the brunette mused.

"Saved if you'll hire him," Hollis grabbed the opening.

"To do what?" Miranda asked. "Does he have any skills?"

"No," Hollis admitted. "But he could do maintenance, or maybe be a guard."

"He looked like a pretty big guy." Miranda was clearly considering it.

"I already asked if the hospital's social worker could help him with paperwork."

Miranda nodded. "That's good."

"And…" Hollis gave Miranda a tentative smile. "I sorta told them that if they did, we'd hire him so he could start paying his bill."

Miranda laughed. "I bet they'll jump on that."

"I hope so." Hollis's mood dimmed. "I don't know how else he'll survive living in this century."

Miranda's head tilted. "What an odd thing to say."

Hollis sucked a quick—and painful—breath. "You know what I mean. He's already living in this century, but completely off the grid."

"Oh. Right." Miranda stood. "Hopefully by the time he recovers this will all be sorted and he can start working."

Relief flushed Hollis's body. "Thank you, Miranda."

The tall brunette leaned over and kissed Hollis's cheek. "Get better. And take this whole week off. I don't want to see you in the office until next week. Am I clear?"

Monday
January 11

Though Sveyn had regained the ability to taste just before he got his body back, he was not practiced at actual eating. Yesterday's lunch and dinner were excruciating ordeals, requiring hours of his time.

First off, twenty-first century silverware was not familiar to his hand. Luckily he had watched it being used often enough to know what to do with the various utensils, but knowing and doing were not the same thing.

Once he managed to portion a suitable bite and lift the food to his mouth, the explosion of full flavor made him stop to fully appreciate it. He held the bite in his mouth and breathed past it to allow his nose to enhance the taste.

Then came the chewing.

He kept biting his tongue—and with his nerves still zinging at each new sensation that *really* hurt. The damned thing had a mind of its own and kept getting in the way. More than once he tasted blood.

Sveyn felt every morsel, every crumb, every hint of temperature and pressure against his teeth. The ache of a tired jaw long unaccustomed to use soon slowed him even further. If it wasn't for the insistent rumble in his belly he might have given up.

Swallowing, however, was worse.

Sveyn thanked God that he was alone in his room as he forced the food to move down his throat. He gagged with every bite at first, and the heaving spasms in his gut pulled achingly at his wound.

But when he ate dinner, swallowing without gagging became mercifully more frequent, until about every third or so bite went down without incident.

I am making progress.

Now he stared down his breakfast, daring it to defy him and willing his body to take the nourishment without objection.

He was fifty-percent successful, swallowing every other bite without gagging or choking. At this rate, he should be able to complete this meal in forty-five minutes, leaving him a quarter of an hour before he would be required to walk.

What will walking feel like?

He didn't have his boots any longer and his feet were thankfully bare—he doubted he could stand the constant rubbing of leather against his soles. The sheets resting on the tips of his toes were bad enough.

The man who was to assist him was late, which only ratcheted up Sveyn's anxiety.

Please, Father God, do not let me fall.

"Good morning, Sveyn. My name is Pete and I'm going to help you take your first post-surgical walk today." Pete was a thick, robust man who looked to be half-a-head shorter than Sveyn. "Are you ready?"

He was not. "Yes."

"Great. First we are going to disconnect a few things. I think you'll feel better once we do."

The first thing Pete did was lift the bottom of the sheet. "I see you've been drinking liquids and passing them adequately. Your bag is full." He smiled at Sveyn. "Let's remove that catheter."

What's a cath—"Ow!"

"Sorry, buddy. There's no way to make that pleasant." Pete held up a translucent bag filled with pale yellow liquid.

"Is that piss?" Sveyn had been wondering why he never felt the urge to empty his bladder.

"Yep. From now on, you'll use the bathroom." Pete pointed at the door closest to the bed.

He nodded, still unsure about how that bag had been attached to his now very-tender member.

Pete went into the bathroom and returned with an empty bag, which he placed inside a red container on the room's wall. He returned to Sveyn's bedside.

"Now let's take out the IV."

What's an—"Ow!"

Pete pulled the flexible needle from the thick vein in the back of Sveyn's hand. Then he pressed against Sveyn's hand to keep it from bleeding.

"Yeah, that stings. But it hurts less than the catheter, eh?"

Sveyn nodded. "What more?"

Pete grinned at him. "Nothing. You are now free of hospital paraphernalia."

He didn't recognize the word, but understood its meaning nonetheless. "Thank God."

Pete laughed. "Can you sit up and swing your legs over the side of the bed?"

That is an excellent question.

When his body first reappeared, Sveyn reacted out of the instinct of an animal in pain, writhing and curling without thought. Now that he was expected to be deliberate with his movement he wondered if his muscles would obey him.

Sitting up was not a problem; he had been doing that since

the damned constrictors were removed from his legs. He threw aside the sheet and blanket rather than slide his skin against them.

"Whoa. You're going to need another gown to cover your backside. And a pair of booties. Let me get those."

Pete left the room and reappeared a minute later. He handed Sveyn a tunic like the one he was currently wearing. "Put this on like a coat."

Sveyn grasped the point and obeyed, assuring that his arse would not be on display when he got off the bed.

Pete slipped blue booties over Sveyn's feet. "Okay. You're set."

Sveyn clenched his jaw, an ancient habit that now caught him by surprise. He relaxed it.

Left leg first.

There.

Now his right leg.

Sveyn heaved a sigh with real breath, noticing that his lungs no longer burned when he did so. He looked at Pete, ridiculously proud of himself.

"Put your hand on my shoulder." He did. "Now slide off the bed and just stand. Don't try to walk yet."

Do not worry—I will not.

When his feet hit the floor, Sveyn's long legs were still bent.

"You're a tall guy," Pete said. "Can you stand?"

Sveyn focused his energy and leaned forward, shifting his weight from the mattress to his slippered feet. Then he straightened his legs.

Pete looked up at him. "You okay?"

He hated admitting any kind of weakness, but he said, "A little dizzy."

"That's normal. Let me know when it passes."

Incredibly, it already had. "I am good now."

"All right. When you're ready." Pete put his arm around Sveyn's waist. "Use me for balance."

Again, he moved his left leg first. Forward.

Transfer my weight.

He pulled his right leg past the left.

Transfer my weight.

He pulled his left leg past the right.

Again.

Sveyn gradually picked up speed until he was walking at the rate of a man past his prime. But that was not the point. The point was that, for the first time since the year ten-seventy, Sveyn Hansen was in control of his own body.

"Again?" he asked once the circle around the nurse's station was completed.

Pete rested his fingers against Sveyn's wrist. "How is your energy level?"

"Good."

"And your pain level? One to ten."

Sveyn had already considered that question, having been asked it repeatedly over the last forty-eight hours. They weren't asking about the pain that was especially his—the scratch against his skin, the burn in his lungs, the ache of his jaw. They wanted to know about his wound.

"My wound is not a bother," he answered truthfully.

"Give me a number, Sveyn."

His brow twitched. "What number lets me walk again?"

Pete laughed, though he clearly didn't want to. "Your pulse is steady, not elevated. And if you can make jokes, I guess you aren't in too much pain."

"No. Not too much," Sveyn agreed.

"Okay." Pete faced forward. "But squeeze my shoulder if you get dizzy again. You don't want to fall and rip your incision open."

Chapter Six

Sveyn was exhilarated after his two circles around the nurse's station. He eased himself back onto the bed, removed the extra tunic and booties, and then stretched out on the almost too-short mattress.

"When can I walk again?" he asked Pete.

Pete pointed at the bathroom. "Every time you need to go."

Sveyn grinned his understanding. "And outside this room?"

Pete shook his head. "Wait a few hours, Sveyn. You don't want to push too hard or you'll actually slow down your recovery."

Though he doubted that was true, he agreed. Then he asked how to call Hollis's room.

"Do you know her room number?"

"Three-oh-five."

Pete lifted the handle-looking part and handed it to Sveyn. "All you have to do is hit pound and dial her room number."

Sveyn frowned. "Pound?"

"This one." Pete pointed at the hash mark. "Like this." He

pushed the hash mark, the three, the zero, and the five.

Sveyn heard a rumbling buzz through the handle.

"Hello?"

He knew that voice. "Hollis?"

Pete waved and left the room. Sveyn raised one hand and waved back.

"Sveyn—you called me!" She sounded very pleased.

"Yes. And I walked."

"Really?" Hollis sounded awestruck. "How'd you do?"

"It was hard at first," he admitted. "But it came back to me. I went around the nurse's area twice."

"I'm so glad."

He nodded though he knew she couldn't see him. "My body is becoming mine again. One piece at a time."

Ӂ

Hollis rested and waited for Doctor Khan to make his rounds. While he said he might release her today, she wasn't feeling strong enough to be on her own. Her head still hurt and there was no way she could put a seatbelt across her chest.

Might be weeks for that.

Besides, she had no way to get home. Thankfully Matt had brought her purse when he followed her to the hospital on Saturday, so she had cash to pay for a taxi. But the thought of calling one exhausted her.

In fact, almost everything exhausted her.

Hollis curled on her side with her back to the door and let her recently frequent tears flow again. Her life had gone through so many sudden and unexpected changes in the last seventy-two hours that she barely had time to process it all.

New job, promising a great future.

New hopes, smashed to smithereens.

New love, suddenly possible.

New lies, the truth being completely impossible.

And all of this resting on an unknown future with an

eleventh-century man now living in a twenty-first century world.

Who wouldn't be exhausted?

A soft knock on the door. "Ms. McKenna?"

Hollis rolled over. "Hi, Dr. Khan."

He approached her bed. "How are you feeling?"

"Not great," she admitted.

He punched a few buttons on the heart monitor, peering at the LED screen. "Your heart rate has been exceptionally boring since you were admitted. I see no reason to continue to pay it any attention."

Hollis smiled a little. "That's good to hear."

Dr. Khan turned off the monitor and unsnapped the leads from the pads on Hollis's chest. "You can remove those now."

Hollis peeled the square-ish pads from her skin and handed them to the doctor, who dropped them in the trash. He reached for the thermometer attached to the wall above her bed, slipped a clean cover over the business end, then pointed it at her.

Hollis opened her mouth and guided the implement under her tongue. In a few moments the wall beeped behind her.

Dr. Khan nodded and returned the denuded thermometer to its holder. "You have a low-grade temperature. This is very common after the sort of injuries you sustained, and is nothing to be worried about."

"Can I stay another night?" Hollis didn't realize until that moment how badly she wanted to remain in this safe cocoon and not face the outside world just yet.

"It is a reasonable request." Dr. Khan looked at her kindly. "I believe, because of the fever, that you should be watched for the next twenty-four hours."

Hollis relaxed muscles she didn't know were tensed. "Thank you."

He gave her a knowing look. "This is the most I can do, Hollis. Tomorrow you must be released."

"I understand."

Dr. Khan nodded again, then turned and left the room.

Hollis curled on her side once more and slid into a deep sleep.

Ӝ

Two hours after finishing a lunch where he only gagged on every fourth or fifth bite—the secret lay in not eating faster than his gullet could move the food downward, apparently—Sveyn walked three circuits around the nurse's station. Two hours after that, someone knocked on his door.

"Yes?"

Stevie Phillips, Hollis's coworker and best friend, stepped into his room. Her eyes widened and her jaw fell slack.

"Oh. My. God."

Stevie's fiancé George stepped past her and into the room. He stood beside the petite blonde, wordless and staring.

Sveyn forced a shaky smile. "Hello, Stevie."

Then he turned to the lawyer. "Hello, George. Thank you for helping Hollis."

"How did you—oh, right."

Sveyn knew everything that had happened in Hollis's life since he manifested to her on Labor Day weekend.

And just five days ago, after watching the *Ghost Myths, Inc.* program starring Hollis and him, Hollis told Stevie, George, and that damned idiot Matt everything about Sveyn.

She was prompted to do so by Stevie, who had begun seeing and hearing Sveyn on her own.

The museum Registrar approached his bed now, her eyes still resembling saucers. "It's you, Sveyn. It's really you."

"In the flesh," he quipped.

Her eyes fell to his hand. "Can I touch you?"

Sveyn extended his hand towards her.

Stevie's grasp was tentative at first, but when she encountered his warm and solid flesh, she grasped it wholeheartedly. "Oh my God. You feel like a real man."

"I am a real man, Stevie."

George stepped up beside her and extended his hand as well. "It's an honor to meet you, sir."

Sveyn assumed George wanted to feel his solidity as well

but Stevie wasn't loosening her grip. He held out his right hand. "Thank you, George."

As George shook his hand, Sveyn confessed, "It was my fault Hollis was rude to you on your first date."

George blinked. "What?"

"I was jealous and I made her say that rude thing."

Stevie seemed to have regained her composure. "What rude thing?"

Sveyn shook his head. "No. It is done."

George looked anew at Sveyn. "Thank you for telling me. You are a true gentleman."

"As are you."

Both Stevie and George stepped back and their gazes moved over Sveyn.

"You look just like when I saw you in Hollis's office," Stevie said, "Only without the leather and fur."

"Those are gone," Sveyn said. "Though I do not think I will mourn for them."

George looked around the room, the walked to a door and opened it. On the floor of the closet was a plastic bag. He lifted it and turned to Sveyn. "Might they be in here?"

"I do not know."

George set the bag on the end of the bed and opened it. He wrinkled his nose. "I think these used to be your clothes, but honestly? They reek."

Sveyn reached for the bag. George handed it to him and he looked inside. Those were indeed his clothes.

And they did, indeed, reek of leather and sweat and dirt and blood, aged over time.

Thank God I could not smell myself.

Sveyn closed the bag and handed it back to George. "Will you dispose of this for me?"

"Of course." George set the bag by the door after twisting it tightly. "What will you wear when you leave the hospital?"

Sveyn stared blankly at the lawyer. "I have no clothes."

He nodded. "I'll get you some. What size?"

Stevie elbowed him. "He wears a Viking long."

George laughed and slapped his forehead. "Yes, that *was* a stupid question."

"When will you be released, Sveyn?" Stevie asked.

He shrugged. "I think tomorrow or Wednesday."

"Then we'll shop tonight," she said with authority. "We just have to figure out what to buy you."

"Stevie?" Sveyn ventured.

She looked at him, eyes bright at the prospect of shopping. "Yes?"

"My skin hurts. Please buy me soft clothes."

"Your skin hurts? Oh!" George nodded slowly. "Of course. You haven't felt anything since you die—*didn't* die in ten-seventy."

Sveyn was glad George understood. "Yes."

"That makes it easy." George turned to his petite fiancée. "We'll get him sweatpants and a t-shirt. And flip flops."

"It's January," Stevie countered. "How about a sweatshirt and shoes and socks instead."

"He's a Viking." George grinned. "He's not going to be cold."

Sveyn watched their exchange, fascinated that there were now three people in his life who knew where he came from, what happened to him, and how he suddenly was alive, and none of them questioned that any of it was true.

He refused to count Matt because that man should be gone, never to return.

Stevie huffed a sigh. "Fine. You win."

George faced Sveyn again just as his dinner tray was being delivered. "We'll go shop now and bring the clothes back later."

Grateful that he would not need to eat in front of them, Sveyn smiled broadly. "Thank you."

Stevie walked toward the door. "I want to see Hollis before we go."

Ӝ

Hollis was awakened by the clack of her dinner tray on the rolling tray table. She stretched and rubbed her eyes before she opened them, surprised to see how dark it was. The clock said five thirty; she'd slept for three hours and she felt immeasurably better for it.

Hollis sat up in bed and pulled the tray table close. She uncovered the dinner plate. Meatloaf. Hollis sighed.

I wish somebody would bring me a pizza.

Someone knocked on her door. Could it be… "Yes?"

Stevie hurried into the room, sadly pizza-less.

Darn.

"Oh my god, Hollis—we saw Sveyn!"

"We?"

George walked into her room behind Stevie.

"Hi, George." Hollis tried to smooth her unruly curls out of reflex. "I look awful, I'm afraid."

"You look good for a woman who almost died, Hollis," he said. "And that's all that matters."

"Thanks." George always was a nice guy. "So you saw Sveyn?"

"Yes!" Stevie sat on the end of her bed. "And he looks *exactly* like when I saw him in your office that one time!"

George leaned toward her in a sort of courtly half-bow. "And he said *he* was the one who put certain words in your mouth on our date."

Hollis's jaw slackened. "He did?"

"He did."

Hollis bounced her gaze to Stevie and back. "Not that that changes anything, of course."

George caught her intent. "No. You and I weren't, um…"

"Right for each other," Hollis finished the sentence. "No chemistry."

"None." George straightened and looked lovingly at his fiancée. "And when we leave you, we are off to buy Sveyn a set of comfortable clothes to leave the hospital in."

Hollis gasped lightly. "He doesn't have any clothes!"

"Not a stitch." Stevie giggled.

Hollis pointed at George. “What’s in the bag?”

“Sveyn’s destroyed leathers.”

“Can I see them?”

George shook his head. “I wouldn’t recommend it.”

“They stink to high heaven,” Stevie stated. “And I’m not exaggerating.”

That was disappointing. “What are you going to do with them?”

“Sveyn asked me to dispose of them.”

Hollis was horrified. “Absolutely not! Those things were made almost a thousand years ago!”

Stevie wrinkled her nose. “What do you want to do with them?”

She didn’t know for sure; only that she couldn’t bear to part with the clothes, destroyed or not.

“I’ll get them un-stinky somehow and decide after that.” Hollis pointed at her closet. “Put the bag in there for now.”

George squinted at her. “Are you sure?”

“I’m definitely sure.” Those are the clothes Sveyn was wearing when she first saw him. And for months afterward.

George complied with Hollis’s request, then spoke to Stevie. “We should go buy the clothes so we can get back here before visiting hours are over.”

Stevie hopped off the bed. “Good idea.”

“Hey guys,” Hollis began. “Can I ask a couple favors?”

Stevie nodded. “Shoot.”

“I need a ride home tomorrow.”

“Stevie has to work, but I can drive you,” George offered. “Sveyn might be released, too, so I’ll plan on driving you both.”

Stevie’s eyes twinkled. “He’s staying at your house, I assume.”

“Yep.” Hollis looked at George. “Thank you, so much.”

“What’s the other favor?” Stevie asked.

Hollis put the lid back on her cooled and bland meatloaf dinner. “When you bring Sveyn his clothes, could you bring me a pizza?”

Chapter Seven

Tuesday
January 12

Hollis let Sveyn sit in the front of George's BMW because it was easier to get in and out of the passenger door. Sveyn was still a bit unsteady on his feet, and bending over and straightening was difficult with his stitches.

"The doctor spoke with me, but I only understood part of what he said," Sveyn confessed when she and George went to his room to collect him. "These are the papers."

Hollis read over the instructions which were pretty straight forward: rest, walk, drink. If temperature or pain level increases call. Use pain meds as prescribed.

She looked at the surprisingly robust Viking. "Do you want pain medication?"

"No."

"Have you been taking any?"

He frowned. "Yes. But it makes me dizzy."

Hollis nodded. "Then we'll try you with just ibuprofen when you get uncomfortable."

"I do not mind being uncomfortable, Hollis."

She gave him a kind smile. "I mean, when the pain gets too uncomfortable."

Sveyn wagged his head. "My entire body has been hurting these three days."

"It has?" A surprised George looked at Hollis, then back at Sveyn. "Why?"

"I have not felt anything for so long," Sveyn explained to the lawyer. "And now I feel everything."

"Is it getting better?" Hollis asked.

Sveyn nodded. "My lungs no longer burn, I am not aware of my heart beating, and these clothes do not scratch my skin."

George was able to find a store at the mall which carried clothes for tall men. Sveyn was now attired in black sweatpants and a soft gray t-shirt.

George said Stevie also insisted on a sweatshirt, so Hollis carried the blue one Stevie selected.

"To match Sveyn's eyes," George explained with a roll of his.

"You can park next to my car," Hollis said to George once they were in her condo's parking lot..

He pulled into the empty slot. "Let me carry something," he said as he opened the driver door.

The entire car shook as a *thunk* and a loud grunt emanated from the front passenger seat.

Hollis leaned forward and asked Sveyn, "What happened?"

The Viking rubbed his head. "I forgot."

"Forgot what?" He didn't have any possessions *to* forget.

He glanced over his shoulder with a very odd look on his face. "I forgot to open the door."

Hollis gasped and burst into excruciating but unavoidable laughter.

George stared at her. "What's so funny?"

Hollis waved at Sveyn to explain because she was trying not to laugh so hard, even though that man's expression hovered precariously between embarrassment and irritation.

"I always moved through things," he grumbled. "I forgot that I cannot do this now."

George was clearly struggling to contain his own surprised amusement. “Do you know how to open the door?”

Without saying a word, Sveyn grabbed the level and pulled. The door popped open.

“Great.” George climbed out and shut his door.

“Are you all right, Sveyn?” Hollis wiped her eyes. “Do you need help?”

The tall figure in front of her swiveled to his right, grabbed the edges of the door frame, and heaved himself out of the vehicle.

Hollis disembarked with her purse, the sweatshirt, and the plastic bag with Sveyn’s leathers. George took everything but the purse, and Hollis walked up the path to her door.

She fished out her key, unlocked and opened the door, and went inside.

George followed and set the stuff on the bar-height portion of the kitchen counter. “Do you need anything? Do you want me to bring you something to eat?”

Hollis watched Sveyn, his pace slow but determined, walk the last few yards to her front door. She turned back to George.

“Pizza and garlic bread knots. I’ll write it down.”

Ӝ

Sveyn stepped into Hollis’s familiar condo, though nothing about it felt familiar. He was embarrassed that he banged his head on the car window when he tried to move through the door out of habit.

New habits were clearly required.

He was glad when Hollis asked George to bring their favorite meal, and anticipating the full flavors of the pizza and knots made his mouth water.

Perhaps they could have wine as well.

I want to taste the white one.

There were still two matters of significant importance that he needed to discuss with Hollis. One could wait. One could not.

After George left, Sveyn took Hollis's hand. "I must talk to you."

Her brows pulled together. "Is something wrong?"

"Yes," he said. "But now I will fix it."

Hollis looked frightened; there was no other word to describe her expression. "What is it?"

"Can we sit?"

"Yes. Of course." Hollis walked stoically to the sofa and sank into the cushions.

Sveyn wanted to kneel in front of her, but was afraid he might not be able to stand back up if he did. So he sat in the chair next to the couch and faced her.

He spoke slowly, concentrating on using the English words which were coming more easily every time he spoke. "For many years, Matt did not do what a man should have done."

Hollis's expression darkened. "Do we have to talk about Matt?"

"Yes," Sveyn said. "Because I am not Matt."

"Obviously."

Sveyn pinned Hollis's gaze with his. "For this reason, I *will* do what a man should do."

Hollis looked confused. "What are you talking about?"

Sveyn winced a smile. "Do you remember when I said I had something to ask you, but I would not ask you when I could not see you?"

"Yes." She drew a quick breath. "It's bad, isn't it."

Sveyn tilted his head. "Why would you think this?"

"Because good news can be shared over the phone," she stated. "But bad news is always delivered face-to-face."

Sveyn huffed a laugh. "I do love you, Hollis. You are so interesting."

"I love you, too. Sveyn." She scowled. "So just ask me, already."

"Do you love me?" he asked just to hear it again.

"Of course I do." She waved her hand over his frame. "And now that you're fully here, that's not so crazy."

Sveyn felt a pleasant warmth flush his chest. "No. It is not crazy at all."

Hollis raised her brows and glared at him. "Speak."

This was not the mood Sveyn hoped for, but knowing Hollis as well as he did he knew this was going to be the best he could get for now.

"Hollis McKenna, you are the greatest love of my overly long life." Sveyn slid off the chair, unable not to. "Will you please become my wife?"

Hollis's eyes rounded and her lips formed a silent O.

Then she began to cry.

Big gulping sobs shook her shoulders and she covered her face with her hands.

"Hollis?" Sveyn pulled her hands down. "What is amiss?"

"Noth—nothing," she wailed. "I just—I didn't…"

Sveyn's gut clenched painfully against his incision. "Do you need time to think before you answer me?"

"No!" she yelped.

Sveyn frowned. "No, you will not marry me?"

Hollis shook her head, sending unruly red waves tumbling across her shoulders. "No—I don't have to think about it, Sveyn." She sniffed wetly and ran the back of one hand under her nose. "Of *course* I'll marry you."

Sveyn leaned in and kissed her. Nothing in their dreamt encounters could prepare him for the impact of actually claiming her lips with his in the real world. She responded fully, huffing little breaths against his still-bearded cheek. He felt a vibration in his throat and knew he had moaned his pleasure.

He was undeniably her captive and he would serve her for the rest of their lives.

Hollis pulled away and stared into his eyes. "I love you, Viking."

"This is why I could never live with you the way Matt did. Promising a future but denying it at the same time," he said.

Hollis blushed beautifully. "I'm so happy."

Sveyn touched her cheek. "How soon can we marry?"

ӜК

How soon, indeed.

Sveyn looked happier than she had ever seen him—and with good reason. His immortal existence was ended at last and in the most surprising way. Now reunited with his body, he should be able to finish his life span like any normal man.

Any normal man born in the eleventh century and living in the twenty-first, that was.

"We have a few problems to solve first," Hollis said.

His brow twitched. "What problems?"

"First you have to recover from your surgery."

He nodded. "Yes. This will not take long."

"And then we have to get you a birth certificate and social security number." Unfortunately the social worker at the hospital was stymied by Sveyn's situation and hadn't gotten back to the former Viking with a solution.

I should ask George for help.

"After that, we can get a marriage license."

"So we can marry in perhaps one month?" His tone was so hopeful that Hollis hated to continue.

But she had to. "We've told everyone that we just met, remember? If I tell people that I'm marrying a man I've only known for a month—and a gypsy at that—there's going to be a lot of push back."

Sveyn's expression turned serious. "Ah. I understand."

Hollis reached for his hand, so glad to finally be able to. His long fingers wrapped around hers and his skin was warm to her touch. "I will marry you, Sveyn. As soon as we are able to do so without raising all sorts of red flags."

"Red flags?"

Hollis thought about how to explain a common expression that she really didn't know the origin of. "Warning flags are usually red. I guess."

Sveyn seemed to accept that. "So we will marry as soon as the people whom you love have no objection."

"Yes."

Sveyn peered into her eyes. The blue in his was brighter than when he was an apparition. "Where will I sleep?

Hollis ran her fingers through his hair. It needed washing, but she didn't care. "Please sleep beside me, like you did after the incident with Sage."

"And what about intimate relations?" he pressed.

Hollis felt a stab of trepidation. "Let's wait until you're better and talk about that again."

"I will be your second lover. Is that correct?"

"Yes." She felt her cheeks heating. "And you?"

Sveyn tipped his head. "I laid with three women before I was stabbed. And I loved another."

"Linge."

"Yes. But I never loved her as much as I love you."

Hollis smiled. "And truthfully, Matt could never be the man that you are."

Ӝ

When George returned with the pizza and garlic knots, Sveyn thought he would burst from the explosion of sensations.

First was the fragrant aroma of the garlic, yeast, sausages, tomato sauce, and cheese. So much more intense than before. So much more enticing.

Then came the tastes. When he bit into a garlic knot and the butter ran down his chin, he thought that even Heaven itself could never be this good. He moaned a little.

"This is better than I imagined it could be," he said when George looked at him, amused.

But then he tried the pizza.

He moaned again, but louder. "*Å min gud…*"

Hollis grinned. "Took the English right out of your mouth, did it?"

Sveyn chewed slowly. He had no more words in any language.

Hollis stood. “Would you like a glass of wine, George?”

“Sure.” He looked at his watch. “I’m picking Stevie up in an hour.”

“White, please?” Sveyn forced the word past a fresh bite of pizza.

“That’s right. You wanted to try the chardonnay.” Hollis opened the refrigerator and pulled out the bottle.

“Let me open that. You sit down.” George took the bottle from her hands. “Where’s the opener?”

Hollis opened the drawer holding the corkscrew, collected three wine goblets from a cabinet, and returned to the table.

George uncorked the wine and poured the three servings. “I’d like to offer a toast.” He lifted one of the half-filled glasses. “To true love conquering the impossible.”

Sveyn claimed a glass and lifted it as well. “And to marriage. May ours follow closely upon yours.”

A sudden and wide grin split George’s cheeks. “Did you propose while I was gone?”

A sweetly smiling Hollis pulled the third glass toward her. “He did. And I accepted, of course.”

“Spectacular!” George cried.

Their three glasses clinked in clear crystal chimes.

Sveyn sniffed the wine before he drank it. The scent was smoky and floral at the same time. When he drank it and breathed in, his head was filled with the complex mix of flavor and aroma.

“I like this,” he said. “I like this very much.”

Hollis smiled. “You have so many new experiences in front of you. This’s going to be fun.”

George faced her. “When will you marry, do you know?”

“After people get used to the idea of Sveyn’s presence and us dating.” Hollis set her glass down and reached for Sveyn’s free hand. He held hers tightly in return. “And we need to get Sveyn documented.”

Hollis turned to George. “As my very favorite attorney, can you help us with that?”

George stood and gave her a perfect Regency bow. Sveyn

smiled.

I should know.

"It shall be my great pleasure to assist both you and the good gentleman in this worthy endeavor."

Hollis giggled and looked happily at Sveyn. He smiled back.

My heart is wholly hers.

Chapter Eight

When George left, Hollis turned to Sveyn. "It's time for you to take a shower and wash your hair."

He combed his fingers through his tangled shoulder-length locks. If he was truthful, he could smell himself: stale dirt and a hint of underarm sweat. "I agree."

"Good." She looked pensive. "Will you need help?"

He wanted to say no, but he honestly wasn't certain. Lulled by a belly full of pizza, garlic knots, and delicious chardonnay, Sveyn was about to fall off the chair into a dead sleep.

"I think yes," he admitted.

Hollis nodded. "Let's get started. And then we'll get you to bed."

Sveyn rose to his feet and slowly followed Hollis down the hall to her bedroom. Hollis went into the bathroom and turned on the water while he removed his t-shirt and sweat pants.

Getting clean will feel good.

Sveyn walked into the bathroom and stopped. Hollis turned to look at him, her eyes moving over his body from scalp to toes.

"You have old scars," she murmured.

That was an unsettling comment. "Is my body unpleasant to you?"

Her cheeks pinkened. "No, not at all. I just never saw them in our dreams."

Sveyn shrugged a little. "I do not think about them. But I believe the new ones will not be so obvious. The skill in stitching a man back together has vastly improved since my last manifestation."

Hollis looked at the neat incisions on Sveyn's belly and back. "Now that they do all the stitching on the inside you're probably right. Makes showering easy, anyway."

Hollis stuck her hand under the running water. "You can't change the pressure of the spray I'm sorry to say, but this lever adjusts the temperature. Cold to the right, hot to the left."

"Yes. I have seen this."

She withdrew her hand and dried it on a towel. "Adjust it a little at a time. It's pretty sensitive."

"Yes."

Hollis stepped out of his way, but she had an odd look on her face.

"What is on your mind, Hollis?" he asked.

The pink in her cheeks darkened. "I've never seen a flesh and blood man who wasn't circumcised."

Sveyn looked down at his member. He knew what she meant, but circumcision was not common in any era in which he had manifested. Was it now?

"I saw a few Jewish soldiers in the war with Germany, so I know the difference," he said before meeting her eyes. "But you saw me in your dreams."

The pink was now full-on scarlet. "Yes, but it wasn't like it is now. All calm, and everything."

That made Sveyn laugh. "This is true."

Hollis waved toward the steaming shower. "Go on, get in."

Sveyn stepped over the little ledge that kept the water inside the doorless shower. The spray hit his feet first.

Too hot.

He reached through the stream and adjusted the temperature.

Better.

The water hitting his skin as he moved under it was both painful as needles and pleasurable as a hot bath. Sveyn drew a deep breath and stood still, hoping his body would adjust to the new sensation and begin to let go of its over-sensitivity.

"You're too tall."

Sveyn looked at Hollis. "What?"

"You'll have to duck down to get your hair wet and I don't think you should try to. You'll stress the incisions. Hold on."

Hollis left the bathroom and Sveyn returned to his previous pose. He turned slowly, allowing the water to pummel his arms, shoulders, neck, and back. Water streamed over his arse and down his legs.

The heat was heaven in spite of the pain.

He picked up Hollis's soap—lavender scented—and began to wash his body. The slipperiness of the soap mercifully eased the sensation of his hands scrubbing his skin, because scrubbing was required. His last bath was eight days before he was impaled.

Sveyn's non-physical body had no odor, thankfully, nor could it get dirtier. A blessing, considering that the bath was nine-hundred-and-fifty years ago. Give or take.

Sveyn took special care washing his privates, pulling back his foreskin and cleaning the rim. He lathered the soap and continued, cleaning himself front and back. The last thing he wanted was for Hollis to sniff anything unpleasant as he slept beside her.

As the centuries passed, Sveyn noticed that people grew increasingly concerned with cleanliness. Running water and flushing toilets had truly changed the world for the better.

Hollis returned, carrying a stool. "I see you've tried my soap." She giggled a little. "Not the most masculine scent. But I love it."

Sveyn placed the soap back in its dish. "Any scent is better than lye," he observed.

"I suppose." Hollis set the stepstool inside the shower. "Can you sit on this to wash your hair?"

Sveyn used his leg to slide the stool under the water. Then, bracing himself against the shower walls, he lowered himself onto the stool. When the spray hit his scalp it felt like a thousand fingers massaging his scalp.

He closed his eyes and let out a little moan.

"Feels good?" Hollis asked.

Sveyn nodded. "Each minute that passes hurts a little less."

After another minute, he pulled a deep breath and opened his eyes. "What should I use to wash my hair?"

Hollis handed him her shampoo. "Use this first to clean it, and then we'll use conditioner after you rinse the shampoo out."

"Conditioner?"

"Takes out the tangles and keeps your hair from getting dry and flyaway."

Sveyn looked at her, wondering if she was jesting with him. "Keeps my hair from flying away."

"You know—when your hair gets static electricity."

Electricity in my hair?

"And it stands out from your head."

Understanding arrived, along with half-a-dozen questions. Sveyn settled on, "The conditioner stops that from happening?"

"Yes."

"How?"

"I have no clue." She grinned apologetically. "But it does. You'll see."

Sveyn had no recourse but to test her words. He squirted shampoo into his palm and worked it through his hair, using his fingertips to clean his scalp.

Thank God I did not have lice when I transformed.

Once the shampoo was thoroughly rinsed from his hair, Hollis had him turn his back toward her. She took off her jeans and sweater, and stepped inside the shower stall in her bra and panties.

"I'll do this for you. Let me know if I hurt you."

At that moment, with the love of his life in the shower with him, nearly naked, and combing her fingers through his hair,

Sveyn could have been run through again and doubted he would feel it.

The only upsetting factor was the dark red and purple bruise blooming outward above and below her bra. The sign of her life-threatening injury, however, was also the reminder of how Hollis saved him.

"Okay, rinse." Hollis stepped back out of the shower and grabbed a towel.

Sveyn turned around and leaned his head back, under the shower's stream.

After a minute, Hollis said, "Now squeeze out the water."

Sveyn straightened and did as she said.

"Now lean forward."

Hollis wrapped the towel around his hair, then reached in to turn the water off. "Sit up."

He did and she handed him another towel. "You're done. If rubbing hurts, just blot your skin."

The towels were unbelievably soft. "How do they make these tiny loops?"

Hollis laughed. "You ask so many questions about things I never thought about. I don't know. They just do."

Sveyn leaned forward and used his weight to help him stand. He carefully dried his body, trying not to irritate his skin. Then he exited the shower and stood on the cushioned rug.

Hollis smiled up at him. "My turn."

ӜК

Why am I suddenly shy?

"You can hang your towels on that rack." She pointed to the one over the toilet. "I'll use this one."

I mean, in his imagination we've done all sorts of intimate things. In all sorts of interesting places.

Hollis opened a drawer. "Use this comb."

But Sveyn wasn't imaginary anymore; he stood right in front of her now. Six-and-a-half naked feet of muscled masculinity, solid, warm, and drop dead gorgeous.

And he's mine.

Sveyn draped his body towel over the towel rack's bar then unwrapped the towel from his head and hung it there as well.

She'd straighten them later.

He looked at himself in the mirror and lifted the comb to the top of his head. When the comb slid effortlessly through his shoulder-length hair, he stared at her image next to his, his eyes as wide as they could be.

"There are no snarls or knots!"

"I told you." Hollis raised a warning finger. "Don't ask me how. Just enjoy it."

Sveyn continued combing his hair for longer than the task required. "I am amazed."

Hollis moved to the side and turned the shower back on. "I think you're gonna like twenty-first century life."

Sveyn leaned forward, peering into the mirror. "I have some white hairs in my beard."

"I noticed. They appeared about a week ago or so."

His startled glanced jumped to hers. "I changed?"

Hollis nodded. "They showed up when your abilities to taste and smell got stronger. And when your hair started to move."

"I did not notice."

"Do you want to shave?"

Sveyn shook his head and dropped the comb back into the drawer. "No. I want to go to bed."

Hollis left the water running and walked into the bedroom. She pulled the covers back on the side that she didn't sleep on.

"Go on, get in. I'll bring you a bottle of water."

Sveyn followed her and eased himself onto the mattress. When she returned with the water, he was lying on his back and covered to the waist.

Hollis twisted the top off and held the bottle toward Sveyn. "Do you want a drink?"

"No. Thank you."

She set the bottle of the night table. "Are you okay sleeping naked?"

His brow wrinkled. “How else should I sleep?”

Nope. No other way at all. “I, um, don’t want you to get cold.”

“I am fine.” His eyelids drooped. “Go have your shower.”

Hollis didn’t take off her bra and panties until she was behind the mostly closed door of the bathroom. Her relief that Sveyn wasn’t going to see her naked just yet started to relax her.

She stepped under the hot stream and let the water run over her shoulders and back, allowing her relaxation to be completed by its gentle ministrations. She washed with the lavender soap as well, moving her hands gingerly over her bruised chest and cracked breastbone.

If Sveyn was disturbed by the stark discoloration, he didn’t say anything. And it was going to get much uglier before it faded away.

Six weeks was her expected recovery time. Hollis figured that was optimistic.

As she stood under the flowing water, she finally allowed herself to contemplate Sveyn’s shocking marriage proposal. His reason for asking her *before* he accepted her offer to live here touched her deeply.

He was right. Matt never followed through, even when she gave him this disappointing second chance.

In glaring contrast with her ex-boyfriend, Sveyn was a man of deep-seated integrity. He fell in love with her when they had no future, and now that a future was possible he didn’t hesitate to set things right between them.

Hollis said she would marry him without thinking about it because she was so taken by surprise. Now, with a quiet moment to consider the question, she realized that she was glad the ceremony was going to be delayed by Sveyn’s lack of a modern identity.

Hollis would need time to ease the Viking into her life and into her world, at least as far as everyone but Stevie and George was concerned. And while the ruse of Sveyn coming out of the gypsy culture answered a lot of questions, it certainly raised several others.

No one she knew would be happy if she traipsed down to the courthouse on Sveyn's arm and pledged until death do them part right after meeting him. And there was no acceptable way to explain the truth.

Hollis reached for her towel, her mind spinning through other obstacles to their marriage. Would Sveyn adjust to modern life? Would his personality change now that he could interact with everyone around him?

What if he's attracted to another woman?

Women will certainly be attracted to him. Hollis had no doubts about that. The man was spectacular. And her gut told her that the rough warrior edge he had was not going to be tamed by her soft world.

Sveyn would always exude a sense of unpredictability. Maybe even danger. That's who he was.

A real Viking.

Hollis dried off and donned a t-shirt to sleep in. She shut off the bathroom light and climbed into bed by the light of the full moon seeping around her curtains.

The rented condo came furnished with a king-sized bed and until tonight she thought that was a waste. Not now. Sveyn completely filled his half.

The man was sound asleep, and snoring. Hollis smiled in the dark.

I guess that comes with the breathing part.

She slid closer, until her hip touched his forearm.

The snoring stopped momentarily while Sveyn lifted his very warm and heavy palm onto her thigh, then it resumed its languid rhythm.

Hollis sighed as deeply as her injury would allow.

My Viking.

Chapter Nine

Wednesday
January 13

Sveyn was in the bathroom using one of Hollis's razors and her shaving cream to remove his beard. She told him that facial hair was very popular these days, but he insisted.

"I have always wished that I shaved before I was transformed," he said. "And now that I am able to clean my face, I shall do so."

She wasn't worried he would cut himself after he laughed at the tiny blades safely encased in their disposable pink plastic handle.

He looked down at her, amused. "As an historian, you must realize that I always shaved with a knife. A very sharp one."

Hollis put up her hands in surrender. "I'll leave you to it then. I'll go check my email."

Her work inbox was out of control. The exponentially increased requests from ghost hunter types were obviously a result of the *Ghost Myths, Inc.* episode that aired a week ago. Hollis moved all of them to a folder to be dealt with later. Once she informed them that the museum charged two hundred dollars an hour with a four-hour minimum, most of them would disappear anyway.

Hollis clicked a new tab and opened her personal email. The newscast on Sunday evening had alerted the world that she was nearly fatally injured, and everyone she knew in Arizona had sent their good wishes.

Even Tony Samoa, the museum's permanent collections manager, who spent the last nine months deriding her, the new collection, and the wing that was built to house it.

"Good thing we buried the hatchet at Christmas," she said to herself as she typed a quick *thank you* in reply. "Hope you still feel that way when you find out I'm permanent."

Oops.

The contract.

Hollis switched back to her work email and opened Friday's close-of-the-day email from Mr. Benton with her new contract attached. Even though the boss man knew everything that was going on, she thought it would be wise to reply that she actually was accepting the position. She copied Miranda, her curator, and blind-copied Stevie, her registrar, just because.

Send.

Sveyn walked out of the bedroom, clean shaven. And naked.

Hollis sucked an appreciative breath deep enough to hurt.

"How do I look?" he asked. His expression said the question was serious.

"You look amazing…"

"It looks odd to me after all this time." His brow twitched. "Do you like my face this way?"

Hollis chuckled and her pulse sped up a little. "I like all of you this way."

Sveyn looked down at his bare frame. "I should put the clothes on."

Darn. "That's probably a good idea."

He looked at her again. "I need more."

"Clothes? Yes, you do." Hollis bit her lower lip.

"Will you send George again?"

Hollis shook her head. "He doesn't have time. Plus, you

should be able to choose your own." She pointed at her laptop. "I'll take your measurements and we'll order you some clothes online."

A slow smile spread across Sveyn's face. "And they will come here, will they not?"

"Yep." Hollis walked to the junk drawer in the kitchen to get her tape measure. Never mind that it was a metal one.

An inch is an inch.

Sveyn was patient with her while she wrapped the cold metal band around various parts of his battered body and wrote down the results. His hair was soft from the conditioner and he smelled so clean, like the shaving cream.

Good stuff, that.

When she finished, he went into the bedroom to don the sweatpants and t-shirt while she searched the internet for tall men's clothes.

The ring of her phone startled her after being silenced while she was in the hospital. "Hi, Miranda."

"Hi, Hollis. I didn't want to disturb you while you're recovering, but I saw your email so I knew you were thinking about work."

"Oh, no." Hollis slumped in her chair. "What happened?"

"Nothing bad," Miranda assured her. "But interesting."

"Okay…"

"When the *Ghost Myths, Inc.* guys filmed you in the collections storeroom, with the hoard in the background, there was a painting behind you of a young girl."

"In the pink dress?"

"Yes. Well…" Miranda inserted a totally unneeded dramatic pause. "A man named Gerhardt Kunst saw the news story on Sunday night, and he called the museum afterwards and left a message."

Hollis waited. "And?" she prompted when Miranda didn't continue.

"And—he said that painting was his, and he wants it back."

"Was there a bill of sale with the painting?"

Miranda paused. "I don't know."

"All right." Hollis dragged her hand through her curls and took as deep a breath as she could. "Have Tom take pictures of the painting front and back and send them to me. Then have him look around and see if there's any kind of receipt or notation from Ezra about it."

Hollis heard Miranda's keyboard clacking. "I'm on it."

"As soon as I get the pictures I'll do some research."

"Great." More clacking.

"Have you called him back?" Hollis asked.

"I did."

"What'd you tell him?"

"First I told him that painting was under your jurisdiction." The clacking stopped. "Then I reminded him that you had that accident, and then I told him you would call him when you came back to work."

Hollis hadn't thought past today. "Did you say when that was going to be?"

"Not this week."

Hollis nodded even though Miranda couldn't see her. "Okay. That's good. Is there anything else?"

"Nope. Just I'm thrilled beyond words that you're staying."

Hollis smiled. "I am, too."

Ӂ

Sveyn sat with Hollis as she selected clothes for him from a couple of different sites. "You are spending a lot of money."

Hollis finished typing in her credit card security number. "Thanks to you saving my life, I have a lot of money to spend."

She turned her head and looked at him; he felt like he could drown in the blue sea of her eyes. "And if you walk around naked, no one in Phoenix will be safe. Consider it my civic duty."

Sveyn shifted in his seat to ease the piercing ache going straight through his side.

Hollis noticed. "Oh for heaven's sake, take some ibuprofen

already."

She got up and grabbed the little white bottle on the kitchen counter and set it in front of him, next to his water bottle. "I promise it won't make you dizzy. Cross my heart."

Sveyn weighed the possibility against his discomfort. "I will try it once."

"Good. But when you feel better, remember that you won't be healed for at least six weeks," she warned.

He gave her a patient look. "I have been injured before." Another thought popped up. "And the blood doctor says my blood has cells like a baby. Regency."

Hollis appeared stumped. "Regency? What does that mean?"

Sveyn opened the bottle. "How many?"

"Four is prescription strength."

Sveyn took three.

Hollis rolled her eyes. "Tell me about this baby 'regency' blood."

"Babies have regency cells because they grow so fast."

Hollis's confused expression stilled, held, and then washed away. "Regenerative?"

Sveyn felt his cheeks grow warm and realized at that moment that he had no beard to hide behind.

Maybe I will grow it back.

He frowned a little, acting nonchalant. "Yes. That might be the word."

"Because your body is new?" Hollis huffed a laugh. "Well, sort of new."

"I think so."

She capped the ibuprofen and put it back on the counter. "That would be great. Because I go back to work on Tuesday, and you'll be recovering here alone."

Sveyn shook his head. "No, I will go to work with you."

Hollis looked at him like he was crazy. "And do what? You can't hang out in my office anymore. People can see you now, remember?"

No. He forgot.

He had experienced so many years and so many people, and

all the while he could do or say whatever he wanted because he existed outside of their world.

Not any longer.

“You are right. I did forget,” he admitted.

Hollis sat beside him again. “Once you’re well enough I can take you to the museum with me, and you can do training until you get your identification stuff and get on the payroll.”

Sveyn lifted one brow. “What will I do there?”

“Maintenance maybe, but I’d rather have them make you a guard.” Her lips quirked and made him long to kiss them. “Your size works in your favor there.”

That made sense. “Will I work the same time that you do?”

Her eyes narrowed. “I’d have to work on that. Maybe.”

Sveyn felt his belly rumble and he looked at the clock on the microwave. “Will we eat soon?”

Ӝ

Sveyn needed to lie down. He hated that he felt so weak, but there was nothing he could do about it. His body was abused before it transformed, and everything he experienced then impacted his body now that it was recovered.

“Go rest, Sveyn,” Hollis urged. “You need to after all you’ve been through.”

He peered at her, trying to discern her recuperation. “Do you hurt?”

Hollis rested her hand over her heart. “My chest does, obviously. It’ll take weeks to heal.”

“And are you using the air thing?”

She looked guilty. “I’ll do that now.”

“The doctor says you must, or you might become ill,” he chastised.

“I will.” She gave him a rueful smile. “I promise.”

Sveyn walked down the short hallway to the bedroom, refusing to put his hands on the wall for support. His balance was not quite steady, but he knew he only needed to work at it and all would come to rights.

Well, not all.

Not one single element of his existence was the same as it was four days ago. When Hollis's spirit appeared beside him, Sveyn did not think about what he said to her, he just acted on instinct. When he told her not to die, but to go back and take him with her, he did not know if such a thing was even possible.

And the next thing he was aware of was lying on the ground, bleeding, and with every fiber of his body in agony.

I believe I was even more surprised than she.

Now he was here. In this century. Living with Hollis for the rest of his unexpectedly restored and natural life.

Sveyn lay down on the bed and curled on his left side. He hated to admit it, but he was miserable.

Gradually his nerves were calming down. The ibuprofen worked and thankfully he was not dizzy, but he still felt random and painful twinges in his healing core. And if rubbed too much his skin still felt like it was burning. But his lungs no longer stung with every breath, and he was mostly unaware of the beat of his heart.

How odd it was to know that he would never again close his eyes and open them to a new setting and a new time. He would never again manifest to an unsuspecting and startled person, to whom Sveyn would be tethered for as long as he was there.

This century was his last to experience. This city was his home. And Hollis was to be his wife.

Sveyn proposed before he moved in, because that was the right thing to do. And because she was the love of his life, of course.

I will be her husband.

And there was the problem.

Husbands were supposed to protect and care for their families, providing food, shelter, and clothing. That was how Sveyn was born and raised, and it was right.

And yet Sveyn's ability to hunt and fish, clean the carcasses, and cook them over a fire was obviously unsuited for this era and this city. Food here came either packaged in huge stores, or cooked so it was hot and ready to eat.

That is a good thing as I have not seen a single deer or a suitably flowing river anywhere.

As for shelter, homes were now built by construction companies and sold to the people who wanted to live in them. And clothing was premade and purchased from stores—or ordered on the internet.

All that was required was money.

How will I earn enough money to care for Hollis?

And what about children?

Sveyn knew Hollis won her civil lawsuit against Everett Sage and received seven hundred thousand dollars, but Sveyn did not know what that amount of money would buy or how long it would last.

He also knew Hollis loved her job, but when the babies came he wanted her to be able to stay home to care for them. That was still how families operated in his last manifestation.

I will need to get a good job.

One that paid more than guard duty at the museum, of that he was certain.

In spite of Hollis and Stevie's fabrication of himself as a captain of a modern boat, there was nothing in the desert that remotely resembled the ships Sveyn helped build. It appeared that his life's training was useless to him now.

Sveyn rolled onto his back with an irritated sigh and covered his eyes with the pillow.

Father in Heaven, what shall I do?

Chapter Ten

Hollis was resting on the couch and mindlessly watching home improvement shows while she listened to Sveyn snore in the bedroom, when her phone pinged the arrival of email. She swiped the phone to life and saw that the email was from Tom.

And it had attachments.

Hollis got off the sofa and retrieved her laptop from the dining table. Resettling back where she was, she opened the computer and logged into her work email.

Here are the photos you asked for. Let me know if I can do anything to help.

Tom

Hollis downloaded the photos of the painting in question and opened the first one. It was a portrait of a beautiful girl, probably in her mid-teens, who sat perched on a stool. One bare foot was on the ground and the other rested on a rung of the stool, barely visible beneath the hem of her mid-calf skirt.

The girl had auburn hair, which hung past her shoulders in richly colored waves. Her olive-colored eyes had a glint of mischief, and Hollis had the feeling that if she met this girl she would like her.

The girl was wearing a plain pink dress with a belted waist and a white lace collar. Simple, fitted elegance. The stool was in a formal living area of the house, based on the fireplace and sculpted mantel behind her, and the Persian rug on the floor.

Hollis zoomed in to look at the signature: *Benjamin Meyer '38.*

"Nineteen thirty-eight, judging by the clothes. That's a good start." Hollis clicked on the next photo—a close-up of the signature. "Good thinking, Tom."

I told Benton he was right for this job.

Photos number three and four were of the back of the painting, one of the entire back, and the other a close-up of a message. Scrawled in what looked like charcoal were the words *For Wilhelm, B Meyer.*

"Interesting." The signatures were not exact matches, but then signing a painting with an oil brush versus a quick note in charcoal could easily explain the subtle differences.

"Who are you, Benjamin Meyer…" Hollis whispered as she started an internet search. She made a face when she saw the results. "Dang, there are a lot of Ben Meyers out there."

Benjamin Meyer painter.

Hollis scrolled through the first three pages of hits. Nothing.

"Hmm. That's weird. How about, *Benjamin Meyer artist.*"

Still nothing helpful.

"Might as well go all in," she muttered. "Benjamin Meyer painting nineteen-thirty-eight."

What topped the list sent a shock through Hollis's languid day. A link on StolenJewishArt.com listed a painting called *Rachel* by Benjamin Meyer, and dated nineteen-thirty-eight, as Nazi-looted property in Berlin. Unfortunately there was no photo or estimated value, but there was a claim number on the listing and a toll-free contact phone number.

"Well, I'll be." Hollis screen-captured the page for her own reference, then sent the link to Tom with her thank-you email.

Great job, Tom! But don't tell Miranda or Benton about

what I found until I have a chance to do more research. No sense in getting everyone all in an uproar yet. When I come in next week I'll make the calls.

H

ӁK

When Sveyn woke up the sky was already darkening. He stretched gingerly and ran his hand over the tender incision in the front of his body. He was still amazed that it was possible to make the stitches invisible and even more amazed that they would simply dissolve.

He swung his feet to the ground and stood. Hollis appeared at the bedroom door and switched on the light. "Oh good, you're awake."

"I am. Is there something you needed?"

She shook her head and walked to the room. "I just had an interesting thing happen with Ezra's hoard."

Sveyn walked carefully around the bed and toward the bathroom. "Tell me."

Hollis stayed in her room while Sveyn relieved himself. "It turns out that one of the paintings in his collection was stolen from a Jewish painter in Berlin."

Sveyn flushed and stepped to the sink to wash his hands. "Why was it stolen?"

"The Nazis stole everything the Jews had, especially if it had any value."

Yes. I remember this now. "Is the painting valuable?"

"Don't know yet."

Sveyn stopped in the doorway and looked down into Hollis's beautiful blue eyes. "I love you."

"I love you, too." Her smile faded. "What's wrong?"

Sveyn hesitated, wondering how honest he should be. "I am worried about earning enough money to take care of you."

Hollis flipped her hand. "I can take care of myself. Don't worry about that."

"But I will be your husband," he said slowly. "It will be my duty to protect you and provide for you."

"Sveyn—this is the twenty-first century. We aren't concerned about who makes the money anymore."

Sveyn wagged his head. "No. When we have children, I want to be able to provide for my family."

Hollis's eyes widened at the mention of offspring. "How many children?"

"I do not know. I never considered being a father since Linge." He thought back to his previous manifestations and what he saw in those bedrooms. "There are ways to prevent conception, if that is what worries you."

Hollis smiled. "Yes, there are. And much better ones than you ever learned about."

That was surprising—preventing pregnancy had not changed for as long as he could remember. "Better condoms?"

She laughed now. "Come on. We'll do some research on the internet and I'll show you."

Sveyn followed her out of the bedroom. "Can we eat first? I am starving."

Ӝ

Hollis tamped down the panic that surged through her when Sveyn mentioned children. It's not that she didn't want any—it's that she was still in the *let's make sure we're compatible now that you have a body* stage.

She loved the Sveyn she knew, that wasn't the issue; but this new Sveyn was a big adjustment. Having the former Viking as a flesh-and-blood roommate was completely different than having an apparition who never ate or slept.

This old-fashioned view of women was probably just the first of many conflicts they would have to overcome as they blended viewpoints forged a millennium apart.

Hopefully they would be successful.

After Sveyn's enlightening and humorous lesson on modern-day birth control, Hollis ordered Chinese for dinner.

Sveyn sat at the table tasting everything and enjoying his second glass of chardonnay. He wasn't very talkative, which was unusual. Something was on his mind.

Hollis reached out and laid her hand over his, glad that urge was finally possible to fulfill. "What's on your mind, Sveyn?"

His eyes met hers, his expression drawn. "You say I will work at the museum?"

"Yes. Probably as a guard." She tilted her head. "Is that acceptable to you?"

"How much money will I make?"

Hollis sucked a shallow breath. Sveyn was still worried about providing for her.

Of course he was.

He is a man of honor.

The sharp ache in her chest reminded her it was time to blow in the plastic thing. "I believe that's an hourly position,"

"This means I am paid for each hour?" Sveyn clarified. "Not like you."

"Right. I'm on salary, so I get paid the same amount twice a month, even if I work extra hours, or if there are days I don't work."

"How much money will I be paid for each hour?" he asked.

"I'm not sure," she added truthfully.

"Would it be enough to buy a house?" He was really pushing the point now.

As much as Hollis wanted him to let it go for the time being, the strength of his convictions—a trait he displayed from the beginning—always impressed her. And the Viking was stubborn. There was no point in trying to deflect him because she wasn't going to succeed.

"No," she admitted. "I don't think so."

Sveyn nodded like that was the answer he expected. "And so I will need another job."

This was going to be moment of truth, and Hollis braced herself. "Sveyn, you don't have any training or skills. Or maybe I should say, there isn't a use for the skills you do have."

"I could work at the Renaissance Faire," he suggested. "I could train men to be careful where they throw their hammers."

Hollis smiled at that. "That would be helpful—and possible. But the Faire is only in Arizona for two-and-a-half months."

His expression sobered. "I did not know this."

"It's too late for this year. Maybe you could do that next year," she offered. "We could look into it."

"Perhaps. But that does not help me now." Sveyn combed his fingers through his hair.

Hollis noticed the bulge of his biceps when he bent his arms and another idea occurred to her. It was unusual, but… "When I first saw you, I thought you were a model, remember?"

His hands dropped to his lap. "Yes."

"Maybe you could actually be one."

Sveyn looked skeptical. "What does a model do?"

"They get paid to be in catalogs, advertisements, or on anything really." This idea was showing merit. After all, Sveyn was tall, trim, and gorgeous. "You get paid by the hour to be photographed wearing or doing whatever it is that the company is promoting. Sometimes you get paid to appear in public as their representative."

He leaned forward. "Does this pay more for an hour than being a guard?"

"Yeah—a *ton* more. Like hundreds of dollars an hour to start. But you'd work less hours, of course." Hollis leaned forward as well. "You could probably do both. Work at the museum, and then take modeling jobs around that schedule."

Sveyn's brow wrinkled. "Are you certain someone will want to take my picture?"

"Oh, yes." Hollis sighed. "I've told you before that you are a very handsome man. And you're tall. Nicely built. And your long hair gives you a great look."

Sveyn ran his fingers through his hair again, looking a little self-conscious. "How do I start this modeling?"

"You have to find a modeling agency and sign a contract with them. Then they get a percentage of your pay in exchange for finding you jobs." Hollis reached for her laptop. "If you're finished eating, we could look now."

Sveyn nodded and scooted his chair closer. "How much percentage?"

"Fifteen or twenty, I think." Hollis typed in *Phoenix modeling agency* and hit enter. "The key is to find a legitimate agency, which is one that doesn't require you to pay them for classes or whatever."

While Sveyn looked over her shoulder, Hollis clicked on several websites. Together, they narrowed his options to three that looked promising.

"This one has an open call every Thursday. You should start there." Hollis tapped the screen. "And it's close."

Sveyn winced. "Tomorrow?"

"No—wait a couple weeks until you're more recovered. And hopefully by then, George will have made you legal. You'll need that paperwork to take any job," she reminded him.

"Yes." Sveyn smiled. "I will do this."

"Good." Another thought occurred to her. "If you're going to get a job, you're going to need a phone. And an email address."

His brow lifted. "Will my phone be smart like yours?"

Hollis nodded. "There is no reason for it not to be. You're smart enough to use it."

"And you must show me how to use your computer," he said.

Sveyn's expression was finally eager and hopeful and it warmed her heart to see his spark returning. "Let's start now. I'll show you how to create your email address, and then I'll have you send me an email."

Hollis closed out of the internet and slid her laptop in front of Sveyn "This screen is called the desktop. Start by moving the cursor—which is the arrow—over the icon—picture—of the program you want to open."

"Here?" Sveyn swirled his index finger over the mousepad in the laptop. "Which icon?"

"The internet."

He moved the arrow there. "Now what?"

"Click—which means push until it makes a noise—on the

left button here."

He did. The Google homepage filled the screen. "That is easy."

"Yep. Now let's create your email."

Hollis walked Sveyn through each step and created his account under his actual name. They had to add an underscore between Sveyn and Hansen because he wasn't the first man with that name to want an account.

"There is another Sveyn Hansen?" He shook his head. "Someone else has my name?"

Hollis chuckled. "There are well over three hundred million people in this country now. And not that many names."

"Hmph."

"Now, let's have you send me an email."

Sveyn had never typed anything before, so he employed the index finger hunt-and-peck method. "Why are the letters not in order?" he grumbled.

"Because when they first created typewriters—you know what those are?"

He nodded. "War with Germany."

"Right." Hollis kept forgetting that Sveyn's last manifestation was in the nineteen-forties, so he was familiar with the original form of much of today's technology.

She laid her hands over the keyboard in home position. "Well, the ladies could type so fast that they kept jamming the keys. So the most commonly used letters, like E and O, were put where they would be hit by the weakest fingers on our hands."

Hollis moved her fingers to demonstrate. "That slowed them down enough that they weren't always getting the keys stuck."

"But this is no longer a problem, because nothing on this can get stuck," Sveyn pointed out. "So why do they not change it?"

Hollis shrugged one shoulder, careful not to tug at her cracked breastbone. "People are creatures of habit. And the transition from typewriters to computer keyboards took a couple decades to become universal."

Sveyn grunted again. "I am finished."

Hollis pointed to the send button. "Click there."

Her phone pinged an incoming email. She opened the Gmail app and then opened Sveyn's message. Smiling, she held it up for him to see.

"And I love you, too." She kissed his cheek. "Now I'll email you back."

Sveyn waited, opened the email, and read it out loud, "You are going to do well in this century. I am sure of it." He faced her. "Thank you."

I could drown in those eyes.

If that sultry look transferred to the print page, Sveyn would become a supermodel. "I'm glad I can help you."

"I do have one more question…"

"What?"

He laid his hands over the laptop's keyboard. "When you go back to work, can you leave this here for me?"

Chapter Eleven

Tuesday
January 19

Hollis drove into the employee parking lot at the Arizona History and Cultural Center for the first time since the accident at the Renaissance Faire. Stevie had come over on Friday and drove both her and Sveyn to the doctor for their follow-up appointments.

Hollis was cleared to drive as long as she didn't wear the seatbelt across her chest for a few more weeks. Sveyn, on the other hand, surprised the doctor with how well he was healing.

"I told you," he whispered as they left the office. "Regency blood."

Hollis laughed at his self-deprecating joke.

And the laptop which she ordered for him on Wednesday was waiting on her doorstep when they returned.

Hollis and Sveyn spent the weekend huddled together on the couch, eating delivery food and exploring the world of modern technology. By the time she left the house this morning, she was very confident that she had created a monster.

Stevie laughed when Hollis told her about the week with Sveyn. "That's hilarious. But I'm glad he's adjusting to technology."

Hollis nodded and added, "Next I need to add him to my cell plan and get him a phone."

"Who are you adding to your cell plan?" Miranda asked as she walked into the staff lounge.

Oops.

"Um, Sveyn Hansen."

Miranda frowned at her. "The gypsy? Why would you do that?"

Hollis glanced at Stevie who was sipping from her oversized coffee cup and staring at the floor.

No help there.

"Until George gets his situation straightened out, he can't set up anything on his own. And until we can hire him as a guard—" might as well get that suggestion out there now "—he has no income. But he can't get a job without a phone."

Miranda poured herself a cup of the always-strong coffee. "You're right, I guess," she admitted, her concern still clear.

"And it's my account," Hollis continued, building her case. "So I can shut him off if I need to."

Miranda added five half-and-half creamers to her cup. "What about the phone itself? Just a flip phone?"

Hollis shook her head. "I'll give him mine, which is paid for, and I'll take my upgrade." That's actually a great idea.

Glad I thought of it.

"That way I know the phones features and can teach him."

"I suppose that makes sense." Miranda took a sip of coffee. "So where is he living?"

Ӝ

Hollis sat in the chair in front of Miranda's desk and listened to her boss's harangue about how stupid she was being, putting her life and livelihood at risk by inviting a stranger—and a gypsy at that—into her home as a single defenseless woman still recovering from a nearly fatal injury.

Not only that, but Sveyn had sent her seventeen emails since she left the house.

Thank God he can't text yet.

Her phone pinged.

Make that eighteen.

It was time to take control of this situation and change the subject, so she could get away and deal with the other one. "The painting is stolen Jewish artwork."

Miranda stopped her diatribe and stared at Hollis. "Which painting?"

"The one the guy called about."

The tall curator dropped heavily into her chair. "Are you sure?"

"Yep." Hollis explained how she searched for the artist and found the listing. "So now I have to call the guy and tell him he can't have it back."

Miranda wagged her head. "Good luck. That's not going to go over well at all."

Hollis stood. "Then I better get to it."

ӜК

Hollis dialed the number she was given for a Gerhardt Kunst, the supposed owner of the painting.

I wonder if he's related to the Nazi who stole it.

"Hello?" The voice crackled with age but was still strong.

"Mr. Kunst? This is Hollis McKenna from the Arizona History and Cultural Center."

"Hello, Ms. McKenna," he said politely. "I have been waiting for your call."

"I'm afraid I don't have good news for you, sir," she began. "Did you know that painting was stolen?"

"Stolen? No. That's not possible."

"I'm afraid it is. It's listed on the site StolenJewishArt.com."

"It might be listed, but that listing is inaccurate." He cleared his throat. "If you look at the back of the painting, there is an inscription."

Hollis startled. How did he know that? "What does the inscription say?"

"It's good that you are testing me." He cleared his throat again. "It says *For Wilhelm, B Meyer*."

Well that was certainly compelling. "Forgive me, sir, but how do you know that?"

"Because Wilhelm Kunst was my father."

Ӝ

Three hours later, an older man with a shock of pure white hair and clear brown eyes was sitting across from Hollis.

"This is my youngest daughter, Amelia Kunst," he introduced the thirty-something blonde who took the seat beside him.

Hollis shook her hand. "Thank you both for coming in."

"He thanks you for finding the painting," Amelia said. "We both do, actually."

"Let's not get ahead of ourselves," Hollis warned. "There is a claim on the painting which legally cannot be ignored."

"But it's wrong," Gerhardt insisted. "That painting was a gift."

Hollis folded her hands on her desk top and kept her tone encouraging. "Why don't you start from the beginning, Mr. Kunst. Tell me the whole story."

Gerhardt settled back in his chair. "My father, Wilhelm Kunst, was born in Berlin in nineteen-twenty-one, after my grandfather returned from the Great War."

"World War One," Hollis said.

"It was not called that at the time," Gerhardt corrected.

Hollis smiled her acknowledgement. "Go on."

"When he was seventeen he was in love with the girl next

door, Rachel Meyer."

Hence the name of the painting.

Gerhardt's expression softened. "She was sixteen. They were so young."

Hollis did the math. "Rachel Meyer? In nineteen-thirty-eight in Berlin?"

Gerhardt nodded. "Yes, she was Jewish. You can see the difficulty."

Totally. "Go on."

"Her father, Benjamin Meyer, spent many years as an art restorer for the Neues Museum in Berlin. But in his lifetime, he only painted one original painting."

"The portrait of his daughter, Rachel."

"Yes." Gerhardt cleared his throat; Hollis wondered if it was a habit, or if the man had some sort of condition. "And it hung in their drawing room."

"Would you like some water?" she asked him.

"No. Thank you."

Hollis glanced at Amelia, but the silent daughter didn't seem concerned. "So how did you get the painting, Mr. Kunst?"

Gerhardt looked down at his gnarled hands. "One night, the Meyer family simply disappeared."

Hollis felt the sting of tears; this man in front of her was just one generation removed from the Holocaust. "Your father must have been devastated."

"He was." Another throat clearing. "He went into the Meyer's house and it was completely destroyed. Everything of value was gone."

"But the painting was still there?"

Gerhardt nodded. "They tossed it into the fireplace, because who would want a portrait of some filthy Jew girl, painted by an unimportant museum employee?" He lifted his eyes to hers. "Thank God it was summer and there was no fire."

"Your father wanted it," Hollis whispered, totally captivated by the story. "Because he loved Rachel."

"With all of his heart." Gerhardt spread his slightly-trembling hands. "So imagine his surprise when he turned the painting over and saw the inscription."

"Benjamin must have known what was coming." That thought pushed a tear down her cheek. She grabbed a tissue. "I'm sorry."

"No." Gerhardt dropped one hand and pointed at her with the other. "Never, *ever*, be sorry."

Hollis blew her nose and waved for Gerhardt to continue.

"When my father returned to his own house with the painting, my grandfather told him to pack a single suitcase. 'We are leaving Germany tonight,' he said."

"And they did? And the painting fit in his bag?"

"Yes."

"How did the painting end up in Arizona?"

Gerhardt shifted in his chair as the story shifted to his own. "My father moved to Arizona after the second World War. He'd had his fill of cold weather when he fought in Europe. He settled in Mesa. I was born there in nineteen-forty-six."

Hollis smiled. "The first baby-boomer."

"Yes." He turned to Amelia. "Show her the picture."

Amelia opened her purse and handed Hollis a four-inch square, glossy, black-and-white photo with white ruffle-cut edges. The year nineteen-forty-six was stamped in the white border.

The happy couple in the picture sat on a couch. The woman was holding a tiny, blanket-wrapped infant.

And the portrait of Rachel hung over her head.

"I am glad that my grandfather wasn't good at aiming the camera or the painting might have been cut off." Gerhardt gestured toward the photo. "As you can see, the painting has been in my family since Benjamin made it a gift."

Hollis nodded; the man had a very strong case. "So how did Ezra Kensington end up with it?"

"Unfortunately, my father Wilhelm died of a stroke in nineteen-ninety-nine. I was traveling through Germany at the time, searching for any surviving family members." Gerhardt's expression turned sour.

Hollis waited in silent expectation.

"My younger sister, whose life was always a mess, and was always short of money, immediately held an estate sale."

Hollis straightened, horrified. "No…"

Gerhardt nodded. "She cleared out the entire house before she told me. By the time I was able to return, the painting was gone."

"That's terrible." *It really, really was.*

The older man managed a tremulous smile. "But when I saw you and the painting on the news, I was more surprised and relieved than you can imagine."

"Ezra Kensington must have bought it at the estate sale," Hollis guessed.

"We assume so, but all sales were in cash and untraceable."

"God bless Ezra and his obsessive collecting," Hollis murmured. "If he hadn't willed all of his hoard to the museum, the painting would have been lost to you forever."

Gerhardt relaxed then. "I so glad to hear you say that."

Hollis titled her head. "Say what?"

"That I have provenance over that painting."

Chapter Twelve

"But he doesn't necessarily have provenance," Hollis said to Sveyn after she related the story.

She had talked for so long that he had finished his deli-made dinner of poached salmon and something called broccolini—all drenched in delicious garlic butter.

"We still have to pursue the claim before we can release it to him."

"I looked that up today," he managed to slip his words into her narrative. "The claims against the Nazis are very strong."

Hollis lowered her fork, the chunk of salmon untouched. "Judging by the number of emails you sent me, you looked everything up today."

"Yes." His eyes widened. "The internet is so interesting. Who put it together?"

"Al Gore."

Sveyn was impressed. "He must have been a very smart man."

"Let's go with that." Hollis ate the salmon and spoke with

her mouth full. "I'm giving you my phone."

That was surprising. "What will you use?"

"I got a new one." She stabbed a forkful of broccolini. "That way, if something happens to it—"

"You do not trust me?" Sveyn interrupted, offended by the implication.

"I trust you, yes, of course," Hollis stated. "But as with any new habit, sometimes we forget. And my phone is paid for, so there's no contract issue."

Sveyn didn't understand all the words of that sentence, but Hollis seemed certain of her stance. This was not a battle that needed fighting, so he let it go.

"So now you have your own phone number. You need to memorize it." She waved a hand toward her purse. "I already programmed my number and the museum number into it and set them on speed dial."

"Speed dial?"

How quickly do people in this century need to speak to each other?

"If you press the two and hold it, the phone will automatically dial my number," Hollis explained. "And if you press and hold three, it calls the museum."

"Ah. I see." That *was* easier.

And easier seemed to define the goals of the current society.

"How are you feeling?" she asked.

"Good. I am good." Sveyn grinned. "No ibuprofen since yesterday morning."

Hollis peered at him. "No pain?"

"Tender. Not pain."

"Good." Hollis's new phone rang and she dug it out of her purse. "Hello, George."

Sveyn's attention focused on trying to hear both halves of the conversation.

Hollis glanced at him. "Hold on, say that again on speaker."

George's voice sounded better on this phone, Sveyn noticed. "I said that I climbed seven levels up in the Department of Records today until I found someone who could handle Sveyn's situation."

"What did they say?" Sveyn asked.

"They said we have to do a fingerprint check and bring back a clean and certified record," George said. "In other words, prove that he isn't trying to hide from some crime elsewhere in the country by creating a new identity."

"How long will that take?" Hollis asked.

"With the rollout of unified databases last year, we could get an answer in twenty-four hours."

Sveyn looked at Hollis, stunned. "That is fast."

George laughed. "I said *could*—I'd bet on a week at the soonest."

"That's fine," Hollis said. "He can't work yet anyway."

"Sveyn, I'll pick you up tomorrow at ten and take you to the police department to get fingerprinted."

"Thank you, George."

"Maybe after that we could score a couple of hot lunch dates at the museum."

Hollis found Sveyn's blank expression quite funny. "I'll explain that sentence to him when we hang up," she told George. "And thanks for helping us out on this."

"It's not every day you witness an apparition brought to life," he replied. "See you tomorrow."

Sveyn looked at Hollis as she set her new phone—which looked quite a bit like her old one—on the table.

"I must assume that scoring hot dates for the midday meal has nothing to do with cutting slits into the fruit of a palm tree."

"That's really funny!" Hollis grinned. "But no. Scoring is like winning—remember the football games on television?"

Sveyn nodded.

"And in this case, hot means sexy."

The light dawned. "Winning sexy dates—he means with you and Stevie. For lunch."

"Yes."

Sveyn nodded. "I will wear my new clothes." He rubbed his prickly chin. "And I will shave again."

Hollis looked around as she carried her now-empty plate to

the sink. "Was there any mail today?"

Sveyn did the same. "Yes. I put it beside the bed."

Hollis disappeared into the bedroom while Sveyn poured the last bit of chardonnay into his glass. She returned with the stack of various envelopes.

"Most of this is junk." Hollis opened the lid of the trash can and tossed all but one envelope inside. "This one is from the hospital. I hope it's not a bill."

"Will you give me my phone?" Sveyn asked.

Hollis stuck her hand into her purse, pulled out the phone he was familiar with and handed it to him before she opened the hospital's letter.

Sveyn considered the sparkly pink covering. "Does this come off?"

Hollis looked up from the paper. "Yeah—give it to me."

Sveyn did and she peeled the flexible covering away from the phone, exposing a black phone underneath. "They only had black that day and I couldn't wait for a white one. So I covered it."

Sveyn was pleased to see the dark and sober color of the actual phone. "This is good."

Hollis went back to reading. "Huh."

"What is it?"

"They don't miss a trick." She looked into his eyes. "Seems my blood type is the universal donor. They are encouraging me to donate blood and as often as I can."

"What is blood type?"

"There are different factors in our blood, so if we need a transfusion we need to get blood that has the same factors."

Interesting. He knew about transfusions from the war. "What is universal donor?"

Hollis shrugged. "I guess they can use my blood for anybody." She looked again. "It's O-negative."

I wonder if mine is the same. "Have you donated your blood before?"

"No." She wrinkled her nose. "Not a fan of big needles."

Wednesday
January 20

Hollis left for work with Sveyn sitting at his laptop. Before she walked out she reminded him that he could put a dozen thoughts into one email, not one thought each into dozens. She also left him her credit card so that he could order food when he got hungry.

"Food only, please," she said. "No big purchases until we talk about it."

"There is nothing I am in need of," he replied and winked. "With the exception of modern cooking lessons, perhaps."

Hollis grinned; having someone cook for her would be grand. "Look on YouTube."

As Sveyn's physical discomfort eased, his mood lifted in proportion. He had only been in his body for eleven days and was doing remarkably well, considering.

Hollis walked into the staff lounge.

"I got a marketing letter from the hospital yesterday," she said to Stevie and Miranda, who were pouring their morning energy. "Apparently my blood type makes me the universal donor, and they are encouraging me to donate. Often."

Miranda looked concerned. "O-negative?"

That took Hollis by surprise. "Yes. How did you know?"

"I'm a regular blood donor." Miranda turned away from the coffee pot and leaned back against the counter. "Depending on whom you marry, having children might present some risks."

"What kind of risks?" Stevie asked.

"If the mother is negative but the father is positive, the child is likely to be positive as well," Miranda explained. "During birth, if the baby's blood mixes with the mother's, then the mother forms antibodies against the negative blood."

Hollis was stunned. "Does the mother get sick?"

"I don't think so." Miranda gave Hollis a compassionate look. "But another positive fetus could be attacked by the mother and expelled."

"Miscarriage," Stevie murmured.

Miranda nodded. "And the antibodies build with each exposure."

"I'm an only child," Hollis blurted, her eyes widening. "I always wondered why my parents didn't have more."

"Did you ask your mom?" Stevie asked.

Hollis nodded, trying to pull up the memory. "When I was little. She gave me some vague answer about God giving them all their children wrapped in one perfect little girl."

"I'm sorry," Miranda said. "But she does clearly love you."

"And there were some hospital trips, I remember." Hollis closed her eyes to entice the memories. "She had a hysterectomy when I was twelve."

Stevie frowned a little. "I'm surprised she didn't say anything to you."

"Me, too." Hollis pondered that a moment. "She probably would have if I married Matt. Or got pregnant."

"My guess is your mom is RH positive and your dad is RH negative." Miranda pointed with her coffee cup. "You might want to call and ask."

Ӝ

George knocked on the door and Sveyn let him in. "Nice clothes," the lawyer said.

Sveyn looked down at his jeans, sweater, and athletic shoes. "Hollis ordered them on the internet."

"She got you talls, then." George smiled. "And she has good taste."

Sveyn touched his pocket to be sure he had the condo key. "Do I need anything?"

"No. I have the order from the Department of Records excusing you from having to provide any identification."

"Then I will lock the door."

The men stepped outside and Sveyn used the little key to turn the little lock. "In my time, keys and locks were massive things."

George looked at him as if in awe. “I can’t imagine all that you have seen, Sveyn.”

Sveyn grinned. “I will tell you. But only one story at a time. Nine hundred and fifty years is a long time.”

The downtown Phoenix police station was a massive and imposing concrete structure. Both uniformed officers and people in normal clothing streamed in and out. George led Sveyn to the area where the fingerprinting for non-criminals was done.

“There are a lot of occupations which require fingerprint clearance and background checks,” George explained in the car. “So they set up a special area and certain hours for those people to come in.”

Sveyn stared at his fingertips. “I wonder if mine will be different.”

George glanced at him. “It’ll be interesting to find out.”

When Sveyn was next, George filled out the paperwork for him. “When you’re ready, you’ll have to learn how to write English,” he said casually. “I know you can read, so that’s the first step.”

Sveyn nodded. “I will ask Hollis to show me. But I can use the laptop keyboard.”

George looked up at him. “Can you?”

“Yes.” He chuckled. “I asked her to leave her laptop with me when she went to work, and instead she ordered one for me.”

“You have your own laptop?”

“And email.” Sveyn reached into his back pocket and pulled out his latest treasure. “And phone.”

“I’m impressed.” George handed the paperwork to the clerk.

She glanced over it and then gave Sveyn what must be described as an appreciative head-to-toe gaze. “Over here, Mr. Hansen.”

Sveyn relaxed his hands as the woman efficiently rolled each finger over a small pad and watched as their grooves and swirls appeared on a screen.

“Okay, you’re done.” She tapped several keys in quick succession. “And now you’re in the database.”

She looked up at George. “You’ll be sent the results in about seventy-two hours, Counselor."

"Thank you." George looked up at Sveyn. "Shall we go collect our lunch dates?"

As the men left the building and walked toward George's car, Sveyn said, "You are helping me, and I can help you."

"Oh?" George looked skeptical. "How's that?"

"I know you are interested in the Regency period in England," he said. "And Jane Austin in particular."

George stopped walking. "What do you know?"

"Everything." Sveyn stopped walking as well and turned back to face the clearly gobsmacked attorney. "I manifested in southern England in the early nineteenth century."

"Did you meet Jane?"

"No, I do not believe so. But it seems that I was near where she was."

"Clothing? Food?" George stepped closer. "Entertainment?"

Sveyn laughed. "Yes. All of that. I will make you the most knowledgeable man in the Jane Austin Society."

Chapter Thirteen

"Hi, Mom," Hollis said into her phone. "How are you?"

"Hi, sweetie. I'm afraid I can't talk long. Our movie's about to start."

Hollis was actually glad—now she could ask her question and run. "That's okay. I just have a quick question. What's your blood type?"

Her mom hesitated before she answered the admittedly odd question. "A-positive. Why?"

Hollis noticed, and instinctively hedged her next question. "The hospital sent me a letter saying that I have type O and they want me to donate. I was just curious."

"Ah." Her mom sounded relieved. "Your dad has O-positive. It's the most common type. He's *always* getting calls from the blood banks."

Hollis's hands began to shake. She tried to keep her voice light as she changed the subject. "So what movie are you seeing?"

"The new Sandra Bullock one. I have to go, honey. The

lights are dimming."

"Okay. Love you, Mom. Let me know how the movie was."

Hollis stared at her phone, too stunned to hang up. The phone disconnected the call when her mom did.

She had done some brief research on blood types after her discussion with Miranda and Stevie, and had learned one absolute fact.

The chances of two positive-type parents having a child with the negative factor was less than one percent. Add in her red hair, and the obvious conclusion was shattering.

Ӂ

Something was wrong with Hollis. Sveyn noticed the minute he saw her, and though she was putting on a brave face he was not fooled.

"Come meet Miranda," she said. "I told her you were staying with me and I want her to see that you're not a threat."

Hollis left her office obviously expecting Sveyn to follow.

"I'm going to grab Stevie," George said. "We'll catch up."

Sveyn wanted to pull Hollis aside and ask her what had occurred, but her actions screamed that she did not wish to speak of it. Not as yet, anyway.

Hollis knocked on the open door and strode into her boss's office. "Miranda, this is Sveyn Hansen, my ex-gypsy roommate. I wanted you to meet him so you can stop worrying about me."

Miranda stood and her smile slowly fell from her face. "Have we met before?"

Sveyn shook his head. "No, we have not. I certainly would remember such a beautiful woman."

Her eyes narrowed and she ignored the compliment. "But you look so familiar…"

"Maybe you saw him when he came to apply for the job?" Hollis suggested the impossible scenario.

"No. That's not it."

"I'm sure you'll think of it. In the meantime, we're going to lunch with Stevie and George," Hollis deflected. "George just took Sveyn to get a fingerprint clearance so he can start getting documented."

"Oh. That's nice." Miranda's confused stare remained unmoved. "How are you recovering?"

Sveyn touched his side. "Very well. Thank you."

"He should be well enough to start work as a guard as soon as his paperwork is completed." Hollis turned to Sveyn. "Shall we go?"

Sveyn gave Miranda a small bow, careful not to strain his wounds. "It was my pleasure to meet you."

"Mine too."

Hollis looped her arm through his and led him out. They met Stevie and George in the hallway.

"Where are we going?" Stevie asked.

"I'm tired of Mexican," Hollis said flatly. "Let's get burgers."

Ӝ

Hollis looked at the strong-jawed man sitting beside her, surprised again not to see a beard. Even though current man-styles involved facial hair, Sveyn looked very good clean-jawed.

She wished they were alone so she could talk to him about what she learned, but that would have to wait until tonight.

She considered telling Stevie, but changed her mind. The information that her parents could not *be* her parents was too new, too raw. She wanted to curl up in Sveyn's arms—now that she could—and cry.

"So you need to teach me to write English."

Hollis startled. She hadn't been paying attention to the conversation. "What? Oh. Sure."

"You can get some of those primary workbooks where you trace the letters," Stevie suggested. "There's a couple of teacher supply stores not too far from ASU."

Hollis nodded. "Yes. Good idea."

"I was impressed that Sveyn is surfing the web on his new laptop," George said. "And that he has email and a smartphone."

"Really?" Stevie grinned at the Viking. "Are you on Facebook?"

"No!" Hollis blurted. "That can wait. Maybe forever."

Sveyn turned to her. "What is Facebook?"

"I'll show you later." Hollis set her cheeseburger down. "I guess I'm not as hungry as I thought."

Sveyn rubbed her back. "Does your chest hurt?"

Hollis looked into his eyes and realized that he knew something was wrong and he was giving her a way out.

"Yes," she accepted his excuse. "It does."

Stevie waved for their waitress. "We need to-go boxes."

Hollis shook her head, touched by her friend's kindness. "We can stay until you finish."

"I have to drop Sveyn off and get back to my office anyway," George said. He handed the waitress with the boxes his credit card. "I'll get lunch."

ӜК

Back at the museum, a suspicious Miranda was waiting for Hollis. "I figured it out."

Hollis dropped her purse in her desk drawer. "What?"

"I figured out where I've seen Sveyn before."

Oh crap. "Where?"

Miranda closed Hollis's door then approached her desk. "He looks like your ghost."

Crap crap crap.

Where should she go with this?

Be as truthful as you can.

"Now that you mention it, I guess he really does," she admitted. "How odd."

Miranda leaned on Hollis's desk. "I don't think it's odd. And I don't think it's a coincidence."

Hollis huffed a breath against the painful tightening in her chest. "What do you mean?"

Miranda sank into the chair that was always on the other side of Hollis's desk. Her expression was a blend of supplication and fear. "If I ask you something weird, would you be honest with me?"

Here it comes.

"Yes." She owed Miranda that much.

"Is Sveyn your angel, ghost, or whatever, come to life?" Miranda winced. "I *do* know that sounds crazy, but…" She left the sentence hanging,

"Yes." Hollis swallowed, her throat gone dry. "He is."

Miranda's jaw fell slack and she leaned back in the chair. "How in the *hell?*"

"Hell has nothing to do with it, I assure you." Hollis tried to smile at her boss but only succeeded in grimacing. "It's a long story."

"I don't believe it." Miranda's face paled, then flushed. "Tell me everything—and don't leave anything out."

Telling Miranda Sveyn's story was a welcome distraction from her other concern. Hollis started at the beginning and explained everything, including her out-of-body experience.

"And then there he was?" Miranda's tone sounded as incredulous as the story. "Lying on the ground beside you?"

Hollis nodded. "And bleeding and bellowing."

Miranda sat silent, processing what Hollis told her. "This is unbelievable."

"I know."

"But the proof just walked into my office."

"Yep."

The curator's gaze cut to hers. "Who knows?"

"Stevie was first. She actually saw him and heard him when he was gaining his senses back." Hollis looked apologetic. "I didn't know then that he was beginning to get his body back. That those were the first steps."

"If Stevie knew, did George know?"

"I told them both the whole story that night we watched the *Ghost Myths, Inc.* show."

Miranda nodded. "And George believed Stevie, of course."

"That's why George was so eager to help Sveyn get what he needs to be part of the twenty-first century."

Miranda's mouth twisted. "He never was a gypsy, was he?"

"No," Hollis admitted. "But that was the only believable excuse as to why he's so far off the grid."

Miranda remained in the chair, but Hollis was at the end of her composure. "I'm not feeling well," she said. "My chest hurts so I'm going home to rest."

"Yes. Go ahead." Miranda stood. "Take a pill and take a nap." She walked to the door, opened it, and left Hollis's office without looking back.

Hollis grabbed her purse and her jacket and locked up. She walked past Stevie's office and stuck her head in.

"Miranda knows about Sveyn now. And I'm going home."

Ӝ

Sveyn looked up from the laptop when he heard the front door being unlocked earlier than usual. "Hollis?"

"Yeah." She stepped through the door and closed it with her backside before dropping her purse and briefcase on the carpet.

Sveyn stood. "What is wrong?"

When he saw the corners of her mouth tug downward, he held out his arms. Hollis ran into his embrace and grabbed onto him as if her life depended on his strength. Sveyn held her close, careful of her battered chest, and rubbed her back.

"Let it out," he murmured into her sweet-smelling red curls.

She cried harder, then, and Sveyn grew concerned. He did not dare ask her to speak before she was ready, but whatever had occurred seemed to shake her to her core.

Even more than the kidnapping.

Sveyn decided to push himself because the situation called for it. He reached down and lifted Hollis, cradling her in his arms. She curled into him with her face pressed against his shoulder. He felt the wetness of her tears seep through the t-shirt he had changed into.

With carefully measured steps, Sveyn walked to the couch. He lowered himself to the cushions and settled Hollis in his lap.

"You will tell me when you are ready," he whispered. "Until then, I will keep you safe."

Hollis's sobs came in waves. Just when Sveyn thought she might calm herself enough to speak, a fresh spasm claimed her composure.

Sveyn held her, kissed her hair, rubbed her back, and whispered, "I am here. You are safe."

When she reached the point that her breath came in jerky spasms Sveyn shifted her off his lap. He went into the bathroom and came back with tissues and a small towel which he soaked with cold water.

He gave Hollis the tissues first. After she blew her nose he pressed the cooling towel against her eyes. "Take this."

She grasped the towel and used it to wipe her face and soothe her swollen eyes.

Sveyn went into the kitchen and poured her a glass of sweet white wine and added a couple of ice cubes. He walked back to the couch, squatted in front of her so his eyes were level with hers, and pressed the glass into her hand.

"Drink some," he urged. "It will ease your throat."

Hollis did as he said, taking two long pulls of the wine.

"Thank you," she croaked.

Sveyn collected the used tissues and stuffed them in his pocket. He folded the towel and laid it across Hollis's forehead. Then he waited.

Hollis would not look at him. Her eyes fixed on the wine or the floor or she squeezed them shut and rubbed her lids.

She seemed unable to talk about whatever had come about. But she was here, with him, and safe. Sveyn could not think of one single thing that they could not conquer together.

Look what we have overcome thus far.

He rested his hands on her knees. "Can you speak yet?" he asked gently.

Her eyes met his then, blue irises in seas of red. "Maybe."

Sveyn asked the obvious. "Did someone die?"

She gave a tiny shake of her head. "No. Not really."

Not really? "Are they mortally wounded?"

"No." She heaved a jagged sigh, winced, and put her palm over her chest. "It's nothing like that."

"Good," Sveyn said firmly. "This is good."

Hollis stared at the wine glass again. "I guess."

"Shall I continue to guess?" he asked in his most sincere tone. "Would that be easier for you?"

Hollis's features twisted. "You won't ever guess this."

"So you have not been removed from your job, and the museum still stands."

Hollis rolled her eyes. *There is her spunk.* "Right on both counts."

"So tell me."

She looked at him again and her eyes filled with fresh tears. "My parents lied to me."

That was surprising. "About what?"

"About *being* my parents."

Sveyn sat back on his heels. Hollis's comments about not looking like either her mother or her father, and how no one else in her family had red hair, slid neatly into what he knew about her.

He watched her carefully. "How did you discover this?"

"My negative blood type." She sniffed and reached for another tissue. "Both my par—both of the McKennas are positive."

"Two positive parents cannot ever have a negative child?" Sveyn did not fully understand what that meant, but he put the logic together.

"Less than a one percent chance." Hollis blew her nose before she looked at him again. "I have no idea who I really am."

Sveyn took her hands in his and stilled, staring soberly into her eyes.

"What?" She looked scared.

"There is something about my manifestations I never told you," he admitted. "Now is the time."

Chapter Fourteen

Hollis felt like the punches to her battered breast just kept coming. "Now, Sveyn?" she moaned. "What does this have to do with me?"

"More than you can imagine." The Viking shifted his position on the floor in front of her. "And it might help your situation to know."

Hollis threw her hands up. "How is that even possible?"

"Just hear what I have to say."

Hollis took another gulp of the wine and waved her hand in an irritated *go ahead* motion.

Sveyn pinned an intent gaze on hers. He spoke slowly and emphatically. "In every one of my manifestations, it is important for you to understand that I only manifested to Hansens."

Hollis frowned. "I don't understand your point."

"Hollis." The muscles in Sveyn's jaw rippled. "You are a Hansen."

That sounded ridiculously random. "How many Hansens are there in the world?" she asked. "Must be at least a million."

Sveyn tipped his head in acknowledgement. "This is very probable. But not all of them descended from my father."

Hollis nearly dropped her wine. "Wait—what?"

"I have only manifested to direct descendants of my father." Sveyn gave a small shrug. "You are a Hansen, originally out of Arendal, Norway."

Hollis's hands began to shake. She set her wine glass down before she spilled it. "How can you possibly know that?"

"I could see it when we met."

"What? Was there some magical glow around me?" she snipped.

Sveyn nodded. "Something like that."

"You're kidding me."

"I am not."

The ramifications of the Viking's claim shot a trill of dread through her core. "You're saying we're related."

"Distantly. Yes."

"Is this—" Hollis wagged her finger between herself and Sveyn, "Incest?"

Sveyn rubbed his mouth and Hollis thought he was hiding his amusement.

"It's not funny!" she cried.

"No, it would not be funny if that were truly the case," he agreed. "But there are nine-hundred-and-fifty-years of generations between you and my father."

Hollis sagged back against the couch cushions. "You never married or had children."

Sveyn shook his head. "No. I did not."

"So how *are* we related. Exactly."

The Viking ran his hand through his hair. "I cannot be certain, of course, but if there was a generation born every twenty-five years—"

"At least," Hollis interrupted. "If you were going to get married in your teens." She was grasping at straws and she knew it. To think there might be something inherently wrong with her deep love for this man was more than she could handle at the moment.

Sveyn spread his hands in agreement. "And if we are being conservative, there are at least thirty-eight generations between you and my father."

Hollis nodded and her dread began to dissolve. "That's a lot."

"It is." Sveyn smiled. "And I have manifested to—now—twenty four of them."

Hollis reclaimed her wine glass and drained it. The wine's warmth flowed through her veins and soothed her raw edges.

"This is too much information for one day," she murmured.

"It is quite a lot, indeed." Sveyn seemed to relax a little.

Hollis scowled at him. "Why didn't you tell me this earlier?"

Sveyn drew a deep breath. "I was so surprised to see that you were a woman, I did not think of anything else."

"Yeah, but you got over that," she pointed out. "Why didn't you say anything then?"

"You were so certain of your ancestry I did not want to confuse you." The Viking looked sincerely apologetic. "Until I came back to my body, I believed I would leave you some day and it would not matter."

Hollis retrieved the cool towel and pressed it against her aching eyes again. "I don't even…"

What?

Know what to do now.

"And when I came back to my body, I did decide to tell you."

Hollis lowered the towel and glared at him.

He huffed a laugh. "It has only been eleven days. I was waiting for the right time."

She made a wry face. "I'll have to give you that one."

Sveyn climbed to his feet and sat beside her on the couch. He looped one arm around her shoulders and gently pulled her close. Without thinking about it, Hollis curled on her side and rested her head on his lap.

"What will you say to your parents?" he asked as he rubbed her neck and shoulder. His hand was large and strong and warm.

That was today's million dollar question. "I don't know."

"You are going to visit them after George and Stevie's wedding, are you not?"

"Oh, crap!" She turned her head to look up at him. "I only have one plane ticket!"

Confusion followed quickly by realization played over Sveyn's handsome face. "I did not require a ticket before."

"But now you do." Hollis sat up. "I better buy it right now, before I miss the twenty-one-day price!"

"Stay here," Sveyn said. "I will bring you your laptop."

Hollis handed him the wine glass. "Would you mind getting me another?"

He looked at her so tenderly that her tears returned. "It is my pleasure, my love."

Hollis pressed the damp towel to her eyes and let the hot tears flow into it. As shocking as the discovery was, she could not deny its reality: the people she thought were her parents had lied to her.

For all of my life.

And now Sveyn claimed that she was actually a Hansen, descended from a dynasty in Arendal, Norway. Everything about her identity was shaken. She felt like the earth beneath her had crumbled and she didn't know where to stand anymore.

"Here you are."

Hollis lowered the towel and looked up at the big man who held her laptop in one hand and a glass of wine in the other.

"Thank you." She reached for the laptop and he set the wineglass on the coffee table.

Sveyn settled beside her and watched while she pulled up her plane reservation, then went to the airline's website to book a second ticket. "I'm moving us to first class," she said as she made the changes. "You need the legroom, and I'll need the comfort."

"I have one more thing to show you," Sveyn said when she finished and closed her laptop.

Ugh.

Hollis winced. "What?"

Sveyn took her laptop and carried it to dining table. He

returned to her side with a white paper in his hand.

"What's that?" she asked.

"Mine came today," was all he said.

Hollis unfolded the letter—a twin of the one she received from the hospital, labeling her as the universal blood donor and asking for donations.

She turned to Sveyn, incredulous. "You are O-negative, too?"

"I looked it up on the Google," he said. "Only eight percent of all people have that blood."

Hollis snorted. "And all of them are Hansens, no doubt."

Ӂ

Sveyn was back in Arendal. And Hollis was with him.

They walked along the bluff where Hansen Hall stood, built of solid stone. He was holding her hand until they were out of sight of the house. Then he turned to face her.

His mouth covered hers and his kiss deepened. His hands reached under her cloak sliding effortlessly to the warmth between her thighs.

A jolt of pain in his groin jerked Sveyn awake.

He curled into a ball, agony radiating from his crotch, and wondering if he had been castrated in his sleep.

He must have groaned out loud because Hollis flipped on the light. "Sveyn? What's wrong?"

"My… my cock…" he grunted.

"Let me see." Hollis began digging through the sheets and blanket and throwing them aside. "Can you lie on your back?"

Sveyn rolled over, his eyes squeezed shut and his knees still at his chest. His breath came in short gasps. "It feels like I am on fire."

Hollis put one hand on his chest and the other on his legs. "Can you unfold?"

Sveyn managed to straighten his legs, though the intensity of his pain made him want to yank them back. He groaned again, hating to look so weak in front of Hollis.

"Wow," she whispered.

"What has happened?" he croaked.

"I'm not sure how to explain it."

Sveyn opened one squinting eye. "Have I exploded?"

"No, of course not. But…" Her eyes moved from his groin to his face. "Have you had an erection since you got your body back?"

Sveyn's breath left him in a whoosh. "I—I…" He shook his head, unable to speak.

"Well you have one now." Hollis's mouth twitched. "And it's impressive."

Sveyn opened both eyes and looked down, terrified of what he would see.

What he saw was a perfectly normal cockstand.

"Why…" he gasped.

"I can't say why it hurts," Hollis answered the assumed question. "But you said everything hurt at first."

Sveyn laid his head back down, wondering if that was all that was happening to him. He was dreaming about making love to Hollis. A sexual dream usually left a man with an erection at the least, and often with actual ejaculation.

"It's been so long…" he rasped.

"And it's long now," Hollis joked. Her voice turned wistful. "Really long."

Sveyn closed his eyes again and risked touching himself. What his fingers felt seemed normal, though their tips left a searing trail on the engorged organ.

"It's starting to go down," Hollis said. "Is the pain less?"

He nodded and concentrated on releasing the tension in his body.

Hollis still sat on her knees beside him. "Is there anything I can do?"

"Do not touch me," he growled.

"I won't." She sounded irritated.

"I was dreaming… about you…" he explained. "And then… this…"

"Ah. I understand."

Sveyn gradually relaxed and the pain dissipated. He opened his eyes, staring only at the ceiling at first. Hollis gathered the covers back into some semblance of order then leaned over and turned off the light.

She curled up beside him, but said nothing.

"I am sorry," he murmured.

"It's not your fault."

"It took me by surprise, is all." *That—and it hurt like hell.*

"I guess it'll be like everything else and get better over time."

"God in Heaven, I hope so."

Hollis huffed a little laugh. After a pause, she said, "We haven't talked about sex."

She was right. As he adjusted to all the other issues involved with regaining his body, he had not thought about having physical relations with Hollis as yet. He assumed that when the time came, their situation would progress naturally.

He had not anticipated his body would react this way.

"Sveyn?"

"No, we have not," he replied.

"I'm fine with waiting."

He turned his head toward hers. "It seems that we will have to wait a while longer at the least. Until I can adjust to the sensation."

He felt Hollis nod against his shoulder. "It's a pretty sensitive area. I can't imagine what that rush of blood felt like."

Sveyn snorted. "Be glad that you cannot."

He reached for her hand under the covers and held it firmly.

"I will tell you this, Hollis. When the day comes that we join together in this world, as we did so many times in my other world, I will worship you with my entire body."

She kissed his shoulder. "I love you, Sveyn Hansen."

"And I love you, Hollis." He sighed his contentment. "You are the fulfillment of my very odd life."

Chapter Fifteen

Thursday
January 21

Hollis could not avoid tackling the backlog of requests to visit the museum any longer.

"That's my goal today," she told Stevie. "To answer every one of them."

"Are you feeling better, then?" Stevie asked.

Hollis made the decision at about five-thirty that morning that she wouldn't tell anyone about what she found out about her identity until after she returned from Wisconsin. By then, she would have a full explanation from the McKennas about how she came to live in their home.

"Yeah. It comes and goes."

Stevie gave her a sympathetic look. "How's Sveyn doing?"

Hollis felt a little thrill in her belly at the reminder of last night's disruption and the beauty of Sveyn's aroused form. That was a good sign—her affection for the man really was transitioning into reality.

"He's actually doing great. And—he's already a fiend on the internet so he's catching up to this century amazingly fast."

"Really?" Stevie grinned. "Who would have thought?"

Hollis rolled her eyes. "There is so much about Sveyn that I bet not one single person *ever* thought about."

"Touché." The petite registrar sipped her coffee. "Have you heard back from anybody about that painting?"

"Not yet. Hopefully I will soon. Mr. Kunst doesn't strike me as an overly patient man." Hollis looked at the calendar on her phone; Stevie and George's wedding was approaching fast.

She faced her friend. "You're getting married two weeks from Sunday. Do you need help with anything?"

Stevie's expression turned thoughtful. "Since we're getting married on stage at the Glendale Chocolate Affaire, we don't have to worry about decorations or anything there. And Natalie at Virginia's House has the reception all taken care of." Her glance cut to Hollis. "Do you have your dress?"

Hollis saluted. "Yes, ma'am. I went back to the shop and bought the yellow gown I wore at the Jane Austin Regency tea."

"You look so pretty in that. What about Sveyn?"

Hollis startled. "You want *him* in costume, too?"

Stevie nodded. "Sure. George will probably want him on stage with you."

"I guess I'll take him to the shop, then…" Hollis hadn't considered that possibility any more than she remembered his airline ticket.

The fallout from Sveyn regaining his body just kept coming.

"Good. And you'll be at the shower on Sunday?"

Another surprise.

Oh, goody.

"What shower?"

"The one Miranda's throwing at her place." Stevie suddenly looked horrified. "Did she forget to invite you?"

"I doubt that, Stevie," Hollis assured her. "It's more likely my invitation got lost in the ruckus of the last couple weeks."

Stevie nodded. "Probably. Anyway, it's tea at her house at three."

Hollis considered not asking the next question and claiming ignorance on Sunday, but she knew how excited Stevie was about details.

"Are people wearing costumes?"

Stevie laughed. "No, silly. We're saving that for the big day."

Hollis blew a shallow sigh of relief. "I'll talk to Miranda, then. See if she needs any help."

"I'm so glad you said something," Stevie said. "I would have hated for you to miss it!"

"Me, too.' Hollis refilled her coffee. "I guess I better get on with my scheduling the crazies." Hollis lifted her cup and turned toward the door. "Wish me luck."

Ӂ

Sveyn looked at the map on his laptop. The open call for the modeling agency—Robert Ford Unlimited—was at a hotel just four-and-a-half miles away.

Dare he try to walk that far? He felt stronger every day, but his surgery was less than two weeks past. In spite of what he jokingly thought of as his 'regency' blood, he was not feeling entirely back to his former self.

"I must learn to drive," he said out loud. He found the sound of his own voice comforting in the silent apartment and was beginning to understand Hollis's quirky habit. "For today, I must find another way."

Unafraid of breaking either his phone or the internet, Sveyn was accustomed to clicking on pictures or words that seemed as if they might answer any question which came to his mind.

When that failed, YouTube was his tutor.

On the map's display he clicked the figure of a person in the square called directions. An alternate route appeared, and the blue line showed a diagonal path along what looked like a canal.

Now the distance was listed as three and a quarter miles.

Sveyn nodded, satisfied. "I can do that."

ӜК

Hollis's office phone rang. "Hello?"

"Hollis McKenna—is that you?"

Well, no, as it turns out.

"Yes. Who's this?"

"Mary Oberman. From Chicago."

"Mary! Oh my gosh!" Hollis greeted her former colleague warmly. "How are you?"

"I'm fine. And I'm in Milwaukee now."

"There's got to be a story there," Hollis said.

"There is. But that's not why I'm calling." Mary's voice held an amused and mysterious tone. "You filed an enquiry regarding a missing painting by Benjamin Meyer."

"I did. But why are you calling?"

"Because the family who listed the painting as 'lost' lives in Tomah, and my current employer, the Milwaukee Museum of History, is their agent for its recovery."

"How fun is that?" Hollis grinned. "And weird."

Mary hesitated. "Why weird?"

"Not weird, exactly. But my grandmother lives in Sparta, the next town over."

At least, the woman I thought *was my grandmother does.*

More damned fallout in her life, but for an entirely different reason. Hollis shrugged though Mary couldn't see it. "So close to home, you know?"

"Yeah. Because you're in Arizona now?"

Hollis chuckled. "There's a story there as well."

"Maybe we can get together sometime and catch up."

"Actually, I'm coming to Milwaukee on February ninth. Staying a week." The next logical thought occurred. "I can bring the painting with me."

"Hollis, that would be fantastic!"

She could hear the smile in Mary's voice and hated to dampen the moment, but dampen it she must. "I have to tell you, though, there's another claim of ownership."

"Really?" Mary's tone darkened. "From whom?"

Hollis gave her colleague a brief outline of Gerhardt's story.

She ended her account with, "But I don't know if your people know about the inscription on the back, so—"

"So don't tell them," Mary finished the sentence. "I totally get it. This is going to be a bit sticky."

"Yep." *What will I tell Gerhardt?* "We'll hear them out first, and then decide what to do next."

"Good call. Oh, Hollis—I can't wait to see you again."

"Me, too. It'll be fun catching up." And a nice distraction from the catching up she'd be doing with the McKennas. She gave Mary her email address. "Email me and I'll keep you in the loop."

Ӝ

In spite of the cool day, Sveyn was a little sweaty when he reached the hotel. He ducked into the men's room to wash his face and comb his hands through his hair.

He considered his reflection in the mirror. A day's worth of beard sprouted on his jaw, but Hollis said that was preferred at times.

"Take me as I am," he murmured. "Or do not take me at all."

He left the restroom and followed signs to the room where the open call was being held. Inside the door was a long table with sheets of lined paper clipped to boards.

"Fill this out and go sit over there until you're called," a woman said without looking up. She pointed at rows of sparsely occupied chairs.

Sveyn gripped the pen and forced his hands to draw out the letters in his name. They were uneven and odd, but they were readable. He walked toward the chairs before she noticed his scrawl and asked him any questions.

Sveyn sat in the back row and mentally evaluated the two-dozen other people already in the room. The variety in their looks surprised him, though when he considered the advertisements he saw on the television, a variety of looks was clearly required.

At the front of the room was another long table with a man and a woman, both very well-dressed, sitting behind it. They spoke earnestly to a young woman who sat facing them. Sveyn thought she was attractive enough, but she was crying.

"I'm sorry," the man said kindly. "Not at this time."

The woman gathered her purse, phone, sunglasses, and papers before she stood and hurried out of the room.

The woman by the door called out a name. A young man in the front row rose to his feet and approached the table.

Sveyn stretched out his legs and leaned his head against the wall behind him. This was going to be a long afternoon.

Ӝ

There was no point in delaying the call and every reason to catch the German man off-guard. "Hello, may I speak to Gerhardt Kunst, please."

"This is Gerhardt," he replied, his words softly accented.

"Hi. This is Hollis McKenna—" She faltered; was the name going to stab her every time she said it? "From the Arizona History and Cultural Museum."

"What have you discovered about my painting?"

Germans are blunt, she reminded herself.

Sort of like Norsemen.

"I received a call from the museum in Milwaukee which is handling the claim that the painting was stolen."

She heard a muffled curse. "What happens now?"

"I'm actually going to Milwaukee to meet with the family at the museum there to hear their side of the story."

"When?"

Hollis held her temper. Barely. "I leave on February ninth and I'll be there for a week."

"I will go as well."

Awww, crap. "There's no need—"

"Yes there is," he interrupted. "I want to meet these people who want to take my painting."

Well... they think your father stole *their painting.*

"If you make your own arrangements, Mr. Kunst, I certainly can't stop you from going," Hollis began. "And I will inform the Milwaukee Museum of History that you wish to be heard as well."

"Thank you."

"How do you want me to contact you?" Hollis asked. "Do you have a cell phone?"

Gerhardt gave her his number and Hollis did the same. Before she hung up, she promised to keep him informed of her dealings with the other museum.

"Oh, and I'll be taking *Rachel* with me."

Ӂ

"Sven Hansen?"

Sveyn opened his eyes, assuming the slightly mispronounced name was his. No one else stood, so Sveyn gained his feet and walked stiffly around the rows of chairs to the front table.

The woman's eyes traveled over his body so intently that he felt as if she had disrobed him. He stuck out his hand to distract her.

"I am Sveyn Hansen," he said, pronouncing it as *Svain.*

She shook his hand. "You certainly are." She heaved a sigh. "I'm Rochelle and this is James. And it *is* a pleasure to meet you."

"Shall I sit?" Sveyn asked.

"Not just yet," James said. "Would you mind doing a slow turn?"

"Like this?" Sveyn turned in a circle.

"Yes, thank you. How tall are you?"

He decided to err on the lower end, since no one else in the room was as tall as he. "Six feet and five inches."

"Thanks, you can sit now."

Sveyn lowered himself into the chair, wondering what was next.

"Have you done any modeling before?" James asked.

"No."

Rochelle stared into his eyes. "Are your eyes really that blue? Or do you wear contact lenses?"

"I do not wear contact lenses." *Whatever those are.*

"And your hair—is that its natural color?"

"Yes. Except the sun makes it lighter."

Rochelle smiled. "You have a delicious voice. Have you done any acting?"

Sveyn shook his head. "No."

James leaned forward. "Look at Rochelle like she's a very beautiful woman that you just met, and say *Hi. I'm Eric.*"

Sveyn's gaze jumped to Rochelle. "But she is a very beautiful woman that I just met."

Rochelle gave him a sultry smile. "So say it."

Sveyn took a moment to figure out what these people were asking of him. Then he looked at Rochelle. He imagined she was Hollis and let those raw emotions loose.

"Hi," he said softly and smiling with his eyes. "I am Eric."

Rochelle and James stared at him.

"Can you do that again, but change it a little?" James asked.

Sveyn's brow twitched. *Change it, how?*

He leaned an elbow on the table and stroked his unshaven chin. "Hi. I am Eric." Then he winked like Hollis did with the reporters once.

"Oh. My. God." Rochelle fanned herself with one of the papers strewn in front of her.

"Smile and say it," James directed.

That was easy.

James turned to Rochelle. "He's a complete unknown."

"And he's hot as hell," she replied. "Women will wet themselves to meet a guy like him."

James nodded. "And he takes direction well."

Sveyn watched the back-and-forth comments, wondering what they were thinking about doing until they turned and faced him as one.

James spoke first. "Have you heard of the dating site, *Match Point?*"

That was the one Hollis used.

And where she met Everett Sage.

"Yes." He managed not to growl.

"Well, we don't normally do this." Rochelle folded her hands in front of her. "But we have been asked to cast the face of their brand for a series of commercials."

"We were planning on auditioning for the part," James interjected. "But we'd like to go ahead and do a screen test with you."

Sveyn leaned forward, unsure that he understood their point. "So you want to test me on a screen and see if I can be in television advertisements for *Match Point?*"

"Jeez he's green," James said.

Sveyn looked down at his clothes, wondering what green thing he had brushed against.

"But obviously trainable in our very capable hands," Rochelle countered.

"True."

"Sveyn?" She said it right this time. "We'd like to sign you as talent for the Robert Ford Unlimited agency."

Sveyn wasn't certain of all the words, but he understood the meaning of the sentence. He grinned and stuck out his hand again.

"Yes. I am very pleased. When do I begin?"

Chapter Sixteen

Hollis stared at him like rabbits were coming out of his mouth. “You walked there? And back?”

Sveyn nodded. “I rested when I was there, and when I returned here.”

“I can’t believe it.” She set her purse and briefcase on the dining table. “And you didn’t get lost?”

Sveyn huffed. “My smart phone has walking directions on the Google’s map. It tells me which way to go.”

“It’s just Google,” Hollis said, her stunned expression not connecting with her words. “Not ‘the’ Google.”

Sveyn shrugged. “Whatever its name, I did what it said and I found the open call.”

“How long did it take you?”

“About an hour.”

Hollis walked around the kitchen’s bar-height counter and opened the refrigerator. She pulled out a thawed pre-made lasagna and turned the oven on before she faced him again.

“I’m impressed that you did that,” she said. “Really

impressed."

Sveyn smiled like it was no large accomplishment. "Thank you. But I do need help with one thing."

"What?"

Sveyn pointed at the folder on the coffee table. "I called George and asked him to look at the papers before I sign them. Because that has been a wise thing to do for centuries."

Hollis frowned. "What papers?"

She walked to the coffee table and Sveyn followed her. When she picked up the shiny and colorful folder, he said, "These are the papers from the Robert Ford Unlimited people."

Hollis flipped the folder open. Her eyes moved rapidly over the first page, then she started reading out loud. "Welcome to Robert Ford Unlimited. We look forward to working with you and building your career."

She looked up at him, incredulous. "They signed you? As a model?"

"Not just for pictures," he explained. "So what do you call a person who tests with a screen?"

"Screen test?" Hollis yelped. "You're going to be an *actor?*"

"Only in advertisements."

"Television commercials. You're going to be in television commercials." Hollis sank slowly the couch cushion. "I can't believe it."

Sveyn frowned. "Why?"

"Because so many people try to get jobs doing that." She started to smile. "And you, Mr. Viking, literally walk in and are signed on the spot."

Sveyn sat beside her on the couch. "I have to test well on the screen first. I am not certain what that means."

Hollis's smile widened. "We'll look it up on YouTube. There must be thousands of screen tests posted, so you can watch and see what they do."

"That is a good idea. I will do that tomorrow."

Hollis closed the folder and laid it back on the coffee table. "Did they say who the commercial is for?"

Sveyn snorted. "Yes. *Match Point*."

ЖК

Hollis sipped a delicious Pinot Noir and watched George and Sveyn at the table, poring over the contract while George explained all the different parts.

"This isn't really my area of expertise," he cautioned at first. "But I did some research online and called a colleague to see if there were any red flags to look for."

"There are no flags of any color in the folder." Sveyn's confusion washed away. "I remember. A red flag is a warning. It is a figure of speech."

George grinned. "Yes."

As he looked over the document, George explained the contract was a standard first-timer contract.

"If they use you in the commercial, and there are positive and measurable results once it's shown, then we could possibly renegotiate before they use you again," he said. "But that's a long way down the road."

Hollis took another sip of wine and watched Sveyn as he listened to George. His gaze was focused and intense. When he didn't understand something, he asked clarifying questions.

Intelligent questions.

Hollis always thought Sveyn was a smart man when he was still an apparition. He quickly understood the things that she explained to him, and applied that understanding to similar situations he encountered.

It was helpful that he had watched the world expand and modernize along the way. An awful lot had happened in the nearly one thousand years since Sveyn was born. And his last manifestation was in the nineteen-forties, so things like radios and telephones, airplanes and cars, electric stoves and water heaters were all familiar to him.

But still, so many things had changed since the second World War.

And he's embracing it all.

Some of her friends' grandparents still shied away from

computers and phones that were capable of more functions than just allowing one person to talk to another.

Sure, there were issues with early internet abuses and phishing emails weren't always caught by the first spam filters, but technology today was much easier to use and security software was constantly being improved.

"Just use your brain," she murmured into her glass.

If the English was awkward, delete the email.

Duh.

Today Sveyn looked up an address on the internet, typed that address into Google maps on his phone, and chose an alternative to the default selection of driving directions. Then he followed those directions to the hotel, and presented himself as prospective talent to the agency.

To any one of her friends, that was no big deal. And clearly, Sveyn felt the same way.

Good Lord, but I love him.

Hollis thought Sveyn had a shot at being a print model when she suggested the idea, but she never considered that he might be able to act. While it wasn't a foregone conclusion, Sveyn told her what they asked him to do and he repeated his responses for her. They were surprisingly good.

"If it's a national commercial, which means it's shown all over the country and not just in Phoenix, you can make a lot of money," she told him.

He looked pleased to hear that. "How much?"

"I'm not sure, but maybe George will know."

The two men at the table turned to face her and their movement caught her attention.

"Will you join us?" George asked. "We have a couple logistical things to work out."

"Sure." Hollis unfolded her legs and got up from her chair. "What sort of logistical things?"

"Transportation for one."

Hollis sat at the table. "Yeah, we've already thought about that. But he can't drive yet."

"I will learn soon," Sveyn stated.

"But not in time for next week's screen test," George pointed out.

He returned his attention to Hollis. "I suggest you set up an account with a taxi-type service so he can be driven where he needs to go without having to deal with cash."

"Phoenix has taxis?" Sveyn asked. "I do not think I have seen them."

"They're mostly green cars now," Hollis said. "But according to their signage, you can book them online."

Sveyn smiled. "That is a good idea."

"I'll call the agency tomorrow and explain Sveyn's unusual circumstances with his Social Security number so they don't worry," George continued. "I'm going to buy some time by encouraging them to go ahead with the screen test, since if it's a flop his lack of a number at this point won't matter."

Hollis nodded, but asked, "Will it freak them out that he had a lawyer look at the contract?"

George smiled. "Probably not. But I'll assure them that my role in Sveyn's life is about getting him documented so he can start working for them."

Sveyn extended his hand across the table. "You are a good man, George Oswald."

"Will you send me a bill for your time?" Hollis asked.

George looked a little offended. "No. Absolutely not."

"Why not?"

George pointed at Sveyn. "Do you grasp the impossible reality that we have an eye witness to Jane Austin's environment sitting at the table with us?"

Of course.

It all makes sense now.

"And the information you pump him for will be priceless." Hollis flashed a twisting smile. "You'll be the rock star of the Jane Austin Society of North America."

"Well…" The attorney blushed. "Not a *star*…"

Hollis laughed. "JASNA will never be the same."

Friday
January 22

Hollis presented Miranda with the schedule for the five Mondays' worth of visitations by the ghost crazies, which would take place between today and the implementation of her new and permanent position.

Until March first, she would still receive a hundred dollars an hour to show these people both the Collections Storeroom where Sveyn-the-apparition briefly appeared on the security cameras, and the currently-on-display *velsignelse av gudene*—Blessing of the Gods—whose mythological ability to make its owner immortal pushed Everett Sage to drug and kidnap Hollis in order to steal it.

A large chunk of Everett's funds were now resting nicely in Hollis's bank account as a result of that man's actions. And while that didn't remove the anxiety she still felt when she thought about the ordeal, the civil judgment against the imprisoned abductor-slash-thief was changing her life for the better.

She still wanted to buy a new car—which she planned to start shopping for on the weekend she nearly died and Sveyn came back to his life. With what happened yesterday, she decided to give Sveyn her car and buy a new one for herself.

Like she did with the phones.

Win, win.

Miranda read through the schedule, nodding her approval. "And on Monday, February fifteenth, you'll still be on vacation?"

"Not entirely vacation, as it's turning out." Hollis scooted forward in the chair in front of Miranda's desk. "I got a call yesterday from the Milwaukee Museum of History, who is the agent for the recovery of that painting Ezra Kensington had."

Miranda looked up from the schedule. "That's a happy coincidence."

"Yep. And they're arranging for me to meet with the people who filed the claim to hear their side of the story."

Miranda's brows pulled together. "What will our German think?"

"I'll let you know." Hollis heaved a sigh, glad to note that the pain in her cracked sternum was definitely lessening. "He's planning on flying to Milwaukee to hear their story as well."

"Wow." Miranda leaned back in her chair. "He really wants it back."

"It's the only thing he has left of his father's and it came from pre-war Berlin." Hollis wondered if she had anything of her father's—the real one. "I can understand it."

Miranda tilted her head. "Is everything all right, Hollis?"

Crap.

Her expression must have shifted without her knowing it.

Hollis forced a grin and decided to distract her boss with the latest news about Sveyn. "I'm just tired. George came over last night to read through Sveyn's new modeling contract and it went late."

That did it.

Miranda straightened in her chair. "His what?"

Hollis pointed at the phone on the curator's desk. "Can you call Stevie in? I'll tell you both at the same time."

Stevie walked in a minute later. She looked at the expressions on Hollis and Miranda's faces and froze. "Good news or bad?"

Hollis laughed and waved her closer. "Good. Sveyn has a modeling contract and a possible commercial."

"George told me!" Stevie plopped into the second chair. "But he didn't give me any details."

Hollis gave her friends a play-by-play accounting of Sveyn's story, acting out his different responses to the agents' requests.

"Oh, my." Miranda fanned herself the same way Sveyn claimed that Rochelle did. "I can only imagine."

"Right?" Stevie sighed. "*Match Point's* servers are going to crash if this ad goes national."

"How soon will it be on?" Miranda asked.

Hollis snickered. "As soon as Sveyn does the screen test, and it's exactly what they want, and *Match Point* approves him, and he gets a Social Security card, and he can sign the contract to be legally hired, and the shoot is scheduled, and air time is purchased, and the ad is edited."

Stevie shrugged, her eyes twinkling. "So, next week?"

Hollis's cell phone vibrated in her pocket.

"It's Sveyn." She hit the green *Answer* icon. "Hi!"

"Hello, Hollis." His deep voice sent tingles straight to her gut. "George called the agency."

"George called Robert Ford." Hollis switched her phone to speaker so she wouldn't have to repeat the rest of the conversation to Miranda and Stevie. "And?"

"And he talked to James. James called Rochelle in, and they put him on speaker phone."

"Okay."

"They believed the story that I was gypsy, but they do not want *Match Point* to know."

Hollis nodded. "I can understand that. Gypsies don't have the best reputation."

"So George told them that once I have my papers, no one will ever have to ask about it again."

"Right. Were they good with that?"

"In part." Sveyn paused and Hollis thought he was laughing. "They are going to create something called a back story for me."

"Like a fake history?"

"Yes."

"Do they know what that will be?"

"George suggested that they say I am a Viking descendent from Norway." Sveyn was definitely laughing now. "And they thought he was brilliant to come up with such an idea so quickly."

Chapter Seventeen

Friday
January 29

"Thank God it's Friday," Hollis said to Sveyn as she hefted her purse and briefcase. "I'm exhausted."

All this week Hollis worked closely with Tom to structure the newly created assistant job which he would assume on March first. While her hours would be flexing around paid ghost-hunter types, Tom would work a regular nine-to-five schedule. Assigning specific tasks to his watch was crucial to getting them off her plate but still assure they were completed.

"There will be extra guards when you have these people here at night, right?" Tom asked her. "Especially after… Well, you know."

"Of course."

I certainly hope so.

Sveyn turned her around, rested his big hands on her shoulders and began to knead her knotted muscles. "It is time for us to go out on a date, Hollis. Like we did before."

She moaned as his ministrations sent goosebumps down her back. "Only now you can actually eat the food."

"And you will not have to pretend to speak to me on your Bluetooth."

That would be a relief. While that ruse proved effective, she highly preferred having Sveyn actually with her. Especially in her bed. He was solid, warm, and the way he reached out for her in his sleep made her feel cherished.

After Matt, the change was delicious.

Hopefully they might be able to add physical intimacy to their relationship soon. Sveyn awakened with an erection on five of the last seven mornings, and though he still groaned as he woke, it was nothing like the roars of the first night.

"Was it still painful this morning?" she asked.

"It gets better each time."

So, yes. "You will have to tell me when you're ready," she said softly. "I have no other way to know."

Sveyn leaned down and spoke into her ear, sending additional shivers over her skin. "You will know, Hollis. Because that night I will take you very, very well. The way you deserve to be taken."

While any other twenty-first century woman might be offended at Sveyn's promise to 'take' her, Hollis had grown used to his occasionally archaic language.

She turned her head to his, whispering, "And I will let you, my love."

Sveyn winced and heaved a strained sigh. "This is good," he rasped. "The more it happens, the less it hurts."

Hollis felt his fullness against her hip. The urge to drop everything, including her pants, swamped her. "That day cannot come soon enough, trust me."

Sveyn lowered his hands from her shoulders. "Have a good day, Hollis."

Hollis turned around to face the Viking. The sad-puppy look on his face underscored his obvious boredom. Though only a week had passed so far, waiting for the government bureaucracy was wearing on him.

Bless his heart, George remained in constant contact with the Robert Ford agency, assuring them that everything about Sveyn was legitimate and to go ahead and schedule the screen test. He also fed them an expanded back story suggestion which was as close to Sveyn's actual life as it could be in this century.

"What did they say?" Sveyn asked after George presented it.

"I told them the story was based on one of your ancestors." George grinned. "To be honest, I think Rochelle was relieved not to have to make it up herself."

George told them he expected the fingerprint clearance to come through at any minute, and when it did Sveyn could get a birth certificate. And when he got a Social Security number he could start his previously unanticipated career as pitchman for *Match Point*.

A connection pinged in Hollis's thoughts: Security. A night guard.

Sveyn.

Paid or not didn't matter at this point. It was time to get him started at the museum.

"Get dressed," Hollis said. "You're coming to work with me."

"To the museum?" Sveyn looked confused. "Why?"

"I'm going to get you hired as my personal guard, at least for now," she said getting more excited as she thought about it. "When I'm at the museum after hours with the paid guests, I want you at my side."

Sveyn looked like a kid at Christmas discovering a pile of presents. "Yes! Give me one minute and I will be ready!"

ЖК

Sveyn walked into the museum which was so familiar to him and heaved a sigh of relief. While the internet was fascinating and he was learning so much about the world he now inhabited, he realized that along with this physical body came the craving for human contact.

He followed Hollis into her office while she hung up her jacket, stowed her purse in her desk, and set her briefcase on top of it.

"Let's get coffee," she said, and they walked down the hallway to the staff breakroom.

"Sveyn!" Stevie smiled happily when she saw him. "What are you doing here?"

"I am going to be Hollis's guard when she must stay here at night with strangers," he replied.

"What a great idea!" Stevie looked at Hollis. "You couldn't have a better guard than a man who really knows how to fight."

Hollis smiled up at him. "I'll be safe if he's with me. Especially if I show him where we keep the battle implements."

Sveyn chuckled. "I already know. Remember?"

Stevie was clearly surprised. "Do you already know where everything in the museum is? Like ESP?"

He shrugged. "What is ESP?"

"Extra sensory perception," she explained uselessly. "You know things, like, intuitively."

Sveyn was lost. He shifted his attention to Hollis, who was pouring herself a cup of coffee. "What is she talking about?"

Hollis set pot down. "She's talking about people who seem to be able to identify things that they can't see. It was a big deal a few decades ago."

"Is this ability real?"

"The research was sketchy at best, so probably not." Hollis lifted an empty coffee cup. "Do you want some?"

Sveyn hadn't tried coffee yet, since Hollis never made it at home. "Yes. Thank you."

"So how *do* you know?" Stevie prodded.

Sveyn gave her a sly grin. "Because before now, I could move through things."

Stevie's brow crinkled. "Like walls?"

"Walls, boxes, shelves, doors." Sveyn's grin widened. "I have explored the entire museum."

Stevie giggled. "So if I want to know where anything is, I can ask you?"

Hollis handed him a cup of the hot brown liquid. “Unless it’s been moved. He can’t do that now, obviously.”

Sveyn lifted the cup with its fragrant contents to his lips. He felt the heat in his hands and rising steam tickled his nose.

“You can add cream or sugar if you find it too bitter,” Hollis said.

He lowered the cup. “Yes, I have watched you all do that. You add cream, Stevie adds cream and sugar, and Miranda adds something from a blue paper packet.”

“That’s a different kind of sweetener.”

Stevie tipped her head to the side. “What else did you see when we couldn’t see you?”

Sveyn knew what she meant. “Nothing embarrassing, let me assure you.”

He took a sip of the coffee. It was interesting. Like most things he experienced, it tasted just like it smelled. He sniffed it again, and took another sip.

“What do you think?” Hollis asked.

“I think I will like it.” He sipped it yet again. “And I will not add anything to it.”

“Okay.” Hollis reclaimed her own cup. “Let’s go talk to Miranda about getting your paperwork and uniform.”

“Good.” Sveyn turned toward the closed breakroom door and without thinking walked right into it.

Ӂ

The loud thud of the big Viking’s impact against the solid steel door startled Hollis and she gasped more deeply than she should have. As he staggered backward in shock she wanted to laugh, but poor Sveyn was doused in hot coffee.

He dropped the ceramic mug on the floor where it shattered and frantically pulled his soaked shirt over his head. What had to be Norse curses streamed from his mouth through the knit fabric until he was freed of it.

“Are you hurt?” Hollis asked, ignoring the pain in her own

chest.

"No," he grunted, staring at the mess in stunned evaluation.

Stevie already had paper towels in her hand and she dropped them on the spill. She unrolled another handful, ran it under the faucet, and handed the wet wad to Sveyn.

"Give me your shirt," she said, trading the garment for the towels.

Sveyn used the paper towels to wash the coffee from his chest while Stevie rinsed his possibly-ruined shirt in the sink.

Hollis stood still, concentrating on breathing without stressing her injury further.

"I am an idiot," Sveyn grumbled.

"No you're not," Hollis objected. "You spent over four months walking through the doors and walls here, and you just forgot you couldn't anymore."

The door opened from the outside and Miranda stuck her head in. "Is everything all right?"

"Yes," Stevie said over her shoulder. "Sveyn walked into the door and spilled his coffee."

Miranda entered the room fully then. As she examined the tall, muscular, and shirtless Viking, Hollis could practically hear her boss's lusty thoughts.

"Oh, my…" Miranda breathed. "Are you okay?"

Hollis watched Sveyn try to recompose himself. "My dignity has suffered far more than my body."

"He's used to walking through closed doors," Stevie chirped as she wrung out Sveyn's shirt. "He just forgot."

Miranda slid her incredulous gaze to Hollis. "Am I really having this conversation?"

"Yep." Hollis finally moved, stepping forward to retrieve the paper towels and pieces of coffee cup from the tiled floor.

"Well. Alrighty, then." Miranda shook her head and drew a deep breath. "So, Sveyn. It's nice to have you visiting us today."

Hollis opened her mouth to speak, but Sveyn beat her to it.

"I am here to do what is required to allow me to be Hollis's security guard when she works at night."

"Oh!" Miranda's face clearly displayed the shifts of her

thoughts. "We already do have a guard when she's here at night, you know."

"I do." Sveyn gave her a kind but pointed smile. "And yet she was imprisoned in the Collections Storeroom in spite of the security here."

Miranda blanched. "No one was supposed to be here."

Sveyn clasped his hands behind his back, but said nothing. Hollis took a fresh look at the body she was getting to know and saw the old scars and sculpted muscles of his previous life.

Only a fool would challenge him now.

And Everett Sage was *a fool.*

"He doesn't need to be paid until he can be legally hired," Hollis stated. "But I want my guardian angel with me if I'm going to continue to be here at night with the crazies."

Miranda nodded. "I understand."

"So we need to do some paperwork and get him a uniform," Hollis pressed.

"And a museum t-shirt. Extra-large." A grinning Stevie handed Hollis Sveyn's damp shirt. "Can't have him scandalizing us women by walking around here without one."

Ӝ

George called Sveyn on his cell phone while he was trying on uniforms. "Hello?"

"Great news, Sveyn!" the attorney said without preamble. "Your fingerprint clearance came through!"

"That is good news, George. What do I do now?"

"I'm going to pick you up and we'll go apply for your birth certificate. I don't want to wait until Monday."

"Good." Then Sveyn remembered to say, "I am at the museum with Hollis."

"Oh?"

"Yes. I will be her security guard when she works at night."

"That's a great idea," George said. "I'm sure she'll feel better with you there."

"Yes. And I will feel better as well."

"See you in a few."

He means minutes. "I will be ready."

When George arrived, Sveyn was sitting in Hollis's office. His folded uniform was on her desk and the stained shirt was draped over the coat rack to dry.

George looked at the evidence and asked, "Did you have a mishap this morning?"

Hollis looked up from her keyboard, her brows raised and her lips caught between her teeth.

She's trying not to laugh.

The realization made Sveyn angry. "I spilled hot coffee on myself."

Hollis snorted and reached for a tissue. "Sorry."

George's concern was obvious. "Did you get burned?"

"No."

"That's good." The lawyer approached him. "How did it happen?"

Hollis coughed repeatedly with her mouth tightly closed. She quickly bent down and opened the bottom drawer, hiding her face behind the desk.

George turned to look at her. "Are you okay, Hollis?"

"Mm-hmm." She waved a hand above the desktop. Even Sveyn could see her shoulders shaking.

George looked back at Sveyn. "What's going on?"

In a flash Sveyn saw in his mind what Hollis must have seen: his tall frame walking straight into a steel door as if it were not there.

If he was not so embarrassed by making such a public mess, he might have laughed then as well.

The guffaw that burst from his chest now filled the office.

Hollis straightened in her chair like a jack-in-the-box sprung free. Her wide eyes met his for one shocked moment before her hilarity claimed her without mercy.

"He forgot he couldn't walk through the door!" she squeaked between exhalations of mirth.

George stared at her like she was insane. "Couldn't walk

through which door?"

"No, not through the *door*," she managed between gleeful spasms. "*Through* the door!"

George's eyes cut back to Sveyn. "Through the door?"

Sveyn nodded, wiping his own amusement from his eyes. "I have a body now."

Understanding shifted George's features like a switch had been thrown. "Oh! *Through* the door! You tried to walk through a door?"

"And I walked into it, of course!" Sveyn roared, pressing a hand against his still-tender incision. "With a cup of coffee in my hand!"

Stevie appeared in the doorway, wiping her eyes as well; obviously she overheard their exchange.

"It was the funniest thing I've ever seen!" she cried. "This great big man just walking straight into a closed door without even flinching!"

George stated to chuckle. "Funny, and very unexpected."

"The look on his face!" Hollis wailed from her desk. "He looked so surprised!"

"I *was* surprised!" Sveyn shouted. "*Å min gud!* I shall never forget this…"

"Let's hope not," Stevie quipped, giggling uncontrollably in the doorway. "We don't have that many coffee mugs!"

Chapter Eighteen

Saturday
January 30

Ten days had passed since Hollis discovered that the McKennas were not her actual parents, but she was no closer to accepting that fact than she was on the first day. Most of the time, she buried the unhappy thought under her work, but every time she said her name it impaled her again.

Once she and Sveyn were settled into their table by the window in the revolving restaurant atop a tall Phoenix hotel and had ordered a bottle of wine, Sveyn asked her what was bothering her.

Hollis looked into his beautiful blue eyes. "When you filled out your birth certificate application yesterday, whose names did you use for your parents?"

"I used my mother's real name, Jorun Hansen." His expression sobered a bit. "But in my back story I said I never knew my father, so I was forced to check *unknown*."

"How did you feel about that?"

Sveyn wagged his head a little. “My father is long dead by now, but I know him in my heart. Checking a box does not change that.”

“That’s what’s bothering me.” Hollis drew a shuddering sigh. “I don’t know mine.”

“Yes, Hollis. You do.”

She recoiled, fearful of what he meant. “Is there another Hansen secret you haven’t told me?”

“No, nothing like that.” Sveyn shifted in his seat. “But I want you to tell me what people today believe a father is.”

“Sveyn,” she growled. “Don’t do this.”

The waiter approached with the wine and their conversation halted during the label-checking, uncorking, and pouring. Hollis looked out the window beside their table so she wouldn’t be drawn into any verbal interaction while she thought about Sveyn’s question.

She knew where he was heading.

She just wasn’t ready to go there.

The city below them was lit up like last month’s Christmas trees, sparkling brightly in the night. A pristine and beautiful façade hiding the dirt, crime, and homelessness that any big city experienced.

Pretending to be something it wasn’t.

How appropriate.

“Do the McKennas love you?”

Sveyn’s question pulled her attention back inside the restaurant. She hadn’t noticed that the waiter had left.

“They always said they did,” was the most she would give him. “But do you lie to someone you love?”

“Yes,” Sveyn said. “All the time.”

“What?” Hollis was shocked by his answer. “What do you lie about?”

“That everything will be fine, for a start. We give each other, and especially our children, the assurance that life will not hurt us.” Sveyn sipped his wine while she stared at him. “This is very good. You should try it.”

“That’s not the kind of lie I’m talking about and you know

it." She lifted her glass and took a sip without paying attention.

Sveyn set his glass down. "It is the kind of lie that soothes fears and makes us feel safe and cared for. Is that not what a father does in this century?"

"Well of course he does," Hollis snipped.

"Does he work to support his family, and give up selfish things as he does so?"

"He's supposed to."

"Is he expected to love the mother of his children and care for her as well?"

"Less and less these days, I'm sad to say." Hollis paid attention to her second sip. The deep red wine really was delicious.

Sveyn leaned forward and rested his elbows on the white tablecloth. "What have I forgotten?"

"I don't know; see that his kids get an education?"

Sveyn smiled. "Yes. My father taught me to hunt and fish and tan leather, among other things. He wanted to be certain that I could take care of myself. And my own family someday, had I been blessed to have one."

"A real father doesn't beat his wife or kids," Hollis added. "And he keeps his promises."

Sveyn picked up his wine glass again. "Now tell me which of these things Mr. McKenna failed to do."

Tears filled Hollis's eyes and she dabbed at them with her cloth napkin. She refused to answer the question.

"What about Mrs. McKenna? Did she lie to you?"

Hollis's hands dropped in her lap still clutching the napkin. "Of course!"

"Did she tell you she was proud of you when you did something small? Or tell you that you were pretty when you needed to hear it?" Sveyn made a *tsk* sound. "Such unforgivable deception."

"Stop it."

"When you were ill, did she give you adequate care?"

Hollis recalled the special bedtable that only came out of the closet when she was sick and needed to be still. It was painted with pink roses and held a storehouse of paper, crayons, and other distractions—usually a new toy.

"Hollis?"

She lifted her eyes to his. "What?"

"Did either of them ever say they regretted your presence in their home?"

That did it. The floodgates opened.

Sveyn reached out his hand. Hollis knew what he wanted her to do, and after a rebellious moment laid one palm in his—the one not wiping her tears. His fingers closed over her hand and his voice was gentle as he answered his own question.

"No. They did not. And I believe that they told you many, many times how blessed and happy they were to have you as a daughter."

Hollis nodded, unable to speak.

"Please tell me: how are these not the actions of loving and caring parents?"

She sniffed wetly and croaked, "They still should've told me."

"Yes, they should have." Sveyn narrowed his eyes. "There must have been a compelling reason for them not to have done so. Do you agree?"

Hollis pulled her hand back, wiped her remaining tears, and sipped her wine in silence. She saw their waiter standing a ways off, trying to watch them without looking like he was watching.

"Do you know what you want to order?" she asked Sveyn.

"Yes. Do you?"

Hollis nodded.

Sveyn looked around for the waiter and nodded when he caught the man's attention.

Hollis ordered quickly, knowing that her crying was obvious and trying to minimalize both the waiter's and her discomfort. Once he was gone, Hollis looked at Sveyn again.

"I *hope* they had a compelling reason."

Sveyn looked at his wine glass before asking. "Compelling in whose eyes?"

Damn it.

The path of all his questions was an infuriatingly logical one.

"I reserve the right to call bullshit."

Sveyn gave her his best *what-are-you-talking-about* look.

Hollis huffed. "That means if I think their reason is crap, I get to say so."

"You can certainly say so," he agreed. "But be kind when you do."

That stung. "I will."

"Of course you will. Because you love them." Sveyn smiled softly as he brought the conversation full circle. "And because they are the people who raised you to be the woman that you are."

Then he lifted his wine glass as if offering a toast and gave her a crooked smile. "Please remind me to thank them."

Ӝ

The food in the slowly spinning restaurant was decent. Hollis told Sveyn when she chose this place for their date that the real draw was the three-hundred-and-sixty-degree view of Phoenix from the twenty-fourth floor.

In spite of that, Sveyn's steak was delicious and Hollis said she had no complaints about her salmon. Dessert was a rich chocolate lava cake paired with a sweet white wine.

And coffee. Sveyn decided he liked coffee very much.

Part of their dinner conversation was spent in speculation as to what Hollis's upcoming museum guests would expect to find.

"Before, when you were still an apparition, I was curious to see what they might feel or hear or see," she told him. "But now they won't find anything, so I'm not as interested."

"What about the Blessing of the Gods?" he asked.

Hollis gave him an odd look. "I think the Exor-Clergy guys purged it."

"You heard the screaming?" Sveyn thought he was the only one who could hear that.

"I did. Then it got very quiet."

"If the purging is true—and it very well may be—then your guests will be paying a lot of money for nothing," he warned.

Hollis shook her head. "Almost everybody would say that the Blessing was a myth anyway. And you never were a 'ghost' to begin with."

She made two valid points. "Who is coming on Monday?"

"A group called People Unlimited." Hollis swirled the back of her fork across her plate to scrape up the last of her chocolate. "Why?"

"I am just curious." He copied her actions, retrieving one last mouthful of the dark deliciousness. "This will be my first chance to be a physical guard, so I am trying to anticipate any trouble."

"You saw the rest of them." She wrinkled her nose. "They've been harmless."

"Have you looked up these unlimited people on the—on Google?" he corrected himself.

"Not yet." Hollis pointed her sucked-clean fork at him. "Do you want to look them up on your phone while you finish your coffee?"

Sveyn pulled his phone out and swiped it awake. He clicked on the Google icon—*that time 'the' Google* was *correct*—and entered People Unlimited. He touched the magnifying glass that meant search.

"What is a cult?" he asked.

"Are they a cult?" Hollis reached for the phone. "Let me see."

Hollis touched his phone's screen twice and then read aloud, "People Unlimited stands for physical immortality and unlimited life. Our mission is to provide an environment that supports life extension and physical immortality."

"That sounds suspiciously like Everett Sage," Sveyn grumbled. "I will not leave you alone with these people."

"Yeah, this reporter's source calls them a cult." Then Hollis laughed and her amused gaze jumped up to his. "But their founder died at the age of seventy-nine. So much for physical immortality."

Sveyn shook his head. "Being pinned to this earthly life for eternity is not a goal any man or woman should aspire to. It is miserable. And I know what I am speaking about."

Hollis handed him his phone back. "Your situation aside, it's got to be lonely. If the possibility was true, all your friends and family members who aren't part of the cult would die, and you'd be stuck with the other cult members forever."

Sveyn's eyes widened as he read down the list of things the group charged for. "It seems that immortality is very expensive as well."

Hollis chuckled and took the last sip of her wine.

Sveyn shifted his gaze to hers. "Do you feel better?"

Hollis smiled softly. "With you beside me, loving me, I can face anything."

She sighed and twirled her empty glass. "Even un-compelling reasons, if it comes to that."

Chapter Nineteen

Tuesday
February 2

Though the agency was skittish at first about going forward when he could not be legally hired, George proposed an unusual solution yesterday. "I offered them bail.".

"Bail?" Hollis looked at Sveyn as if wondering if he knew what the word meant.

"Money given as a guarantee that the person in question will appear as required," Sveyn said. "Yes, I am familiar with the process."

George pointed at him, his expression triumphant. "Exactly. I initially offered them five thousand dollars, but they asked for ten."

Hollis waved her hands. "Wait. Are you saying that if we give them ten thousand dollars, they'll go ahead with Sveyn's screen test?"

George nodded. "Yes. And when his paperwork comes through, we get the money back."

Sveyn thought that made sense, except, "I do not have ten thousand dollars."

"I do. It's a drop in the bucket that I won in the civil suit against Sage." Her expression turned mischievous. "Why not use it to help someone who really was immortal?"

So George delivered the cashier's check to Robert Ford Unlimited yesterday afternoon, and Sveyn's screen test was scheduled for one o'clock this afternoon.

Sveyn used the driving service where Hollis created an account to get a ride to the agency for his screen test today. He arrived freshly shaven as requested.

"There you are!" Rochelle strode across the agency's lobby. "Right on time."

She looped her arm through his. "We'll start with hair, then do your makeup."

That was surprising. "Makeup? Like a woman?"

"Wow. I forget what a virgin you are." She opened a door into a dim room with an adjustable-height chair, large sink, and a big rectangular mirror rimmed in lights. "Here you go. Jane will take it from here."

Sveyn assumed the aproned woman with short black hair who waited in the room was Jane, but Rochelle left without making a formal introduction.

"Hi, what's your name?" she asked.

"Sveyn Hansen."

"I'm Jane, as you heard, and I'll be getting you gorgeous for the camera." Her eyes swept over his frame. "Easy work today. Have a seat."

Sveyn sat in the chair. Jane swung it around and lowered the back until the back of his neck rested on the rim of the sink. She turned the water on and let it run over her hand.

"Have you done a screen test before?"

"No."

"Well, don't stress. Just be yourself." She flipped a switch and the water flowed through a rubber tube with a shower end on it. "Relax while I wash your hair and blow it dry."

Just be yourself, she said.

That was not possible. Thankfully Sveyn's new back story was close enough to his real life that he should not trip over it.

The shampooing felt good on his scalp. Jane used shampoo, a conditioner, and some additional product which Sveyn was unfamiliar with, but it smelled pleasant. She wrapped his head in a towel and sat him upright once again.

"You have great hair," she said as she combed it. "Don't ever cut it."

Sveyn smiled. "I will not."

Blowing it dry was awkward, as his hair kept going into his eyes. But when Jane finished and he looked at himself in the mirror, he was amazed.

"My hair looks very good," he exclaimed, reaching up to touch it.

Jane grabbed his hand. "No touching! It'll make it go flat."

She tucked a paper bib around his neck. "I'm going to even out your skin tone with foundation, use a little bronzer low on your cheeks to emphasize your bone structure, and use a touch of mascara on those to-die-for lashes."

Sveyn watched Hollis get ready for work every day, so he knew what the products were. He watched his reflection shift subtly with every layer until even he would declare himself a handsome man.

"You're ready to go, Sveyn." Jane pressed a button on the wall and it buzzed softly. "Remember, don't touch anything."

Rochelle opened the door. "Hot damn," she murmured. "You look incredible."

"Thank you." Sveyn's skin tightened with an uncomfortable blush.

"Let's get this show on the road." Rochelle led him to another dim room scattered with bright rectangle lights. One wall was dark gray, and a single stool stood in front of it. "This is Chad. He'll be behind the camera while you and I have a conversation. Go ahead and get comfortable."

Sveyn picked his way over electrical cords and around the legs of lights and cameras. He made it to the stool without damaging anything, and settled on its ample seat.

Because of the lights, he couldn't see Chad or Rochelle from where he sat. Chad materialized, adjusting the angle of the lights then disappearing again behind his camera. After Chad repeated this action several times, Rochelle said, "Perfect."

She stepped out of the darkness so he could see her. "Okay, Sveyn. You and I are just going to talk, like we met each other at a party and we want to get to know each other."

"I understand."

"What I need to see is your personality. Make love to the camera."

Sveyn laughed. "I do not know how to make love to a camera." *Show your personality.* "But I do know how to love a woman. Very well in fact."

"Nice." Rochelle looked at the stack of white cards in her hands. "What do you want in a relationship?"

That was easy.

Talk about Hollis.

"I want a woman who knows herself well and will not disappear when a strong man comes into her life," he began. "A woman who can be a partner with me, and one whose desires and plans are like mine."

"What are your desires and plans?"

"I want to marry. Have children. Buy a house to raise them in." Sveyn hesitated before continuing, but his conviction was strong. "I want my wife to be able to raise our children without worrying about money."

"What does that mean?"

"I will be considered old-fashioned, I think." *I know.* "But I want to provide for my family so that they feel protected and loved."

"What if your wife wants a career?"

Sveyn thought about that. Hollis will. "If she wants a career because she loves her work, I must accept this."

He tilted his head, trying to make his explanation clear. "But I never want my wife to feel that she must do other work besides managing our home and caring for our children because I have not been enough of a man to adequately provide for them."

Rochelle shuffled the cards in her hand and muttered, "I wish all men felt like that." She looked up again. "Make me laugh."

Sveyn grinned. "Shall I tell you a joke?"

"Sure."

He thought a minute about some things he read about Vikings on the internet. "If the best thing you can say about France is that you left most of it standing, you might be a Viking."

Chad laughed in the behind-the-camera darkness. "Good one!"

"If you finish your trip to England with more money than when you arrived, you might be a Viking."

Chad laughed harder, and Rochelle deigned to chuckle.

"Is this what you wanted?"

"Yes, it's perfect." Rochelle turned to Chad. "Do we need more?"

"A little."

Rochelle read a couple more questions from her cards and Sveyn answered with as much truth as he could. Half an hour after they began, she declared the screen test finished.

"We'll edit it and send it to the *Match Point* marketing department today. They've been chewing my butt to get it 'cause they want to launch the campaign Valentine's weekend."

"So soon?"

"Yes, so if they like it, we'll be filming immediately."

Sveyn shook his head. "The world works so quickly now."

If Rochelle thought his comment was odd she didn't let on. "If you want to see what we send them, I can email you a link."

"I would like that."

"Let's go." She around turned to lead him out of the morass of lights and cords. "Whatever you do, stay by your phone. And leave the ringer on."

Ӝ

Last night's People Unlimited group was less scary than they were creepily weird. Even so, Sveyn stayed near her and well within earshot, and Hollis felt safe from the creepiness in his tall and silently threatening presence.

"They never stopped smiling," she told Stevie as they worked in the Collections Storeroom. "Like if anyone frowned it would break the spell."

Stevie opened one of the blue-lidded boxes they brought from Ezra Kensington the Fifth's hoard. Blue lids meant the objects inside were most likely museum worthy and could be attributed to a specific owner.

"Do we want to switch out Dick Turpin's tricorn for this bottle of Doctor A. B. Seelye's Wasa-Tusa healing elixir from eighteen-ninety-nine?"

"Sure." Hollis was flipping through the photos they had printed from a container of film from Danesfield House. The photos were taken when the house was used by the Royal Air Force as an image intelligence unit. "Let's think of how to display these at some point."

"Okay." Stevie set the brown glass bottle on the stainless steel counter. "How long did they stay last night, the Unlimited people?"

"About an hour. They just wanted to see the Blessing."

Hollis never told anyone about what happened when the Exor-Clergy priest doused the icon with holy water, and if Sveyn hadn't heard the screams Hollis might believe she had imagined it. All she could say about the ancient icon now was that the separated halves no longer vibrated when she held them.

Her lips curved in a crooked smile.

They died.

"Were they hoping the story was true?" Stevie asked.

"Probably." Hollis was relieved to know that even if the promise of immortality for the reconnected icon's owner was true at one time, it wasn't true any longer. "I was just glad that they left early."

"How can anyone believe that if you change your way of thinking, you will never die?" Stevie shook her head. "I mean, death has a one-hundred-percent track record. Their *founder* died!"

"The reporter who wrote an article about them called them a cult, because they isolate their members from everyone else and charge them a ton of money for the privilege."

Stevie lifted the bottle of healing elixir and smiled like a product pitch person. "I guess there really is a sucker born every minute."

Hollis's phone vibrated in her pocket and she pulled it out to see who was calling her. She swiped the green answer icon.

"Hi, Sveyn! How'd it go?"

"Good. I am home now."

Though Hollis and Sveyn had watched screen tests online, there was no way to know if his experience today would be like what they saw. "What was it like?"

"Very much like the films we watched," he said. "A woman washed my hair and dried it, and then put makeup on me, before I talked in front of the camera."

Hollis grinned. "Makeup? Really?"

"I looked good."

Now she laughed. "I bet you did."

He chuckled as well. "You will see. She will send me a link after they edit the film and send it to *Match Point*."

"Oh, good!" Hollis said. "I really want to see it."

"They will send it today."

Hollis shook her head even though he couldn't see her. "I don't think it'll be that fast."

"Yes, it will. They are sending it to *Match Point* today."

"Did they say that?"

"Yes. Rochelle said that *Match Point* wants to launch the campaign on Valentine's weekend."

"What? That's crazy fast."

"This world is fast." He blew an audible sigh. "I hope I am able to keep up."

ЖК

Hollis sat on the couch next to Sveyn, watching the screen test for the fourth time.

"I can't believe that they did this so quickly," she said. "But I guess that if the guy knew what he was doing, the digital editing's not that big of a deal."

Sveyn stared at himself on the monitor. "I never thought to do anything like this."

"Most people don't." Hollis bumped her shoulder against his. "But *dang* you look good."

He had to admit she was right. "Whatever they did, I wish they could do every day," he said. "I never see this man in the mirror."

"It's the lighting," Hollis stated. "See how there aren't any shadows?"

"Why is there no color?"

Hollis's brow twitched. "Something about a person's features being more noticeable in black and white."

Sveyn smiled self-consciously. "Can we watch it again?"

"Sure." Hollis hit the replay icon. "By the way, where'd you get those jokes?"

"One day I asked Google for Viking jokes. I wanted to see what people in this century thought was amusing."

"Well you nailed it."

Sveyn's phone rang and vibrated on the coffee table. He reached for it and looked at the screen.

"It is Robert Ford."

Hollis's eye rounded. "Answer it!"

He did. "Hello?"

"Sveyn? Rochelle. Good news."

Sveyn looked at Hollis. "What good news?"

"The *Match Point* people absolutely love you. We film Thursday morning."

Chapter Twenty

Thursday
February 4

Hollis wanted to take time off and watch Sveyn film the commercial but he said no. "I will be uncomfortable enough, because I will have absolutely no idea what to expect or what to do."

Hollis was clearly disappointed, but how could she argue with such a statement?

"At least let me drive you," she bargained. "And pick you up afterwards."

"This I will agree to. And perhaps you can come inside and look at how things are set up." He was surprised at how soothing that idea was to his nervous excitement.

"Great!" Hollis beamed up at him. "After our experience with *Ghost Myths, Inc.* filming us at the museum, I'm interested in seeing how studio work is different."

Sveyn doubted that was the reason, but he went along with it rather than start a silly argument. Instead, he said simply, "I love you, Hollis."

"And I love you." She backed up her words with a kiss—and while that kiss went straight to his groin, his discomfort was lessening each day. In his mind, he classified it the same way they did in the hospital. The first erection that jerked him from his dream was a ten. Perhaps even an eleven. This one was a six.

I am making progress.

Hollis parked the car outside the agency and followed him inside. They were directed down the same hallway where the screen test was done, but to a much larger room.

James was there, barking orders, while Rochelle conferred with Chad who was apparently filming him again.

When she spied Sveyn, Rochelle hurried over. "Great! You're early. Let's get you to Jane so she can gorgeous you up." She turned a stilted smile on Hollis. "Hello."

"This is Hollis McKenna, my fiancée," Sveyn said.

Rochelle's gaze hardened. "Did you meet on *Match Point?*"

Sveyn stifled a laugh. "No."

"Then don't mention her. Ever. To anyone." Rochelle whirled on one sharp heel and strode toward the door.

"You said you liked her," Hollis whispered as they followed Rochelle's perfumed path.

"She was always nice to me," was his weak explanation.

When they reached Jane's compact hair and makeup room, Hollis grabbed his hand. "I need to get to work."

Sveyn leaned down and gave her a firm kiss, glad that she knew to leave. "I will call you when I am done."

Hollis squeezed his hand. He watched her backside sway as she walked away.

"She's beautiful," Jane said.

Sveyn startled. He didn't know the woman was beside him.

"Yes," he said. "At least I believe she is."

Jane's gaze shot up to his. "Is it serious?"

"We are getting married."

"Oh. Too bad." With a sigh, Jane went back into her room.

Sveyn followed. Half an hour later, he remerged with the same strict instructions to not touch his hair or face.

"I'll be there the whole time and I'll touch up anything that needs fixing," Jane explained. "You just focus on the camera."

When they reached the studio, Rochelle had Sveyn try on several shirts before selecting a blue chambray button-down.

"The color is great with your eyes, and the formality of the shirt offsets your hippy hair."

What is hippy hair?

"You are the boss," he replied safely.

Rochelle's eyes narrowed. "It's not quite right, though…"

"Roll up his sleeves," Jane suggested. "Then he'll look like he's a hard worker."

Rochelle brightened. "Great idea, Jane."

Sveyn straightened his arms in front of him as ordered, while each woman meticulously rolled his cuffs twice, assuring one was not longer than the other.

"Perfect. I love it." Rochelle took Sveyn's arm and led him to the rounded wicker chair waiting in front of a bright green wall. "Go ahead and have a seat."

Sveyn had to ask about the unusual color. "Why is the wall green?"

"We're going to experiment with different background settings and let the *Match Point* marketing guys choose the one they like."

That explanation made absolutely no sense. He would have to ask Hollis about it later. He walked to the chair and sat, ready to see what came next.

Ӝ

Jane was indeed beside him the entire three hours. Each time Chad said 'cut' she stepped to his side and adjusted either his hair or his shirt, or dabbed his nose with a soft pad.

"Don't want you shiny," she chirped.

Thankfully, the words that James wanted him to say were clearly written on a white board and placed at the spot where Chad told him to look.

"We want it to look like you're telling this story to a friend," he explained. "We won't have you look into the camera until the last shot."

Sveyn read the words over and over again about not being able to find the right girl. Bars and workplaces hadn't gotten him anywhere. So he finally decided to try Match Point as a last resort.

"While most dating sites advertise their successful connections, Match Point wants to mention the ways most couples meet," James explained as he made slight changes to Sveyn's words—he called it a *script*. "The obvious message is that since you've been unsuccessful at those, come try us."

"And now I am available on Match Point," Sveyn connected the ideas. "So will they look for me?"

"They'll look for Eric. Match Point is setting up a profile for him."

Sveyn frowned. "But there is no Eric."

James capped the marker. "Right. But when they do look for Eric, they'll find other guys that do exist and hopefully make a connection with some of them."

On one hand, Sveyn thought the plan was a bit diabolical, the way they were deceiving women who were desperate to find a match. On the other, he couldn't wait to see 'Eric's' profile.

For the final shot, Sveyn was to look into the camera with a variety of expressions and say different versions of, "Are you my match?" and "Let's be happily ever after."

"It's a thing," Rochelle explained. "The fairy tale ending."

All the fairy tales Sveyn was familiar with had nothing to do with happy endings. Most were horrifying.

When Chad, Rochelle, and James finished staring at the back of the camera and mumbling to each other, James looked at Sveyn and grinned. "That's a wrap."

"What is a wrap?"

"Green. Got it." *Green again?* "That means we are finished. You're done."

Sveyn reached for the phone in his hip pocket and texted Hollis: *I am finished.*

ӝ

Hollis left the office immediately when she got Sveyn's text three-and-a-half hours after dropping him off. When she arrived at the agency, he was waiting outside.

Oh, well.

No more inside-the-shoot experiences.

Once he was in the car she asked, "How was it?"

"Interesting." He faced her after connecting his seatbelt. "They had me sitting in front of a very green wall the whole time."

"A green screen? So they can change the background?" Hollis shifted into drive. "That saves them a ton of time—which they don't have—and a ton of money, which I'm betting that they do."

Sveyn looked confused. "Can you explain to me how this is done?"

The obvious answer stood up and waved. "Better. I can show you."

Hollis drove to downtown Phoenix, where the channel twelve television station had built a windowed studio by the sidewalk. Hollis parked around the corner of the building, fed the meter, and pulled Sveyn to the windows.

She looked at her watch. "The midday newscast is just ending. Look at the guy standing in front of the green screen. He's about to give an update on the weather, so when he does look at the monitor."

Sveyn's eyes moved from man to monitor and back again. "It looks so real…"

"Yep. The computer replaces the green in the background with whatever image is chosen." Hollis snickered. "No, I don't know how, so don't ask."

Sveyn looked at her. "So you can never know if someone is where they say they are."

"No, but you can usually tell if it's real or fake."

"Eric is not real, but he will have a profile on *Match Point*."

Sveyn's matter-of-fact tone was at odds with his startling words. "Really?"

"Yes." He turned his blue eyes on hers. "In this century, I do not think you can ever believe what you see if you do not see it for yourself."

Sunday
February 7

Hollis got out of her car at Virginia's House and retrieved her yellow Regency-era gown from the back seat. Sveyn did the same with his outfit. As they walked through the back gate, they were met by a pretty brunette woman with a bubbly personality.

"Hi, I'm Natalie. Welcome to Virginia's House." She addressed Sveyn first. "The groomsmen's changing area is inside the guesthouse. George is already in there."

"Thank you." Sveyn slung his garment bag over his shoulder and headed toward the door.

"The ladies are in the house." Natalie fell into step with Hollis. "This is such a fun idea for the wedding, dressing up and having it on a stage."

"Have you heard of the Jane Austin Society of North America?" Hollis asked. "JASNA for short?"

"Not before this, but it does sound like something I would like."

The little white house was charming. Built in nineteen-thirteen, Natalie said she bought it from its third owner, a woman named Virginia, who lived in it for almost fifty years.

"Hence the name." She led Hollis inside. "We had her original wool carpet in here for several years, until the tears in it became a hazard."

Hollis heard Stevie's voice coming through a door. "Is that where we change?"

"It is." Natalie knocked on the door.

It was pulled open from the inside. "Hollis is here!"

Natalie smiled. "Let me know if you ladies need anything."

The horse and almost-period-correct buggy, which Stevie said George insisted on renting, stopped on the street in front of the house forty-five minutes before the wedding was scheduled to begin. There were only six blocks between Virginia's House and the Chocolate Affaire, but they consisted of wide streets and high traffic so walking there in costume did present challenges.

"He wants everything to be perfect." Stevie's eyes glowed with happiness. "And I'm happily going along with it."

The wedding party was small, but so was the buggy. The participants were carried in pairs and dropped off as close to the main stage as was possible in the enormous crowd. Hollis and Sveyn were the first couple transported.

"You look amazing," she told him.

He smiled, his eyes crinkling at the corners. "As do you."

Once everyone in the wedding party had arrived and the band started packing up, the pastor and JASNA member whom George flew in from Ohio to perform the ceremony stepped up to the microphone.

"Ladies and gentlemen, we are about to partake in a Jane-Austin-era wedding, complete with period-correct clothing and ceremony. Please stay and be our guests."

As they climbed onto the stage, everyone took their spots: Hollis, Stevie's cousin, and George's sister stood next to Stevie. George's brother, his best friend from the law firm, and Sveyn stood beside George.

"I will perform this wedding using The Book of Common Prayers, which is the basic text for the Anglican Church," the pastor explained to the crowd. "I'm sure you will find much of it familiar."

He faced Stevie and George, both looking like they were about to explode with glee.

"Dearly beloved, we are gathered together here in the sight of God, and in the face of this congregation, to join together this man and this woman in holy matrimony, which is an honorable estate, instituted of God in the time of man's innocency, and signifying unto us the mystical union that is betwixt Christ and his Church…"

He went on to read the lengthy text, and Hollis was surprised at how much of it really was familiar: marriage is not to be taken unadvisedly… it was ordained for the procreation of children… it was ordained for mutual help, and comfort, both in prosperity and adversity.

"Therefore, if any man can show any just cause why they may not lawfully be joined together, let him now speak, or else hereafter forever hold his peace."

Hollis worried that someone in the crowd might think this was a good time to jokingly object, and was very relieved when no one did.

"George Franklin Oswald, wilt thou have this woman to thy wedded wife, to live together after God's ordinance in the holy estate of matrimony? Wilt thou love her, comfort her, honor, and keep her in sickness and in health; and, forsaking all other, keep thee only unto her, so long as ye both shall live?"

"I will," he answered.

"Stevie Marie Phillips, wilt thou have this man to thy wedded husband, to live together after God's ordinance in the holy estate of matrimony? Wilt thou obey him, and serve him, love, honor, and keep him in sickness and in health; and, forsaking all other, keep thee only unto him, so long as ye both shall live?"

Hollis thought Stevie never looked more beautiful as she did that moment in her pale blue silk gown, a complement to George's navy blue waistcoat and brocade vest.

"I will," she said, gazing onto George's eyes.

Next, they made the actual pledge, repeating those promises and adding, "And thereto I plight thee my troth."

After that came the rings, with an apology from the pastor. "In Jane Austin's time the woman did not give the man a ring. This is an adjustment for our century."

A prayer followed, then the declaration that, "Those whom God hath joined together let no man put asunder."

Until today, Hollis hadn't thought much about where the current traditional wedding ceremony came from. The Church of England, commonly called the Anglican Church, was scandalously founded in the sixteenth century by King Henry the Eighth. Even though he did it so he could divorce Queen Catherine of Aragon and marry Anne Boleyn, it made sense that the Englishmen who formed America brought those traditions with them.

Hearing the words and promises whose origin extended back five hundred years made Hollis's history-loving heart happy.

Hollis's musing was brought back to the present by the words, "I pronounce that they be man and wife together, in the name of the Father, and of the Son, and of the Holy Ghost. Amen."

As the ceremony still continued with blessings and prayers, she slid her attention to Sveyn. He was staring at her with such blatant emotion that she felt her pulse surge.

I love you, he mouthed.

Hollis smiled at the tall Viking, resplendent in his Regency suit.

I love you, too.

Chapter Twenty-One

Tuesday
February 9

Sveyn wondered what flying would be like. He had ridden in planes during his last manifestation to the soldier, but without a body he could not feel the sensations of taking off and landing; all he knew was what he saw.

"Are you afraid of flying?" Hollis asked as they waited at the gate in Phoenix Sky Harbor's terminal four.

He shook his head. "No. But I am curious."

Hollis put him by the window in their upgraded seats so he could watch their take-off and landing and parts in between. Now as the plane rolled down the runway, increasing in speed, he was pressed backward into his seat. With a definite upward movement that pressed him down, the airplane left the ground.

"Is it what you expected?" Hollis asked.

Sveyn nodded. "Yes, it is."

He almost wasn't able to take this flight. Luckily, his new

birth certificate arrived yesterday, so Hollis left work to take him to get a state identification card as well as his Social Security card. Last night, she emailed a photo of his Social Security card to Rochelle, and she responded this morning that Sveyn's paperwork was now complete and the ten thousand dollars would be transferred back to Hollis's account today.

He was beginning to feel like he truly existed here now.

Once the announcement was made that the crew would begin to serve beverages and snacks, Hollis asked for white wine.

"It's free in first class," she told him. "Would you like some?"

Sveyn addressed the smiling woman in a red, white, and blue uniform. "Yes. Red wine please."

The woman returned with their wine and a little plate of cheese and crackers.

"I could make flying up front like this a habit." Hollis put a slice of cheese in her mouth.

All Sveyn knew about flying was that the seats in back looked very cramped. Though the space up here wasn't overly large, at least there was enough room that his knees weren't banging against the seat in front of him.

"It is very comfortable," he agreed. "And I do like the service."

Hollis smiled and sipped her wine. "I do have the money for some indulgences now. This will probably be one of them."

"What do you think will happen with the painting?"

Hollis's glance bounced up to the compartment over their seats where the painting of Rachel Meyer was carefully stowed. "I honestly don't know. I wish you were still invisible and could be in the interview. Then you could give me your opinion about who is telling the truth."

"Perhaps they both are," Sveyn posited.

Hollis looked at him like he just named her worst fear. "And then what? Cut it in half?"

"When Solomon suggested that very thing, the real mother said no. Her son's life was more important to her than which woman raised him."

Hollis rubbed her forehead. "I hope you're right and someone gives it up."

Sveyn finished his wine before he asked, "When will you talk to your parents about what you discovered about your birth?"

Judging by her expression, this fear weighed on her far more heavily than the first one. "Tonight."

Though Sveyn agreed that was the wise thing to do, he still asked, "Are you certain?"

"Yes." Hollis sighed. "I know that the minute I see them it'll be the main thing on my mind."

Sveyn kept his tone gentle. "What do you believe they will say?"

"That they love me. That I am their true daughter, in spite of not giving birth to me." Hollis gave a little shrug. "Stuff like that."

"Will you tell them that we are engaged?"

She winced as she looked at him. "I haven't decided."

Sveyn understood her hesitancy. To everyone around her, he entered her world only one month ago.

"It is one month today since you brought me back."

"Is it?" Hollis looked surprised. "You're right. We went to the Renaissance Faire on January ninth."

He leaned across the wide armrests between them and kissed her. "I will be eternally grateful that you saved me from my fate," he whispered.

Her eyes sparkled prettily. "As will I."

ӜК

Hollis spied her mom and dad immediately, waiting just outside the baggage claim. And though their eyes were on her initially, they quickly shifted to the tall, long-haired blond walking beside her.

"Hi, Mom. Dad." Hollis hugged her mom first. "This is Sveyn."

Her dad stuck out his hand. “Good to meet you, Sveyn. Call me Ian.”

Sveyn clasped Ian’s hand and shook it. “It is good to meet you, Ian.”

“And I’m Brianne.” Hollis’s mom held out her hand but instead of shaking it, Sveyn kissed it.

“I am honored to meet the woman who raised such an amazing daughter.” Brianne blushed.

Hollis felt a stab of trepidation over the coming conversation and wondered if Sveyn chose those particular words intentionally.

Sveyn straightened. “Ian and Brianne?”

Ian laughed. “Yeah, I know. We had one of those celebrity mash-up names long before it was fashionable.”

Sveyn shot Hollis a look which she labeled as his *tell me later* directive.

“Ready to go?” Brianne asked.

Hollis’s mom and dad each grabbed the handle of a rolling suitcase while Hollis and Sveyn put on the warm coats they brought with them—hers from her previous life here, and his from Goodwill. February in Wisconsin was nothing to joke about.

Then Sveyn tucked the package holding the painting under the protection of his arm, while Hollis lifted her briefcase and purse.

Brianne’s expression dimmed when she saw the briefcase. “I thought this was your vacation.”

“I carry my laptop in it for one thing,” Hollis defended. “But I do have a very interesting task to perform while I’m here. I’ll tell you about it in the car.”

ЖК

Sveyn found Hollis’s parents’ home very spacious for the three people who lived in it. They lived in a town on the north side of Milwaukee called Whitefish Bay, and Hollis said the cozy home was built in the late nineteen-fifties.

"It's called mid-century modern now and it's all the rage," Brianne told Sveyn as she showed him to a bedroom "Of course, we've updated the kitchen and bathrooms over the thirty years that we've lived here."

"Almost thirty-one." Hollis shot Sveyn a significant glance. "They moved in right after I was born."

"When is your birthday?" Sveyn asked.

Hollis looked embarrassed. "Um… Friday."

"Friday the twelfth?"

Hollis blushed. "Yep. The same day as yours. I'll be thirty-one the same day that you turn thirty-five."

Sveyn snorted. "Why did you not tell me?"

"I don't want people to make a big deal about it."

"So I should cancel the party?" Brianne asked.

Hollis stared at her mother. "You didn't!"

Brianne's mouth curled at the corners. "No. Your father wouldn't let me."

Sveyn noticed Hollis's eyes dim at the mention of Ian.

"That's good," she said. "I'd hate to disappoint by not showing up to my own party."

"Come to the kitchen and help me with dinner," Brianne said. "Let Sveyn get settled in."

Sveyn didn't know what *settled in* meant, but he knew enough about women to recognize that Brianne wanted some time alone with her daughter—the daughter she raised, that was.

He opened the suitcase and hung his shirts in the closet, then decided everything else could stay where it was. He stretched out diagonally on the full-sized bed and closed his eyes.

ӜК

Half-an-hour had passed since dinner was finished and Hollis's belly threatened to expel every bite if she didn't get to the point soon.

Okay. Here goes.

"I have something I want to talk to you guys about."

Her father's eyes immediately cut to Sveyn. "You want to get married."

Hollis's jaw dropped. "Why would you say that?"

"Holli-hon, we see the way you look at each other," her mom said. "The attraction between you two is obvious."

"We just think you're rushing into things." Her father leaned forward. "You only met a month ago."

Hollis looked at Sveyn. He sat across the coffee table from her with an odd look on his face.

"We met before that," he said, throwing the ball into her lap.

Oh crap.

"Really?" her mother looked relieved. "How long ago?"

Hollis glared at the Viking.

Yes—how long ago, exactly?

"I am a guard at the museum where Hollis works."

Sveyn's brilliant plan became immediately clear to Hollis. She wanted to kiss him it was so good. "Right! He is. He started there in September."

"I was working at the museum the night it was broken into." His gaze slid to hers. "The night of the security video."

Hollis smiled at Sveyn, challenged by his careful choice of words. "That was the night that our relationship began to change."

The Viking looked impressed. "Yes. And that change continued in part because Matt came to visit her a few weeks later."

Ooh, good one.

"Matt Wallace?" Her father's mood soured immediately. "What did he want?"

"He filed for divorce and wanted to begin our relationship again." It was an easier story to tell if she flipped the timeline; the outcome was the same either way. "But the day I was injured I'd already told him to get lost."

Her gaze shifted to Sveyn. "I told him that I chose Sveyn over him."

Sveyn did something startling, then: he slid off the chair and onto his knees in front of her father.

"Ian McKenna, I am asking for your blessing. I wish to marry your daughter."

"I don't need his permission," Hollis objected.

The stern look Sveyn threw at her stopped her from saying anything else.

"Blessing is not permission," he said to her before returning his attention to her father. "And you should wait to know me better before you give it."

"Then why ask now?" Hollis demanded.

She noticed that both her father and mother were watching the exchange in stunned silence.

"Because Ian and Brianne have correctly discerned our hearts, Hollis," he answered tenderly. "Making my intentions clear is the respectful thing to do."

Hollis moved her attention to her father. "Dad?"

He looked like he might laugh. "I will wait, Sveyn, because your counsel is wise. But I'll tell you now, that I've never seen a man handle our fiery girl so gently."

"Thank you." Sveyn shook Ian's hand and reclaimed his chair. He turned his intense gaze on Hollis. "And now I believe you have something to tell them as well, do you not?"

Chapter Twenty-Two

Sveyn was surprised by the sudden shift in this conversation to marriage with Hollis, but he took the opportunity to ask for a blessing when Ian brought the subject up. Now it was time for Hollis to say what she intended to say when the four adults sat down together.

She looked like a wild animal caught by a hunter; wanting desperately to escape but finding no way out.

"What is it, Holli-hon?" Brianne asked.

"Please don't call me that," she managed. "I'm not three anymore."

Brianne shot an embarrassed glance at Sveyn. "Sorry. Old habits."

Hollis looked at the carpet and drew a deep breath. "Remember that day I called you about the hospital wanting me to donate blood?"

"Yes. We were at the movies and I said your dad has O-positive blood as well."

"It's the most common blood type, so I'm always being asked to donate." Ian frowned a little. "Are you afraid to donate, sweetie? You don't have to do it, you know."

"It's not about being afraid." Hollis's voice was so soft it was hard for Sveyn to hear.

"What is it then?" Brianne asked.

Hollis lifted her head. Tears streamed down her cheeks. Sveyn fought the nearly irrepressible urge to leap over the low table and gather her in his arms.

"Are you sick?" Ian asked. "Do you need a blood marrow donor?"

"No, no." Hollis wiped her cheeks. "It's nothing like that. I'm physically fine."

"Then what is it?" The fear in Brianne's voice and the concern on her face tore at Sveyn. If Hollis didn't say it, he would.

Hollis met his gaze with terrified eyes. She gave a little nod of her head.

Message received.

Sveyn took a deep breath to draw Ian and Brianne's attention to him. "Hollis has O-negative blood."

No one moved. No one breathed.

Ian and Brianne stared at each other. Ian's face reddened violently while Brianne's went white. Obviously they both understood the ramifications of the revelation.

Hollis's voice sounded like a rusty spring. "Why didn't you tell me I was adopted?"

Brianne began to cry. "We couldn't."

"Couldn't?" Hollis cried. "The adoption laws were changed decades ago!"

"We didn't become your parents through public adoption." Ian's voice was strained. "It was a private agreement between friends, and we only got you because we promised to keep their secret."

"We couldn't have children, Hollis, and we wanted you so desperately that we would've agreed to anything."

"We even had to move away from Sparta, our hometown,"

Brianne squeaked between sobs. "That's why we moved to Milwaukee. It was part of the agreement."

"Left family and friends behind… I had to transfer jobs." Ian heaved a shaky breath that seemed to reach his toes.

"What about Grandma?" Hollis growled.

"She was my mother," Brianne answered quickly. "And Grandma and Grandpa McKenna were your dad's parents."

Hollis jerked a thumb toward Ian. "*This* dad?"

"Hollis," Sveyn interrupted, his voice low. "Remember what you told me at dinner in the turning restaurant."

Hollis fell back in her seat and glared at him across the expanse of the little coffee table.

"This has been a long day," Sveyn offered. "Perhaps we should discuss this more fully tomorrow."

Hollis drew a steadying breath and laid her hand over her chest, a sign that her injury still ached. "This discussion is not finished. Not by a long shot."

"No, it is not." Sveyn waved a hand toward the softly sobbing Brianne. "But you have had some time to think about this and your parents have not."

Hollis looked at Brianne then and the hard edges of her expression eased. "You're right." Hollis moved to her mother's side and hugged her. "I love you. Mom."

Sveyn caught the hesitation and wondered if Brianne did. Hollis went to her father and hugged him as well.

"I love you, too, Dad."

Good. *No hesitation.*

"See you in the morning, sweetie."

Sveyn said his goodnights and followed a very subdued Hollis down the hall to their separate bedrooms.

ӜK

Hollis opened Sveyn's door, slipped into the bedroom, and eased it closed again. She heard him roll over and saw the shape of him in the dim light as he sat up.

She crossed the room and climbed into the bed, forcing him to move over and make room for her. He didn't ask why she was there, he just curved his body along hers.

"You were brilliant tonight," she whispered.

"I was glad you understood what I was doing," he replied in kind.

"We told the truth."

"Only the truth," Sveyn concurred.

Hollis tipped her head toward his. The streetlight's glow edged around the curtains and she could see a faint reflection in his eyes. "You asked my father if you could marry me."

Sveyn's chest bounced with his soft chuckle. "He mentioned the idea. I only took the opportunity that was handed to me."

"Everything you said tonight was perfect."

"I cannot claim perfection," Sveyn demurred. "But remember that I have spent nearly a thousand years watching countless men make repeated fools of themselves."

He flashed a crooked grin. "If I did not learn from their many obvious mistakes, then in the end I would be the biggest fool of them all."

He made a good point. "That must why you seem so wise all the time," she murmured.

"Not all the time, I am afraid." Sveyn kissed her forehead. "Even so we will be married soon, Hollis. That is the utmost desire of my heart."

Hollis snuggled against Sveyn's bulk. "You make me feel safe and cared for."

"I will always keep you safe and cared for," he murmured.

One of Sveyn's hands cupped her breast, the other her bottom. She felt his physical reaction swell against her thigh.

She slid her hand down and took hold of its length. "Does it still hurt?"

He moaned softly. "Pleasure and pain are so intertwined, that I cannot distinguish one from the other."

Hollis smiled into the dark.

Soon indeed.

Wednesday
February 10

Hollis's meeting with the family who filed the claim for the missing painting was scheduled for eleven o'clock at the Milwaukee Museum of History. Though she slept for several hours in Sveyn's arms, Hollis woke up in her own room as a show of respect for her parents.

"I'm sorry you can't be in the meeting," she told Sveyn at breakfast. "But you can explore the museum while I'm in the interview and then we can go out for lunch afterwards."

Brianne set a plate of scrambled eggs and a rasher of bacon on the table. Her eyes were puffy and her smile nonexistent.

She didn't look at either Sveyn or Hollis, but quietly said, "The toast is in the toaster."

Hollis reached for her mother's hand. "Mom, I'm so sorry."

Brianne lifted her eyes. "No, Hollis. We're sorry and you've a right to be angry. Your father and I talked about it until late last night, and we decided that, in spite of our friends' request, we were wrong. We really should've told you the truth years ago."

Hollis squeezed her hand. "I want to hear the whole story tonight at dinner. Every detail. Promise?"

"Yes." Brianne gave her daughter a watery smile. "Every single one."

"Once Hollis realized that you could not have birthed her, she did tell me what wonderful parents you were to her," Sveyn said. "You do not know me yet, but I do not lie."

Hollis glanced his way.

Thank you.

"Your father said he'd be home early. He's going to grill brats for supper."

Sveyn's eyes moved to the thickly white-coated back yard. "It's a fine day for cooking, I think."

Hollis giggled. "Do you know what brats are?"

"Meat that will be grilled," he replied. "That is all I need to know."

"They are German sausages that we boil in beer and onions

first, then brown over the flames," Brianne explained.

Hollis winked at the Viking. "And then we *drink* beer when we eat them."

Sveyn grinned. "I will look forward to this all day."

ӂ

Hollis carried the disputed painting into the museum lobby and approached the front desk. "Could you let Mary Oberman know that Hollis McKenna is here?"

The girl behind the desk didn't look like she heard a word. Her eyes were fixed on Sveyn, who admittedly looked really, really good in his fitted jeans and the Nordic sweater which Hollis bought him for this frigid trip.

"Hi. I'm over here."

"Oh!" The girl's gaze shifted to Hollis. "Sorry. How can I help you?"

"I'm here to see Mary Oberman."

She picked up the phone. "And you are?"

Hollis spoke slowly. "Hollis. McKenna."

"Is she expecting you?"

"Yes."

Hollis turned around and rolled her eyes. Sveyn covered his mouth but his eyes were laughing.

"Ms. McKenna!"

Gerhardt's voice boomed through the lobby as he strode toward her. Daughter Amelia struggled to keep up in her high-heels. Obviously the woman had not come prepared for a frozen environment.

"Mr. Kunst." Hollis smiled stiffly. "I see you made it."

"I said I would, didn't I?" The older man's consideration moved to Sveyn. "I don't believe we've met."

"This is my fiancé, Sveyn Hansen." Hollis heard a little grunt of disappoint from the girl behind the desk. "He's going to explore the museum while we have our meeting."

Sveyn held out his hand.

Gerhardt shook it. “Do you know what you’re getting into with this one?”

Sveyn laughed. “Yes. And very well.”

“Good luck to you then.” Gerhardt returned his attention to Hollis. He pointed to thc satchel under her arm. “Is that my *Rachel?*”

Hollis had to give the stubborn German credit for tenacity. “It’s somebody’s *Rachel*. Whose *Rachel* it is will be determined soon, I hope.”

Mary Oberman walked around the corner behind the lobby desk. The bubbly brunette looked exactly the same as the last time Hollis saw her.

“Hollis! It’s so good to see you again.” She gave Hollis a quick hug, and then turned to Gerhardt. “And you must be Mr. Kunst.”

“Yes.” He shook Mary’s hand. “This is my daughter Amelia.”

“Pleased to meet you.” Mary moved her appreciative regard to Sveyn. “And you are?”

He gave a little bow. “I am Sveyn Hansen, Hollis’s fiancé.”

Mary’s jaw dropped and she scowled at Hollis. “You didn’t tell me!”

“Trust me, there’s a *lot* I haven’t had the chance to tell you,” Hollis said. “But let’s not waste Mr. Kunst’s time.”

“Mary, would you join Hollis and me for lunch after your business is finished?” Sveyn offered.

Mary looked like she might actually swoon. “Sure!”

“I told him he could explore the museum in the meantime.” Hollis looked at Sveyn and held up her phone. “I’ll text you when we’re done.”

He nodded.

Mary gathered herself and turned back to the business at hand. “The Meyer family is already in the conference room. Follow me.”

Ӝ

Eli Meyer was a soft-spoken man in his eighties with thinning hair that might have been red once. Large wire-rimmed glasses perched on his nose and hearing aids hung over his ears.

"I am pleased to meet you, Miss McKenna," he said in thickly accented words. "And may God bless you for finding our painting."

Gerhardt grunted.

Hollis ignored him. "You can thank a man named Ezra Kensington the Fifth, who we believe bought the painting at an estate sale about twenty years ago."

Eli looked confused. "Then how did you get it?"

"When he passed, Mr. Kensington willed his entire estate to the Arizona History and Cultural Museum. I'm the Collections Manager for his bequest."

Mary stepped forward. "As I told you on the phone, Mr. Meyer, we do have another claim of provenance regarding the painting."

Eli turned to the taller, younger man. "Would that be you?"

"Gerhardt Kunst, son of Wilhelm Kunst."

"I know that name…" Eli rubbed his forehead. "Wilhelm was our neighbor, I think. In Berlin."

A man who looked very much like Eli and was about the same age as Gerhardt spoke up. "So you remember that, Papa?"

"Is this your son?" Hollis asked.

He nodded. "Samuel Meyer. I drove my father here from Tomah."

Hollis looked around the room. "Shall we all take our seats before I reveal the painting?"

Mary sat at the head of the oblong conference table. Gerhardt and his daughter Amelia sat on one side, Eli and his son Samuel sat on the other.

Hollis unlatched the leather case and pulled out the painting, wrapped in cotton cloth. She turned around and set it on the easel someone had thought to provide.

"Here she is," Hollis said softly. "Here is *Rachel*."

Chapter Twenty-Three

"Rachel..." Eli began to weep. "My beloved sister…"

Hollis looked at Mary, shocked.

"Mr. Meyer, are you Benjamin Meyer's son?" Mary asked.

"He is," Samuel answered for his overcome father. "And I am Benjamin's grandson."

Gerhardt looked panicked and opened his mouth to speak.

Hollis held up a hand to silence him. "Mr. Kunst, you will have your chance to tell your side once Mr. Meyer is finished, I promise. Until then, Mr. Meyer has the floor. Please don't interrupt him."

Eli rose from his chair and walked slowly to the easel. "I watched my father paint this. It took him weeks before he was satisfied."

Hollis's eyes welled as she watched the elder Jew stare so reverently at this poignant piece from his past.

"Why don't you start at the beginning, Mr. Meyer," she

suggested. "Tell us the whole story, and don't leave anything out.

Eli nodded. He began his tale, still facing the painting.

"My father, Benjamin Meyer, worked as an art restorer for the Neues Museum in Berlin. All day long he repaired priceless masterpieces." Eli turned to Hollis. "He was so honored to be trusted with these paintings, do you understand?"

She nodded. "We work in museums. We do understand."

"Of course you do."

Eli sighed and faced the rest of the people in the room. "But things in Germany were going very badly. We all know this now, but I was only seven when my father painted this, and I did not understand what was coming."

"No one did, Papa," Samuel reminded him. "How old was Rachel?"

Eli blinked. "Fifteen. Sixteen. I'm not sure. The one thing I do know is that I never saw him paint anything before this." He drew a shuddering sigh. "I think he wanted to leave something of himself behind, something original that came from his hand."

"Did he paint anything else afterward?" Hollis asked.

"I don't know. If I did, I would have listed them as well." Eli looked at Hollis over the rim of his glasses. "Do you know if he did?"

Hollis gave him an apologetic smile. "No, I don't."

Eli nodded and walked slowly back to his chair. "Anyway, some weeks after he painted the portrait, my six-year-old brother David and I were sent to England for our safety. Rachel was already too old, no family would take her in."

"England was bombed," Mary stated, her surprise evident. "How was that safe?"

Eli pinned a gimlet eye on the woman. "They weren't killing Jews there."

Hollis pressed her lips together. Eli made a tragically valid point.

He resettled in his seat. "We were out in the northwestern English countryside, in a little village on a farm. We stayed there until after the war ended and a cousin from Belgium came to collect us."

"Then you moved to America with him," Samuel said. "To Wisconsin."

"I did. But David chose to stay in England." Eli waved an arthritic hand. "He had just turned six when we left Germany in nineteen-thirty-seven, and our cousin came for us nine years later. David didn't remember Berlin, or even our parents, probably. He was happy to stay where we were."

Hollis gave Eli a knowing look. "But you remembered."

He met her gaze. "I did. I was nearly seventeen by then. And I knew what horrific things had happened. I wanted to get as far from the war as I could. Wisconsin was a fine choice for me."

"What happened to your family?" Mary asked.

Eli removed his glasses and wiped his eyes.

Samuel handed him a tissue. "When you're ready, Papa."

Eli sniffed and settled the frames back on his nose.

"Someone in the neighborhood got word to my foster family, I don't know how. They wrote that my parents and Rachel were taken away in the middle of the night on August fourth, nineteen-thirty-eight, and they were never seen again."

Hollis reached into her purse for a tissue of her own. She glanced at Gerhardt, wondering how he was taking the story, but the man's face might have been carved in stone.

"Did you ever find out what happened to them?" Mary asked.

Eli nodded. "I found my parents' names, Benjamin and Rose, on a list of known dead at Flossenburg. But I never found out what happened to Rachel."

"And David?"

Eli pounded a fist softly against his chest. "My brother, still in England, died last year of lung cancer."

Gerhardt leaned forward and glared at Hollis. "Can he prove any of this story?"

Samuel's fist hit the table. "Why would anyone lie about something like that? The painting isn't worth anything to anyone except my father!"

"It's worth something to me!" Gerhardt barked.

"Time out!" Hollis leaned on the end of the conference table. "You'll get your chance to speak, but not until we have heard everything Eli has to say."

Gerhardt flopped back in his chair.

Hollis faced Samuel next. "I'm not calling your father a liar. But since ownership is in question, any additional evidence would be helpful."

Eli pulled a worn envelope from the breast pocket of his tweed jacket and held it out toward Hollis. "I have this."

Hollis walked around the table to accept it.

"My mother packed a few things for David and me as remembrances when they sent us away," Eli explained. "For all those years in England, I looked at this photo every night before I went to sleep."

Hollis pulled the rough-edged photograph from the envelope. "Oh my God."

"What is it?" Mary asked. She jumped to her feet and ran to Hollis's side. "I can't believe it, not after all these years..."

Hollis walked to the other side of the table and laid the photo in front of Gerhardt.

"There is Rachel posing on the stool, and that is Benjamin looking back at the camera." She looked at Eli, the spitting image of his father. "Am I right?"

He shrugged. "Hold it up to the painting."

There was no need. The pose was identical.

"This photograph does prove that this man's father made the painting," Gerhardt allowed. "But he was just a boy and he can't know what happened to it after he was gone from Berlin."

Eli looked at Samuel. "What is he talking about?"

Hollis spoke as gently as she could. "The question of provenance is not whether or not your father painted the portrait, but whether he made a gift of it to Wilhelm Kunst."

Eli stared at Gerhardt. "Is that what you think?"

"It's what I know," he answered.

Hollis took control of the conversation yet again. "Mr. Meyer, do you have anything else to say before we listen to Mr. Kunst?"

The old man shook his head, his eyes tearing once again.

"Only that this simple painting, made by my own father of my beloved sister, is the only thing left of my family and our life in Germany. I want her back for these reasons."

"Fair enough." Hollis sighed. "Let's take a ten-minute break, and then Mr. Kunst will tell us his story."

As the occupants of the conference room rose and wandered out in search of water or a restroom, Mary sidled up to Hollis.

"He doesn't know about the writing on the back."

"And we aren't going to say anything about it." Hollis tapped her chin. "Gerhardt will bring it up, of course. Let's see how that plays out."

ЖK

Fifteen minutes later, all the family members had reconvened in the conference room.

"It's your turn, now," Hollis said to Gerhardt. "Tell us about what happened to the painting after Eli left Berlin."

"Benjamin Meyer gave the painting to my father, Wilhelm Kunst." Gerhardt cleared his throat. "The painting was a gift, because my father—all of seventeen at the time—was deeply in love with Rachel."

"But your father wasn't Jewish," Eli blurted.

"No," Gerhardt said carefully. "My father was a reasonable man and never believed the racist lies."

"But my father would never have allowed Rachel to be with a man who wasn't Jewish," Eli countered.

"Can we please move on?" Hollis interrupted. "We can't speculate today on what *might* have happened, only what *did* happen."

"When the painting was finished, it hung in the Meyer's drawing room." He looked at Eli. "It was the room connected to the dining room, and on the wall farthest from the window."

Eli paled. "I do not doubt that your father was our neighbor Wilhelm, and I do not doubt that he visited the house. But that does not make the painting yours."

Hollis turned to Gerhardt. "So how *did* your father get the painting, Mr. Kunst?"

Gerhardt twisted his hands together on the smooth tabletop.

"As Mr. Meyer has said, one night the Meyer family disappeared."

Though she heard this before, Hollis felt the sting of tears once again. "Your father was devastated."

Gerhardt nodded somberly. "Yes. He went into the Meyer's house and it was completely torn apart. Anything that looked valuable was gone."

"But the painting of Rachel was still there?" Hollis prompted.

Gerhardt looked at Eli. "They tossed it in the fireplace because it was unimportant."

Eli gave a little groan. "Thank God it was summer and there was no fire."

"My father took the painting because he loved Rachel."

Samuel leaned forward and spoke to Hollis. "Wilhelm took the painting *after* Benjamin was gone. It was never a gift. He stole it."

Gerhardt spread his hands, a cocky expression on his face. "So you must understand his surprise, then, when he turned the painting over and saw the inscription."

Eli straightened. "What inscription?"

Gerhardt's gaze cut to Hollis. "They don't know?"

She shook her head.

"What inscription?" Samuel demanded.

Hollis turned the painting over and set it back on the easel.

Eli and Samuel both stood and Samuel let his father approach the canvas first. When they saw the words *For Wilhelm, B Meyer*, both men turned to stare at Gerhardt

"You wrote that!" Eli accused.

"Why would I do that?" Gerhardt stood. "The painting had no monetary value!"

"Then your father did it!" Samuel declared.

"Gentlemen." Hollis used her most authoritative voice. "Sit

down. *Now*."

Once the three were perched on their seats, Hollis delineated the logic. "First of all, that inscription was on the painting before Ezra Kensington bought it."

Samuel glanced at his fathcr.

"Second," Hollis continued. "I believe Benjamin saw the writing on the wall, both with his daughter and with Germany, and when the inevitable happened he hoped Wilhelm would rescue the painting."

Eli's expression shifted as he considered this new perspective.

"Lastly, Wilhelm truly *did* believe that this painting was a gift from Benjamin—one he could never give to Wilhelm openly, considering the rampant anti-Semitism throughout Germany."

Hollis paused, deciding to throw in her own spin on the situation. "And since the painting was found, I've come to believe that this gift was Benjamin's way of acknowledging the doomed love that Wilhelm and Rachel shared."

No one spoke. The only sound in the room was the whir of the heat through the air vents.

Samuel broke the silence first. "How did the painting get to Arizona?"

Gerhardt shifted in his chair. "When my father returned to his house with the painting, my grandfather told him to pack one single suitcase. He said they were leaving Germany that same night."

"And they did?"

"Yes." Gerhardt shifted from Wilhelm's story to his own. "My father moved to Arizona after the war and settled in Mesa. I was born there in nineteen-forty-six." He turned to Amelia, who up until now was a non-player in the discussion. "Show them the picture."

Amelia opened her purse and produced the four-inch square, glossy, black-and-white photo with the year nineteen-forty-six stamped in the border. She slid it across the table to Eli.

"That's me the week I was born." Gerhardt pointed at the

photo. "As you can see, the painting has been in my family since Benjamin made it a gift."

Samuel frowned. "So how did this Ezra Kensington guy end up with it?"

"When my father died I was in Germany. My sister held an estate sale before I could return. When I did, the painting was gone."

"Clearly, your family has taken care of this painting since my family was taken away and murdered," Eli said softly. "And for this, I thank you."

Gerhardt held out his hand and Samuel laid the photo in his hand.

"It was a gift," Gerhardt growled. "Even Ms. McKenna referred to it as such."

Eli shook his head. "Forgive me for saying this once again, but you cannot prove it was a gift."

"And you cannot prove it wasn't."

Hollis heaved a sigh, noticing that it didn't hurt much any more. "I'm afraid that Ms. Oberman and I will need to consult a higher authority before a decision is made."

She flashed a crooked smile. "Unless you want us to cut it in half, of course."

Chapter Twenty-Four

Sveyn grinned. "You mentioned Solomon's solution?"

"Yep." Hollis's mouth twisted. "And both men shouted no, so no help there."

Sveyn held the door to the museum's cafeteria open for Hollis and Mary. After discussing their options for lunch, his rumbling belly prompted the easiest solution.

"We have a staff-only dining area, so it's away from the crowds." Mary smiled impishly. "And we can use my staff discount."

After selecting their meals, the trio sat at a table in the farthest corner. "In case any of the family members decide to eat here as well," Sveyn suggested. "I do not believe you want them to hear your conversation."

"Not only gorgeous, but wise," Mary purred. "I have to hear your story. How did you and Hollis meet?"

Sveyn stuck with the story they told Hollis's parents. "We met in September. I started working as a guard at the museum where she works, and I am now assigned to her when she has the ghost hunting people come after the museum is closed."

He smiled.

All true.

"Ghost hunters?" Mary turned to Hollis. "More than the cable show?"

Hollis stopped chewing her Caesar salad and talked around the lettuce. "You saw that?"

"Well, yeah. Everyone who knows you saw that." Mary leaned forward. "There really was a ghost there, right?"

"There was something that the guys caught on camera, yes." Hollis glanced at Sveyn. "But no one's seen anything since the show aired."

"Did it get scared away?" Mary sat back and shook her head. "No. Ghosts don't get scared of people—it's the other way around."

"I don't have an answer for that," Hollis murmured and took another bite.

Sveyn watched the interaction, glad that he was clean-shaven and wearing modern clothing. Though Miranda caught the resemblance between him now and him on camera, no one else had as yet.

Mary turned to Sveyn. "So what are you guarding against?"

He chuckled. "People who believe that if they think hard enough that they can live forever, then it will happen."

"Oh, no." She looked at Hollis. "For real?"

"Afraid so." Hollis sipped her diet cola. "Did you hear about our icon—the Blessing of the Gods?"

Mary's brow puckered. "Maybe…"

"It was in Ezra's hoard. Well, half of it."

Sveyn stiffened wondering how much Hollis was going to reveal about her ordeal.

Her gaze bounced to his, then returned to Mary's. "Long story short, the museum acquired the other half."

He relaxed.

Good choice.

"The story is that possessing one half will drive the owner

insane, but locking the two halves together makes the owner immortal."

Mary's eyes narrowed. "And people actually believe this stuff?"

"They do," Sveyn inserted himself into the conversation. "So between the apparition on the camera, and the ancient icon halves in a double-locked bulletproof case—"

"What?" Mary squeaked.

Hollis's brows shot up. She gave Mary a tight-lipped *yes-I-know-it's-crazy* smile and nodded.

"The museum receives requests every day," Sveyn continued. "People want to visit after hours and see these things for themselves."

Mary shook her head. "And you let them?"

Hollis grinned. "Sure. For two hundred dollars an hour with a four hour minimum."

Mary laughed. "Well played." She turned to Sveyn. "How did you propose?"

"On my knees. In her living room."

"Aww—no big YouTube surprise?"

Sveyn shook his head. "No. After the way Matt treated Hollis, I wanted her to know that I am sincere. And that I will keep the promises I make to her."

Mary sighed and her expression turned dreamy. "Do you have a brother?"

He laughed loudly at that. "He is married." Well, was.

Still true.

"Damn."

Sveyn shrugged. "Sorry."

Hollis dropped her napkin over her salad bowl. "So what will we do about the painting?"

"I'll contact the people where the claim was filed and see what they have to say, but my gut is that it will go back to the Meyers," Mary said. "But in the meantime, let's x-ray it, just for shits and giggles."

Hollis looked surprised. "Do you think there's something under it?"

"I don't know. But when a Jewish artist paints one painting in his entire life, and does it *when* he did it, it makes me curious about why."

Hollis nodded. "You're the expert. Do you have the equipment here?"

"We share it with the Milwaukee Art Museum. I'll call them when I get back to my office and see how soon we can get in."

Sveyn was familiar with x-rays from the war and his recent hospital experience. "What will this show?"

Mary smiled. "It'll show us if Benjamin painted over another painting."

"Maybe a valuable one," Hollis clarified. "In order to hide it from the Nazis."

Sveyn nodded slowly. "And you will not tell the families what you find until after the decision is made."

"I think that's wise." Hollis looked to Mary for confirmation. "Right now, they both say the painting isn't valuable in and of itself, but they want it for sentimental purposes."

Sveyn realized with a stab in his chest that he would give up any amount of money to have something tangible of his parents and brothers. His father's ring was in Ezra's collection—perhaps when he earned enough money he could convince Hollis to put it up for auction and he would buy it from them.

Sveyn sighed. "In the end, perhaps that connection is more valuable than money."

Ӝ

Hollis and Sveyn returned to her parents' home after she drove him around Milwaukee to show him the sights. True, everything was buried under a blanket of snow and the sky threatened more, but Sveyn's life originated in a cold climate and he didn't seem to mind any of that.

There was something that had been niggling in the back of her mind that she wanted to talk to him about before going back to the house.

"When we talk to my parents tonight, I don't think we should mention that you were stabbed at the Renaissance Faire," she began. "Because I want to avoid the gypsy thing with them."

"I agree." He nodded. "I was there, but only you were injured in that accident."

Hollis glanced at the robust man beside her. "You're healing really well."

"Except for the one last bit of sensitivity…" He grinned and winked at her. "I feel as fit as I ever did."

Hollis's gut tingled. She ached to make love to Sveyn with his real body in the real world. "When we get back to Phoenix we'll try it. I don't want to have sex in my parents' house."

"No, not when they have us sleeping in separate rooms." Sveyn turned in his seat. "Perhaps my new story with Robert Ford will be what we tell people from this point forward."

Hollis smiled. "That's actually a good idea. Going forward, no one needs to know about the whole getting you documented thing, now that you officially exist."

She turned into her parents' driveway. "Dad's home already."

When she turned off the car, Sveyn leaned over and gazed into her eyes. He slid one hand up her cheek and into her hair, pulling her face to his. He kissed her, long and deep, until the windshield began to fog.

Hollis pulled back, feeling a little light-headed, "We should go in."

Sveyn hummed a sigh. "I love you, Hollis McKenna, and we are getting closer to the prize."

Ӝ

Hollis's father was in the back yard dumping what looked like black rocks from a bag into a round basin about three feet off the ground. He turned toward Sveyn as his boots crunched in the snow.

"Call me old fashioned," Ian said, setting the bag on the

ground. "But I'm a charcoal man all the way."

Sveyn smiled. "I am old fashioned too, Ian."

Ian looked over Sveyn's clothes, from the boots to his bare head. "Not too cold for you?"

"No. I come from a long line of Norwegians." *True*. "I love the cold." *Mostly true*.

"How'd you end up in Phoenix?" Ian popped the plastic top on a metal container and squirted liquid over the black rocks.

"I was born there."

"Ah." Ian pulled a red wand out of his pocket. He clicked a button and a tiny flame appeared at the end. He chuckled a little. "Not so old fashioned that I need to use matches."

He touched the flame to the rocks and fire spread over their surfaces. Sveyn and Ian watched them burn in silence for a while.

"How did you come to love the cold?" Ian asked, his eyes still on the burning rocks.

"I have traveled to Norway, Scotland, England, and other places in Europe, spending time with members of my family." *True*. Never mind that he could not feel temperature at those times. "While it is nice in Phoenix, I do miss snow." *True again*.

"Do you have a college degree?"

"No."

Only centuries' worth of experiences.

Ian looked up at him. "How will you support my daughter? You certainly can't make much on a guard's salary."

"What are you men talking about?" Hollis walked up. She didn't have a coat on and hugged her arms across her chest.

Sveyn gave her a smug look. "Your father asks how I will support you. I was just about to tell him."

Hollis rolled her eyes. "Dad, I can support myself. More than you know."

Ian shook his head. "And when there are children? Who will care for them?"

Sveyn grinned. "This was my question to her."

Hollis shivered. "Well come inside and we'll talk. Mom wanted to let you know the brats are cooked."

"Okay." Ian considered Sveyn with a new expression. "Let's go inside and have a beer. It'll take about twenty or thirty minutes for this to get hot enough for the brats."

The four adults gathered in the kitchen and Ian asked Sveyn if he wanted light or dark beer.

"Dark. Thank you." He accepted the bottle labeled Guinness and took a long draught. When he lowered the bottle, he sighed. "It has been a very long time since have I enjoyed a stout brew."

"Don't they have it in Phoenix?" Brianne asked as she used tongs to fish the sausages from their fragrant beer and onion bath.

Sveyn looked at Hollis. "I don't know. Hollis prefers wine."

Her cheeks reddened. "They do. I'll take you."

Ian looked confused. "I thought you were born in Phoenix."

Sveyn felt a zing of panic. "I was. But as I said, I traveled to be with family."

"When did you leave?" Brianne asked.

"The first time I left Nor—my *home*—I was fifteen or sixteen."

Hollis's mother *tsked*. "So young."

"What about high school?" Ian pressed.

"Sveyn was home-schooled, and he's so smart he graduated early," Hollis forestalled Sveyn's answer. "Then like he said, he traveled. Family."

"I have learned so much about the world," Sveyn offered. "Now I am in Phoenix and I have a new life." *True again*. "And I have found the woman who makes me whole."

So very true.

"So, besides working as a museum guard, what are your career plans?" Ian was like a wolf with its prey.

Sveyn looked at Hollis. "You tell them. You can explain it better than I can."

Hollis took a gulp of her light beer, looking like she was about to be shot. "Well, when I first saw Sveyn, I thought he was a model…"

"I can see that," Brianne murmured. When Ian shot her an irritated look, she bristled. "What? Look at him. He's gorgeous."

Sveyn's cheeks felt hotter than the burning rocks.

"So," Hollis continued. "After we had this same discussion, where I explained that in the twenty-first century, women don't need to be taken care of—"

"And I said that mothers of children *do*," Sveyn interrupted, noticing Ian's approving reaction.

"*Any* way," Hollis grumbled. "I suggested that he actually try modeling."

Ian's brow wrinkled. "Really? Does that pay well?"

"It's not steady work," Hollis admitted. "But commercials can provide a nice income."

"Sure, if you can get one," Ian countered. "That's not a foregone conclusion."

"I got one."

All eyes moved to rest on Sveyn.

"I am Eric, the face of *Match Point*. They match people online." Sveyn shrugged, trying to loosen the weight of the elder McKennas' incredulous stares. "We filmed my part on Friday."

"Wha—when will it be shown?" Ian stammered.

Hollis flashed a triumphant smile. "They said they wanted it to be on this weekend because it's Valentine's Day and people are thinking about love."

Brianne's eyes were still wide with shock. "Will we be able to see it?"

"I don't know." Hollis looked at Sveyn. "They didn't say what markets it would be in."

"I guess we will wait and see." Sveyn pointed at the sausages cooling on a plate and turned a hopeful face to Ian. "Is the fire hot yet?"

Chapter Twenty-five

Hollis waited until the brats were cooked, and the rest of supper was on the table, and her father said grace, and everyone had taken their first bite and commented on how good it was before she asked, "Okay. Tell me my story."

"Your mother will tell it better than I could," her dad deferred. "But I'll correct her if she makes a mistake."

"Oh, Ian," Brianne groused. "This is serious. Stop making jokes."

He looked offended. "I'm not making jokes."

"Just start at the beginning, Mom," Hollis urged. "And don't leave anything out."

"Well, as you know, we met in college in La Crosse—"

"Wisconsin," Hollis added for Sveyn's sake.

"Right. And after we got married we moved to my hometown of Sparta."

This time Sveyn said, "Wisconsin."

Ian leaned forward. "Okay, this entire story takes place in

Wisconsin."

Hollis chuckled and wagged her head. "Go on, Mom."

"Well, we tried to have children for years. We just couldn't manage to conceive." Brianne heaved a sigh which carried the pain of all those fruitless years. "We were thirty-eight and thirty-seven when my dearest friend, Karen Mueller, came to me absolutely heartbroken."

"I know them." Hollis looked at Sveyn, then back at her mom. "Didn't he move to a church in Eau Claire?"

"Eventually." Hollis's dad laid his hand over her mom's. His eyes were misty.

"Karen's daughter, Kathleen, who was only fifteen at the time, was pregnant."

Hollis's heartbeat stuttered at hearing the name for the first time. "Was I that pregnancy?"

"Yes. And Karen and Howard were determined to make Kathleen give up the baby. After all, Sparta is a tiny little town and Howard was already the Lutheran pastor there."

"But Kathleen was stubborn," Ian added. "She said she didn't want strangers to take her baby."

Hollis drew a deep breath and tried to imagine how frightened Kathleen must have been. "So you offered to take the baby—me."

"Offered?" Her dad snorted. "We begged. For three solid months."

Brianne's expression turned somber. "Finally, Karen and Howard put our request to Kathleen. She knew us well, of course, and she was thrilled."

"So why did that take three months?"

"Because, as we said last night, there were conditions."

Hollis fell back in her chair. "You had to move and take me away."

Her mom nodded. "And never tell you where you came from."

So many ramifications of the tale bashed around in Hollis's head that she didn't know where to start. "Does Kathleen know anything about me?"

"Probably not," her dad admitted. "But Howard and Karen ask about you now and then."

"Is Kathleen still in Sparta?"

Her parents looked at each other. "She went to college in Madison, I thought," her mom said.

"Did she get married?"

Her dad looked apologetic. "We don't know. We weren't allowed to ask for any information about Kathleen."

"And you won't ask them now…"

"Hollis," Sveyn ended his watchful silence. "They have already broken their promise not to tell you. Please do not ask them to do more."

Hollis's shoulders slumped. "What should I do?"

"Do what everyone else does," Sveyn answered. "Look on the internet."

Thursday
February 11

Hollis's phone rang in the middle of a group discussion about what to do for Hollis and Sveyn's shared birthday the next day. The number on her screen was the Milwaukee museum.

"Hello?" She mouthed *sorry* to her mom.

"Hollis? It's Mary."

"Hi, Mary! What's up?"

"The Art Museum had an opening for their x-ray tech to scan the *Rachel* painting right after lunch today, so I took it over there."

Hollis froze, staring at Sveyn. "And?"

"And I'm going to email you the images."

Hollis hit the kitchen table with a fist. "Oh, come on! Just tell me."

"What did they find?" Sveyn asked.

"Way to spoil my fun," Mary teased. Then she said the name like Hollis should know it, "A Max Lieberman."

Hollis's excitement dipped. "A Max who?"

Mary groaned. "Really?"

"Yeah. Really." Hollis turned a confused expression to Sveyn. "Nineteenth-century paintings aren't my area of expertise."

"Well look him up. I'm sending the images now."

"Okay. Thanks."

"And call me after you see them."

"I will."

Hollis hung up the phone and faced the three expectant faces at the table. "The x-ray of Rachel revealed another painting underneath. One by a Max Liebermann."

"Let's look him up!" Her dad jumped up and handed Hollis her laptop, which was on the kitchen counter.

"Google him," Sveyn urged.

"I am." *I've created a monster.* Hollis read the first thing she found out loud.

"The son of a Jewish banker in Berlin, Liebermann studied law and philosophy at the University of Berlin, and later studied painting and drawing in Weimar, Paris, and the Netherlands. After living and working for some time in Munich, he returned to Berlin in 1884, where he remained for the rest of his life."

Hollis looked up from the screen. "Well, Benjamin was in the right location."

"Now look up how much his paintings are worth," her mom said.

Hollis got lost in trails trying to find solid info. "I think Mary's going to have to use her contacts for that answer."

"What about missing paintings?" Sveyn asked.

She typed in *Max Liebermann missing*.

"MonumentsMenFoundation.org?" Hollis laughed. "I had no idea that's still a thing."

"Look at that," her dad pointed at the screen. "So much artwork is still missing. This many years later, I'm betting it was destroyed."

"Or is hanging in someone's house…" Hollis opened another tab and went to her email. "Let's see what exactly we're looking for."

Mary's email had two large images attached.

"Oh. My. *God.*"

Behind the barely visible portrait of Rachel was the portrait of another girl, in the almost identical pose, but wearing clothing from a completely different era. The painting was clearly signed along the bottom in thc right hand corner: *M Liebermann '89*

Sveyn leaned over her shoulder. "Was it stolen by the Nazis?"

"I don't think so. It's listed as from a 'private collection' and 'whereabouts unknown'..." Hollis scrolled down. "The owners are listed as Elijah and Marion Weichsel."

"So Benjamin got the painting from them," Sveyn posited. "Could he have bought it?"

"Maybe." Hollis looked at him over her shoulder. "The question is, could he afford it?"

Sveyn slid back into his chair. "He was an art restorer. Perhaps he traded for it."

"Hopefully Eli will know. After we tell him, that is." Hollis stood. "I have to call Mary back—this changes the situation."

Her dad spun the laptop around to face him while she walked into the living room and dialed Mary's number.

"So, Hollis. What do you think?" Mary's bubbly personality didn't require a salutation.

Hollis laughed. "This is crazy! What are we going to do?"

"Well, I contacted the mediation committee yesterday and gave them the two stories, both of which were substantiated with additional evidence," Mary said. "They promised a ruling in forty-eight hours."

"So Friday afternoon?" Hollis paused. "Let's have the families come back on Monday. Then we won't have to bum-rush the unhappy side."

"Good idea."

"You know, both sides say the painting isn't valuable but they want it for sentimental purposes. So I don't think either one of them has a clue."

"I think you're right." Now Mary paused. "We shouldn't tell them until after we announce the committee's decision."

"Good call," Hollis agreed. "Do you have a sense of which way they'll go?"

"No, they gathered facts, asked a couple questions and said they'll get back to me. Why?"

Hollis hesitated, trying to coral the elusive threads of logic which were linking in her mind. "What would happen if we disagreed with the committee's decision?"

"You mean because we have new information?"

"Yes."

"We could appeal and present what we've found. What are you thinking?"

"I think I know who should get the painting," she stated. "I think the answer to *was* it a gift is obvious."

"Really?" Mary chuckled. "Care to share?"

"Not yet, I'm still working out the details." Hollis sighed. "Promise you'll call me as soon as you hear?"

"Sure thing."

Hollis walked back into the kitchen. Sveyn's long legs stretched under the table, his Nordic frame so different from her adoptive father's.

Am I really a Hansen?

"I've decided what I want to do for my birthday," she announced. "I want to go to Sparta."

Friday
February 12

"This looks like Norway," Sveyn said as Hollis drove the hundred-and-eighty miles across central Wisconsin.

She smiled. "That's why so many Norwegians settled here, I guess."

"And Germans," Ian said from the back seat. "Lots of Germans."

When Hollis announced that she wanted to go to Sparta and try to find out more about the young girl who birthed her, Sveyn thought it was the perfect way to mark the day. And of course, there was no way that Ian and Brianne were staying behind.

Hollis spent the rest of yesterday searching on ancestry sites, telephone and address listing sites, even Facebook, looking for any reference to Kathleen Mueller from Sparta.

Sveyn asked about Hollis's birth certificate, prompted by his own recent experiencc. "Is the father listed?"

Hollis shook her head. "My legal birth certificate always listed my legal parents, the McKennas. But I do know where and when I was born, so that helps."

"We'll check church records," Brianne offered. "And call some of our friends. Somebody has to know who Kathleen was going around with."

"Teachers at the high school might, if any are still there," Hollis added.

"Good idea," Ian said. "I'll go there."

Hollis huffed a laugh. "I appreciate your enthusiasm, Dad, but we only have one car. We'll all go everywhere together."

"Might we be able to walk?" Sveyn asked.

Hollis shrugged. "Maybe. Depends on the weather."

Sveyn squinted at the brilliant blue sky and the bright white ground beneath the acres of dormant forests that they whizzed past. "If this holds, we will have an enjoyable search."

Ӝ

Sparta was a typical midwestern-America town, with a main street lined with hundred-year-old government buildings and repurposed shop fronts and restaurants. Hollis followed her GPS's voice to the Victorian bed-and-breakfast she found online yesterday. Even though it was Valentine's weekend, the dead of winter wasn't when most people visited rural Wisconsin, so she was able to book three rooms.

"Oh, go ahead and stay with him," Brianne said when Hollis told her. "I'm not that naïve."

Hollis blushed a little. "Believe it or not, we haven't—I mean, we're not—"

Brianne put up a hand to hush her. "That's fine. I don't need to know."

As a child Hollis always felt like she was coming home when she and her parents visited her grandparents here. Their cozy nineteen-forties bungalow always smelled like bacon—her grandfather's favorite food. And when her grandma baked, the sweet and savory aromas mixed into what Hollis thought of as comfort.

I wonder if I could get a room freshener that smells like that...

Hollis parked the car and led the charge up the Victorian's front steps. She looked at her watch; it was only ten-thirty. Thanks to the clear day, they made the drive in good time.

"Let's get settled in and start our search." She looked at her parents. "Most of our targets will be closed tomorrow, so now's our chance."

Chapter Twenty-Six

Their first stop was the hospital where Hollis was born.

"Records are in the basement," the cheery girl in the candy-striped apron said. "Take the elevator at the end of the hall."

This hospital was much smaller and older than the one Sveyn and Hollis had been in. He almost made a comment about that before remembering that his own part in that fateful day at the Renaissance Faire was a secret.

Ian opened the door to the records' room and the four members of their group filed in.

Hollis stepped up to the desk and asked for the records from her birth. The bookish man, who was clearly surprised by the sudden crowd at his counter, had her fill out a paper, show her driver's license, and then he looked at the date.

"Happy birthday."

She gave what Sveyn thought of as her *polite* smile. "Thank you."

"This might take a minute. Our new records are digital, and

we're still working on scanning in the old stuff."

Sveyn pressed his lips together, refusing to smile at Hollis's birth being called old.

"Fine." She looked around the small chair-less space. "We'll just be standing here."

The man returned after a very long eleven minutes. "Here you are. The application for a birth certificate."

Hollis nearly grabbed it from the man's hand. Her eyes flitted over the paper, then she turned a defeated face to Sveyn.

"She wrote that the father is unknown."

Ian reached over and rubbed his daughter's shoulders. "That happens a lot. I'd bet Karen told her to write that."

Hollis asked for a copy of the paper anyway. "There might be other clues. Or it's a souvenir."

"The church next?" Brianne asked as they waited for the elevator.

"What are we looking for there?" Hollis asked.

"Confirmation records. Maybe a name will pop out."

Sveyn looked at Brianne. "Do you believe the father to be the same age as Kathleen?"

Brianne's eyes widened. "No! He's older! I remember Karen saying something about him being a senior…"

Hollis counted backward. "A summer fling before college? Kathleen would have been between her freshman and sophomore year when she conceived."

Ian nodded. "So we'll go back four years, just to be sure."

The church secretary at the Lutheran church was clearly put out by the request. "Those logs are in a closet in the old office building."

"We'd be happy to search through them so you don't have to," Ian told her with a smile. "We know which four years we need and confirmation only happens twice a year."

"Hmph." The woman called somebody on the phone. "Can you come get some visitors and show them to the file closet?"

She hung up. "He's on his way."

The man who escorted them was much cheerier and greeted them with a grin. "I'm Marcus. So what are you folks looking for?"

"Confirmation records," Hollis answered. "I was adopted and I'm trying to find my father."

"Like putting a puzzle together." Marcus nodded. "Or a murder mystery."

Surprised at that choice of words, Sveyn looked askance at Ian. "Let us hope not."

The closet was filled with shelves, and the shelves were filled with binders. Thankfully the dates were on the spines, if not the type of records inside them.

"Do you folks need any help?"

Brianne smiled kindly. "No, we can manage. But thank you."

Marcus looked disappointed. "Are you sure?"

Hollis shot Sveyn a resigned look. "I guess you could hand us the notebooks we need, then put them back when we're done."

Marcus smiled like it was *his* birthday. "Happy to!"

Each of the four took one year, starting with Kathleen's assumed confirmation year. "Found her!" Hollis called out.

"Should we try and get copies made, or just write down the names?" Ian asked.

Brianne handed out pens and tore slips of paper from a shopping-list pad in her purse. "This will be faster."

Sveyn accepted the task, though his handwriting was still rough. He could not wait to find a Hansen.

Ӝ

An hour later, the group cozied into a booth at a diner and ordered a hot lunch. A soap opera played softly on a flat screen TV over the dinette's counter, while two women in business attire and one man dressed like a laborer sat on the red vinyl stools and watched as they ate.

While they waited to be served, Hollis's little group read each other's lists. Hollis was looking for Hansens.

She knew there was no way she could say anything to her parents about Sveyn's contention that she descended from his father—who was born a thousand years and forty generations ago. But after knowing the Viking for these last five-and-a-half months, she believed he knew what he was talking about.

She found six Hansens on the lists, two of which were boys. One of those was three years ahead of Kathleen in school. Hollis put a little checkmark next to his name: Aleksander Hansen.

Then she slid the list under Sveyn's hand.

He gave her a puzzled glance before he looked at the names. Then he smiled, and handed back the paper.

"What is it?" Brianne lifted her teabag from its steaming cup and wrapped the string around the spoon to squeeze it. "Did you find something?"

"Oh, Sveyn thinks it would be funny if I turned out to be a Hansen." Hollis kept her tone flippant. "And there's a boy on the list who's the right age."

The waitress and a busboy showed up with plates of food and began dispersing them around the table.

"I like how people here eat." Sveyn smiled. "It reminds me of home."

Ian's brows pulled together. "Phoenix? Really?"

"Sveyn thinks of Norway as his home," Hollis covered. "He spent a lot of time there, like he said."

The waitress brightened as she set his plate on front of him. "*Snakker du Norsk?*"

"*Ja*," he replied. "*Jeg lærte norsk før jeg lærte engelsk.*"

"*Jeg også!*"

Whatever they were saying, the waitress was clearly flirting with Sveyn. Hollis laid her hand on his arm and interrupted their little Norse party.

"Mom wants to know if the church is still available on our wedding date."

Sveyn coughed a laugh. The waitress whirled around and walked away, hips swaying defiantly.

Her father winked at her, grinning. "Well played, daughter."

"What's mine is mine." She leaned against Sveyn's muscled

arm. "And this hunk of Viking is mine."

A very familiar voice pulled her attention to the television. "Oh my gosh! Look!"

Sveyn's image filled the screen.

She hit his arm with the back of his hand. "It's your commercial!"

Her outburst pulled the attention of the three customers at the counter. They looked at her, Sveyn, the television, back to Sveyn, and back to the television.

"It *is* you—isn't it?" one of the ladies asked.

Sveyn's face was as red as his cream of tomato soup. "Yes."

"We have a celebrity here!" The other woman beamed. "Can I have your autograph?"

Ӝ

Sveyn was glad when they finished lunch and escaped the diner. He hoped that this kind of thing was not going to be a common occurrence—that was not anything he considered when he agreed to do the commercial.

He was especially grateful that Hollis hurried their exit along with the reminder that the high school office would close in a couple hours and none of the staff was likely to stay late on a Friday.

"And it's a three-day weekend. President's Day is Monday.

Hollis entered the office first and stepped up to the counter. "I need to speak with anyone in this school who was working here thirty years ago."

The twenty-something secretary blinked. "Why?"

"Because I'm trying to find my father. And in order to do that, I'm hoping that someone remembers who my mother was dating before I was born."

The woman's brow furrowed rather deeply for someone so young, Sveyn thought. Maybe she was easily confused.

Hollis's well-stated question seemed to have completely discomfited her.

"I don't know…"

Hollis drew a breath. "Then could I speak with the person in this office who has been here the longest?"

"I'm not sure…"

"The oldest person *here*," Hollis simplified.

A stout woman with gray hair, gray skirt, and bright bird-like eyes stepped out of an office to the side of the counter. "I've got this, Heather."

Heather turned around and slunk back to a desk, where she immediately busied herself with organizing pens.

The older woman faced Hollis. "How can I help you?"

Brianne stepped forward. "Polly Carson?"

"Yes—oh my goodness! Brianne!" Her jaw dropped. "What are you doing here?"

"This is my—adopted—daughter, Hollis." Brianne paused. Sveyn could see how hard this was for her. "She is trying to find her father, but to do that we need to know who her mother was dating thirty years ago."

Polly nodded knowingly. "She didn't name him on the birth certificate."

"No."

Polly turned to Hollis. "But you know who your mother is."

Hollis nodded. "I was adopted privately. The girl who birthed me was the daughter of my mom's best friend."

"And what was her name?"

"Kathleen Mueller."

"That name is familiar. Let's pull out a yearbook and look her up." Polly pushed a button and the counter-height gate popped open. "Come on back."

The quartet walked single file behind Polly, past office doors, glass cases filled with dusty trophies, and posters proclaiming something called a Sweetheart Dance. Polly stopped and unlocked a door, which hid yet another room of shelves and books.

"We keep three yearbooks from every year in storage here, for whatever reason comes up." Polly looked up at Sveyn. "You never know when a graduate might become famous."

Sveyn recoiled and looked at Hollis. Did she recognize him already?

Hollis made an *of course not* face and spoke to Polly. "She would have been a freshman thirty-one years ago."

Polly perched a pair of reading glasses on her nose and ran her finger along a shelf until she found the right year. "Here we go. You said Mueller?"

Sveyn watched over Hollis's shoulder as the book's pages flipped by. When she hit the first page with tiny rectangular black and white pictures, Polly stopped and laid the book flat.

"Let's see…" She turned two pages. "Here she is."

Ӝ

Hollis stared at the young teen who was her mother. Her throat swelled and tears stung her eyes. "I look like her."

Brianne put her arm around Hollis's shoulders. "Yes, you do."

Polly flipped to the index in the back of the book. "Let's see if there are any more pictures of her."

There were two. One of her painting banners for a pep rally, and one of her at the Sweetheart Dance. With a tall, light-haired boy.

Hollis pointed at the black-and-white picture. "Who's that? Does it say?"

"No."

Hollis looked at Sveyn and he nodded his encouragement. She turned back to Polly.

"Could you look up a name in the back?"

Polly looked at her over the rim of the pink glasses. "Of course. What name?"

"Aleksander Hansen. With a KS instead of an X."

Polly skimmed the index. "Here he is. And he's listed on that same page." Polly flipped back to the dance photo page. "The boy in the top photo is tagged as Aleksander."

"Not the one at the dance with Kathleen?" Hollis made a sad

face; that was disappointing.

"Is there a picture of Aleksander in the front part?" Sveyn asked.

"Yes. He would have been a senior," Hollis gambled.

Polly turned to the senior class photos, which were much larger and more focused. "This is Aleksander."

It was the same light-haired boy in the dance picture with Kathleen.

"They tagged the wrong photo." Hollis turned to her mom and dad. "On the other page! They tagged the wrong photo!"

Brianne's hands visibly trembled. "This really could be your father."

Hollis faced Polly again. "I have a *huge* favor to ask you."

"You want to borrow the yearbooks."

"Yes. Please? May I? I'll give you a security deposit. A hundred dollars a book." Hollis gave Polly her most sincere and pleading look. "I only want to go through them and scan all the photos. And I'll have them back to you by the end of the weekend. I swear."

"That's Tuesday, you know."

"We are going back to Milwaukee on Sunday," her dad said softly.

"Then I'll drop them at your house. Tomorrow. Please," Hollis begged.

Polly turned back to the shelf. Her smile was impishly conspiratorial. "Which years do you want?"

Chapter Twenty-Seven

Saturday
February 13

Last night in the drawing room of the Victorian house where they were staying, Sveyn watched Hollis turn every page in the four yearbooks that she brought back from the high school and bookmark each page that she wanted to scan.

"Tomorrow we'll go to that big office supply store down the road," she told him as she settled on the floor next to the coffee table. "They do printing so I'm sure we can scan there, too."

"That sounds like a good plan," he replied. "Then we can return the books afterwards."

The pleasant older woman who ran the guest house came in and turned on the television. "I hope you don't mind."

Hollis looked up from the first yearbook and smiled. "Not at all."

She leaned over Hollis. "What are you working on?"

Hollis's tone was much more casual than Sveyn knew her

emotions were. "Finding my father."

The woman looked at Sveyn. "Did I hear her correctly?"

Sveyn nodded. "My fiancée—" He loved that he could finally call her that. "Was adopted. While she knows who her mother was, she is trying to discern who might be her father."

"So the older couple with you?"

"Adopted her."

The woman smiled. "They seem like lovely people."

"This is weird," Hollis said from the floor. She looked up at Sveyn. "Kathleen isn't in her sophomore yearbook."

Sveyn had no answer for that. "Perhaps your mother will know why?"

"What will I know?" Brianna and Ian came into the room.

Hollis turned around to look at her mother. "Why Kathleen isn't in her sophomore yearbook."

Brianne sat on the settee across the coffee table from Hollis. "She was pregnant, remember. And attitudes were different thirty years ago, especially in a small town."

Hollis's face twisted. "So Karen and Howard hid her away?"

"Sent her away, actually." Ian sat beside his wife. "To stay with a cousin in Minneapolis."

Hollis spread her hands in question. "But what about school?"

"Correspondence school. Via snail mail." Brianne laughed a little. "That's what they did before the internet."

Hollis tapped the table top. "But I was born *here*."

"After the Muellers agreed we could adopt you, I transferred to Milwaukee to work, but your mom stayed here," Ian explained.

"We told everyone it was a promotion, so we didn't have to answer a lot of questions," Brianne added. "Your dad got us an apartment and I waited for you to be born."

Brianne squeezed her husband's knee. "Kathleen came back here a couple weeks before you were due, and as soon as you were born I bundled you up and drove to our new life."

"As first time parents in a new home in a new city." Ian blew a heavy sigh. "Let's just say, we survived."

"You did all of that for me." Hollis looked up at Sveyn, her eyes glistening. "I had no idea."

"You said they were good parents," he reminded her. "You were a very blessed baby."

"Oh my!" Their hostess pointed at the television. "Is that you?"

Sveyn whirled around and stared at himself on the screen once again. This commercial was slightly different than the first one they saw. And it was still very odd to watch himself.

"I like this version," Hollis said. "I really love your smile at the end."

As it turned out, that commercial played every thirty minutes all evening as the older woman watched program after program about people with problems. Hollis said this was the same station that had programs about hoarders, and it focused on something she called 'lifestyles.'

Whatever that was, it obviously attracted lonely women.

Now the two of them were in the office supply store, and Sveyn assisted Hollis with the scanning of the yearbooks. It took a few minutes for each photo; after the machine ran its light over the page, Hollis checked the image on a monitor and then saved to a device she called a flash drive.

Sveyn waited for her to admit what he knew she wanted to do next, but didn't have the courage for.

While she was reading the yearbooks last night, Ian asked their hostess if she had a phone book. When she produced one, Ian flipped through it, paused, and motioned Sveyn to his side.

Sveyn looked at the spot Ian indicated.

Aleksander Hansen.

"He still lives here," Ian murmured.

Sveyn looked into his future father-in-law's eyes. "She should go see him."

"I think so, too."

Hollis grinned. "What are you two cooking up over there?"

"Aleksander Hansen still lives in Sparta," Sveyn said.

Hollis's smile faded, replaced by expressions shifting from surprise to joy to fear to confusion. "What should I do?"

Sveyn squatted beside her. "Go see him and ask him if he is your father."

"I can't do that… can I?" She clearly wanted him to say no. And yes.

Sveyn nodded. "We can go tomorrow after you copy the pages."

"Just, what? Knock on the door and say, 'Hi, Dad'?" Hollis was clearly panicking.

Sveyn tucked a strand of unruly red hair behind her ear. "Ask him if he dated Kathleen. If he says no, then you'll know."

"And if he says yes…"

"Then tell him he might be your father."

Hollis did not agree to that plan last night. But the constant crease between her brows this morning told Sveyn she was still thinking about it.

She handed him the last yearbook. "Okay. Done. Let's go pay."

The day was cloudier than yesterday and the intermittent breeze smelled like snow. Once Hollis started the car, she waited for it to warm up before she made any move toward engaging the gears.

"I have his address," Sveyn said softly.

"I'm scared."

"I know." Sveyn laid his hand over hers. "Tell me what you are scared of."

Hollis hesitated. "I'm scared he's my father." She turned wide eyes to his. "And I'm scared that he's not."

Sveyn understood both answers. "What is the worst that can happen?"

Hollis huffed a laugh. "That he's not home."

Sveyn smiled. "Let's go find out."

Hollis shifted the car into drive.

Ӝ

Sveyn wondered if he would still be able to recognize his

father's descendants, now that he was back in a normal body in the real world. Before, when he manifested, he could see the connection. Something intangible always confirmed that he shared a bloodline with his latest victim.

So when Aleksander Hansen opened his front door, what would happen?

Hollis parked in front of the house that the cheerful voice in her phone told her was her destination. "There's a car in the driveway," she said quietly. "So that's good. Somebody's there."

Sveyn pulled the handle on his door. "Are you ready?"

"No." Hollis grabbed her door's handle. "But let's get this over with."

Sveyn followed Hollis up the brick path to the front door. She pressed the doorbell with a gloved finger. They waited, the chime inside sounding softly through the door.

The inner door opened and a tall man with gray temples looked at them through the glass-and-screen outer door. He pushed it open about a foot and asked, "Can I help you?"

Sveyn sucked a breath. His chest tightened. He did know.

This is him.

"Are you Aleksander?" Hollis's voice sounded strained.

"Yes. And you are?"

Hollis was obviously thrown. "Are you in good health?"

He scowled. "Whatever you're selling I'm not interested."

Hollis grabbed the door to keep him from closing it. "We're not selling anything, I just don't want to give you a heart attack."

Aleksander snorted. "Why would I have a heart attack?"

"Because…" Hollis pulled a deep breath. "I think I'm your daughter."

Ӝ

Aleksander squinted at the sky. "Honey, I don't think that's possible."

Hollis felt her chance slipping away, so she threw her very best pitch. "Did you date Kathleen Mueller when you were a senior in high school?"

Aleksander paled. "You better come in."

Hollis stepped inside the cozy and typically middle-class home. "My name is Hollis McKenna, and this is my fiancé, Sveyn Hansen."

"Another Hansen, huh?"

When the men shook hands Hollis felt the air tingle. She stared at Sveyn to see if he noticed, but he didn't look at her.

Instead, he smiled at Aleksander. "It is quite a common name, as you know."

"Especially in these parts." Aleksander waved them to the couch. "Please explain yourself."

Hollis pushed her coat off her shoulders and it rested around her hips like a nest. Sveyn planted himself silently beside her, still not looking at her.

"There is a photo of you and Kathleen Mueller in her freshman yearbook. I just want to know if you two were close."

Aleksander's eyes narrowed. "Very. We dated for several months."

Hollis's heart stumbled and she put a hand against her chest. The idea that her heart might stop sometime still nibbled at the edges of her thoughts, even though the doctors assured her it was unlikely to happen again.

"Then you broke up with her when you went to college?"

"No. She broke up with me."

That was a surprise. "Really?"

He nodded. "In October, right before Sparta's homecoming weekend. She said she didn't like having a boyfriend who wasn't there for all the high school events."

October.

Three months after she conceived.

"Were you upset?"

"Sure, you how it is. Young love." Aleksander's expression turned wistful. "I had hopes it might last."

Somehow, that helped. "Did you see her when you came home?"

"No. She avoided me." He sighed. "After a while, I stopped

trying."

Time to drop the bomb.

"That's because she was pregnant. With me."

Aleksander stared at her, obviously looking for hints she was right. "If that's true, why didn't she tell me?"

"Her parents locked her down. Sent her to Minneapolis to live with a cousin and take correspondence classes."

His skepticism was clear. "How do you know this?"

"Because I was adopted by Howard and Karen's best friends."

"The McKennas?" Aleksander's expression brightened. "Of course. I remember that name. They did hang out with the Muellers. Whatever happened to them?"

Hollis felt a lump grow in her throat as she recalled the lengths her parents went to so they could raise her as theirs. "The Muellers insisted they move away with me so Kathleen could pick up her life like I never happened."

Aleksander nodded. "That sounds like them." He considered her again. "When were you born?"

"Yesterday was my thirty-first birthday."

Aleksander slumped in his chair. "Oh my God."

"Yeah." Hollis pressed her lips together and waited for the man—who had to be pushing fifty—to catch up with what just happened.

"You're my daughter."

"Yep."

His eyes narrowed again. "What do you want from me?"

Hollis gaped. "Nothing! I just found out I was adopted a couple weeks ago, so I wanted to find my birth parents. I promise you—that's the extent of it."

"And to know who she is descended from."

Hollis and Aleksander stared at Sveyn, who had remained silent since their introduction.

"What do you mean?" Hollis asked, knowing full well what he meant.

Sveyn addressed Aleksander. "Would you write down the names of your father, and your grandfather? Great-grandfather as well. If you know it."

"Of course I know it. I have a whole family tree constructed on Ancestry." Aleksander chuckled. "You probably want to make sure you two aren't related before the wedding, right?"

Hollis turned startled eyes to Sveyn. What made him say that?

Sveyn chuckled as well. "That would be awkward, would it not?"

Hollis pulled the men back to Sveyn's initial query. "Would you be willing to share that family tree with me?"

"Sure. Why not. Write down your email address and I'll send you a link."

While Hollis complied with the request, Aleksander asked, "So will I see you again?"

"I actually live in Phoenix now." She handed *her father* the slip of paper. "I'm a collections manager in a museum there. But we can be in contact. If you don't mind, I'd like that."

Aleksander rubbed the paper between his finger and thumb as he considered her, *his daughter*. "You know, Karen has hair like yours."

"No, I didn't. Did Kathleen?"

He shook his head. "And she was glad she didn't. But I always liked it."

Sveyn stood. "Thank you for speaking with us. I know how much Hollis appreciates it."

Hollis stood as well. "I do have one last question to ask."

Aleksander clasped his hands behind his back. "Go on."

"What's your blood type?"

Chapter Twenty-Eight

"O-negative," Hollis said to Brianne. "That's where I got it."

Brianne sat in the drawing room sipping tea and nibbling homemade scones. Hollis sat next to her, her legs tucked under her, while Ian read a newspaper in a nearby chair.

"These are amazing." Hollis turned to Sveyn. "Taste them."

Sveyn obeyed. And Hollis was right.

"I'm going upstairs to get your laptop," he said. "I want to see if Aleksander invited you to the family tree yet."

Hollis smiled knowingly. "Okay."

Sveyn returned with the computer. He set it on the coffee table next to the plate of scones and opened it. He clicked on Google, then on the email icon. Hollis's inbox opened.

"Is it there?" Hope colored her voice as much as it colored his mood.

"No—yes! It just arrived." He looked at her. "May I continue?"

"Sure. You're going to be my husband, so we have no

secrets."

Sveyn wondered what Ian and Brianne would think if they knew the extent to which that statement was true. He opened the email and clicked the icon which opened the site.

He turned the laptop toward Hollis. "You need to create an account."

While she did, Sveyn noticed Ian watching him. "Does something concern you, Ian?"

He set his newspaper down. "How much will you make from the commercials?"

"Dad!" Hollis barked.

Ian's gaze moved to hers. "You mentioned that he's going to be your husband and I have some concerns."

Sveyn looked at Hollis as well. "As your father, he has the right to ask these things."

Then he spoke to Ian. "I do not know what the total amount will be, but I do get paid something each time the commercial is on television, multiplied by the number of stations that show it."

Ian looked impressed. "That could be some serious money."

"I hope so."

Hollis unfolded her legs and leaned forward. "Dad, I need to tell you something."

"Hollis, please don't start an argument," Brianne pleaded.

"I'm not." Her consideration moved to Sveyn. "But something happened that I didn't tell you guys about."

Sveyn knew what that was; as an apparition he heard every word that came out of Hollis's mouth, no matter how loud or soft, and there was one glaring omission in her conversations with Ian and Brianne.

He leaned back on the settee and rested his hand on the small of her back.

"When I was attacked back in November, I was actually drugged and kidnapped," she began. When Ian's eyes moved to Sveyn, Hollis noticed. "Not by Sveyn—he saved me!"

"Were you badly hurt?" Brianne asked.

"I would've been if Sveyn hadn't intervened." Hollis tried to give an explanation that would make sense. "You just couldn't see him on the YouTube video the museum posted."

Hollis then proceeded with a very stripped down version of Everett Sage's actions, ending with his plea bargain while her stunned parents stared at her.

"So because he pled guilty, I was able to sue him for damages in civil court." Hollis shrugged. "And I won."

"How much?" Ian asked. "If you don't mind saying."

Hollis looked like she did mind somewhat. "Enough to pay cash for a nice house in a nice Phoenix suburb, and tuck away a generous retirement fund after that."

"Oh." Ian cleared his throat. "Was this before Sveyn proposed?"

Hollis looked like a mother bear protecting her cub and Sveyn was afraid Ian was about to get the worst of it.

"Yes, Ian, it was," he said to forestall the feminine outburst he anticipated. "And that is why I agreed to do the commercials. I want to bring my own financial worth to the marriage."

"Dad. Sveyn probably saved my life. Do you *get* that?" Hollis growled.

"Honey, I just—"

Hollis swung her arm around to point at him, nearly planting a finger in his eye socket. "I'd give him half the money even if he hadn't proposed! Because he deserves it!"

Sveyn gripped her hovering hand and set it in her lap. He would never have accepted that money, but to say so now would only fan Hollis's fire.

"I believe your point is made," he said calmly.

"Dad?" Hollis prodded. "Do you have anything else to say?"

Ian looked older all of a sudden. "I forget that you're a grown woman, Hollis, and capable of handling your own life. I apologize." His gaze jumped to Sveyn. "To both of you."

Hollis's body relaxed. "Apology accepted."

Sveyn smiled his acceptance. "Ian, I hope that when Hollis and I have a family, that I will be as diligent a father as you are."

Brianne patted Hollis's hand. "I'm sorry about what you went through, but I wish you would have told us."

"I didn't want to worry you, Mom."

Sveyn reached forward, woke up the laptop that had gone black, and changed the subject. "Shall we look at Aleksander's family tree?"

"Yeah. Let's." Hollis leaned against his shoulder. "Click there."

When he did, a sort of maze appeared on the screen. "Here is Aleksander. He has a wife and children." Sveyn slid his gaze sideways to Hollis. "You have two half-siblings."

"Hmm. Maybe I'll look them up on Facebook, but not until I'm sure he's told them about me."

Sveyn moved up a level. "Aleksander's father, Thor Hansen, was born in nineteen-forty-five. His wife, Elsie Baumann was born in nineteen-forty-seven."

"How many children did they have?"

"There are four names."

"And Thor's father?" Hollis asked.

Sveyn moved up a level. What he saw should not have been a surprise, but it was nonetheless.

"Thor's father, Tor Hansen, was born in Arendal, Norway in nineteen-fifteen." Sveyn's throat thickened and he rubbed his eyes before tears could fall. "He died in nineteen-forty-five."

"Sveyn?" Hollis whispered.

He nodded.

He was with Tor when the man died—only six months ago in his own warped existence. Tor was the soldier he had followed in his last manifestation during the war with Germany.

And he was Hollis's great-grandfather.

Sveyn cleared his throat and squinted at the screen. "He was married to Kyle Solberg, an American born in nineteen-nineteen. She passed in nineteen-eighty-nine."

Hollis laid a hand on his arm. He rested his palm over it.

"We have to drop off those yearbooks," Hollis said. "How about we do that on the way to dinner?"

"Dinner?" Brianne laughed. "I'm full of scones."

"I didn't mean now." Hollis squeezed Sveyn's arm. "I want to lie down for a little while. I'm done in."

Sveyn closed the laptop. "I'll come up with you for a while."

"Dinner at five?" Hollis asked as she stood.

"Sounds great," Ian answered. "Let's try the German Haus. I always liked that place."

Hollis crossed the room and kissed his cheek. "Thanks, Dad. I love you."

He kissed the top of her head.

As Sveyn followed Hollis out of the room, he saw his face on the muted television.

Hi, I'm Eric. Are you my match?

Ӝ

Hollis was stunned to discover that Sveyn knew her great-grandfather, and judging by his sudden emotions he must have liked Tor.

She also wanted to ask him about the electrical tingle she felt when he shook Aleksander's hand, though after discovering the direct connection the men had, she assumed that was what caused it.

Hollis and Sveyn laid close on the bed so they could speak softly. This conversation was not one she wished for anyone to overhear and ask her about.

"First of all, did you feel anything funny when you met Aleksander?"

Sveyn nodded. "I wondered if I would still recognize my father's descendants if I was to meet one in this body. But as soon as he spoke, I felt it. I knew."

"When you shook his hand I felt the same kind of electrical tingle I used to feel when we tried to touch—back before all this changed." Hollis frowned. "Why do you think that is?"

"I have no idea. Perhaps I have changed you."

"So." Hollis turned on her side to face Sveyn. "Tor Hansen was your last manifestation?"

"Yes."

"The World War Two soldier who died in Italy?" Hollis looked stricken. "Oh, no! Did he ever see his son?"

Sveyn sighed heavily. "No. I am afraid he did not."

"How long were you with him?"

"I manifested to him when he was getting on the plane to fly from Colorado to Europe."

Hollis wiped away a tear rolling over the bridge of her nose. "Did he say anything to you?"

Sveyn smiled sadly. "He asked if I was his guardian angel."

Monday
February 15

Yesterday's drive from Sparta to Milwaukee was exhausting. The snow which Sveyn said he smelled on Saturday came down in a constant but thankfully windless flurry. Even so, the roads were slippery and Hollis's arms were stiff when she finally pulled into her parents' driveway.

"Not a very romantic way to spend Valentine's Day, huh?" she muttered to Sveyn as she navigated around a slow semi-trailer.

"We have many years ahead to celebrate," he reminded her. "And when we do, we will be married."

Hollis slept late this morning, burrowing under the covers until Sveyn came in and rousted her out just before eleven.

He kissed her soundly before asking, "Do you still have a meeting at the museum about the painting?"

"Yes. At one." She groaned and stretched. "I guess I should get to it."

Sveyn came with her to the museum again, stating that he found it fascinating to explore. "If I am going to spend the rest of my life with a collections manager, I should become familiar with different methods for display, should I not?"

Hollis laughed. "You just don't want to be home where my father can grill you with more questions."

"No, but if he would grill more brats I would be very happy."

Hollis stepped back while he opened the museum door.

"They do sell brats in Phoenix, you know."

Sveyn's cheeks split in a wide grin. "I did not. Now I am even happier to return."

The same gal was working at the front desk.

"Would you please let Mary Oberman know that Hollis McKenna is here?"

"Hello, again." She smiled at Sveyn. "I saw you on TV."

"I'm still over here."

The girl's irritated gaze shifted to Hollis. "Sah-reee," she warbled.

Hollis lifted her cheeks in an admittedly insincere smile. "I'm here to see Mary Oberman."

She picked up the phone with a sigh. "And you are?"

Hollis spoke slowly yet again. "Hollis. McKenna."

"Is she expecting you?"

"Yes."

Hollis shook her head. Sveyn laughed outright.

Mary appeared from a different direction this time. "Oh good. You're here."

Hollis looked at her watch. "I'm early."

"So were they."

"Text me when you finish," Sveyn said. "And take all the time you need." Then he walked toward the twentieth-century wing. World War Two.

Welcome to the current focus of my life.

Hollis returned her attention to Mary. "Have you said anything to them yet?"

"No. I was hoping you would."

"Me? Why?"

"Because you said you figured it out." Mary leaned closer. "And Gerhardt won't argue with you."

"Wanna bet?" Hollis scoffed. "So did the mediation people send anything written?"

"Yeah, it's in my office." Mary linked her arm through Hollis's. "Come with me and together we can brace for the storm."

Chapter Twenty-Nine

Hollis walked into the conference room to find both the Kunst and Meyer family members sitting in the same places as their last meeting. Once again, Mary walked to the head of the conference room table, leaving Hollis standing alone in the line of fire.

"First of all, I want you all to listen carefully to everything I have to tell you, because there is more to the story than any of you know." Hollis pinned her gaze on Gerhardt. "Does everyone understand that?"

Heads bobbed over anxiously clasped hands and not one person's eyes moved away from Hollis.

"First, I will say that I agree with the mediations committee. They made the right choice as to who has provenance over the painting." Hollis drew a steadying breath which did not slow her heart or keep her hands from shaking. "And that choice is the Meyer family."

Gerhardt's fist hit the table while a weeping Eli embraced

his son Samuel. Amelia Kunst looked inexplicably unconcerned.

"It was a gift!" Gerhardt bellowed. "This decision is wrong."

"The thing is, Mr. Kunst, it wasn't."

"What do you mean?" He flung a pointed finger toward the painting. "My father's name is on the back!"

"And that's what gives it away," Hollis said. "Who inscribes a painting like that, and then hangs it back up on their own wall?"

Gerhardt's mouth flapped soundlessly. Eli and Samuel returned their attention to Hollis.

"That is a very good question," Eli ventured. "Do *you* know why, Ms. McKenna?"

Hollis gave him a soft, empathetic smile. "I have a very good idea, Mr. Meyer."

"Please," Gerhardt growled. "Enlighten us."

Hollis tried to maintain her composure as she outlined the only explanation that made tragic sense. "Benjamin knew what was happening to Jews in Germany in nineteen-thirty-eight. First, to the poor and uneducated, and for a while, he believed that his connection to the Neues Museum offered him protection."

"And then, he realized it wouldn't…" Samuel offered.

"He truly held out hope that it would," Hollis said. "But he was a smart man. He knew he had to prepare for the worst."

Gerhardt's shoulders fell. "So he wrote my father's name on the back of the painting in case, well, what happened—happened?"

"Yes. The inscription to Wilhelm was there in the event that Benjamin and his family disappeared. So it was less a gift, than a plan B."

"To save both the painting and Rachel's memory." Gerhardt nodded somberly. He glanced at Eli. "I have to admit, that does make sense."

Hollis switched her tack before revealing the final chapter. "I understand that for both of you, the painting of Rachel has deep personal significance."

Gerhardt and Eli met each other's gaze, and for the first time without any animosity.

"It is the only piece left of our fathers," Eli murmured.

"Our only piece of beauty to survive an ugly time," Gerhardt agreed.

"I don't know if any of you know this," Hollis said carefully, "but with modern technology we can scan a painting and print it with amazingly accurate raised brushstrokes on a new canvas."

"By all means, make one for Mr. Kunst," Samuel said without hesitation. "I'll gladly pay for it. Without his father's intervention, this painting would have been destroyed."

"That's very kind, Samuel. Thank you." Hollis smiled. "And I especially thank you for your words."

"It is true." Eli looked at Gerhardt. "Rachel is here with us because Wilhelm was not afraid to go after her and carry her to safety."

Hollis looked at Mary.

Mary was grinning like a hyena.

Hollis pulled *Rachel* from her leather satchel and set it on the easel which was apparently a permanent piece of the conference room's furniture. Then she faced the family members again.

"When you make the copy, Samuel, you are going to want to make two."

Samuel gestured toward Amelia. "I have no problem with that, but she will inherit her father's you know."

"I do." Hollis wanted to drag the moment out as long as possible; it was just too delicious. "But that's not why."

Eli turned to Mary his wrinkled brow pulled up like purse strings. "Does the museum want to display her?"

"Not the way she is now, no," Mary played along.

Eli frowned. "You are talking in riddles, Ms. McKenna. Please say what's on your mind."

Hollis folded her arms and considered him. "Your father only painted one original painting in his lifetime, is that correct?"

Eli bounced a nod. "Yes."

Hollis turned to *Rachel*. "Yet he seems very competent."

"That was not his passion," Eli countered.

Hollis tapped her chin. "But he went to some lengths to try and save it, even if that meant she went to the neighbor boy."

"My father loved her," Gerhardt said. "Benjamin knew this."

"I'm sure he did." Hollis let her glance drop, and then slowly lift again. "But beyond that, he knew Wilhelm wasn't Jewish."

"So he knew the Kunst family would not disappear." Samuel shrugged. "And so neither would the painting."

"But they did disappear, didn't they?"

Gerhardt looked at her, awestruck. "They were neighbors. They must have spoken to each other. Benjamin would know my grandfather's politics."

Hollis nodded. "And the day after the Meyers were taken, the Kunsts left Germany."

"With the painting." Samuel wagged his head. "That was quite a plan."

"Yep. Quite a plan to save a worthless painting. The only painting ever made by an unknown Jew…" Hollis let the sentence hang in the air before she added, "A Jew who restored priceless masterpieces as a career."

Four pair of eyes locked on hers. The palpable silence in the room was charged with disbelief. Hollis felt the hair on her arms rise.

"Are you accusing my father of stealing a masterpiece?" Eli growled.

"No, not at all."

"Did he paint over one?" Samuel looked from Hollis to the canvas and back.

"Yes, he did."

"Who was the artist?" Eli croaked.

"Max Liebermann."

This is the most fun game of twenty questions, ever.

"Who?" Gerhardt looked at the others in the room. "I've never heard of him."

"I hadn't either, until we were able to match it to a missing post online. Max was a nineteenth-century Jewish impressionist from Berlin."

Mary produced two color copies of the painting's x-ray and

handed one to each of the families. "This is how we found out what he did."

"That looks like *Rachel*." Eli observed. "It is a young woman in the same pose."

Hollis nodded. "I would assume that was where he got the inspiration to paint Rachel the way he did."

"And he would have used the brush strokes as a template for his own composition," Mary added.

Samuel addressed Mary. "She said the painting was listed as missing." He winced. "Was it stolen?"

"No, it was listed as being in a private collection and its whereabouts unknown."

Eli lifted his head. "Whose collection?"

Mary consulted her notes. "Elijah and Marion Weichsel bought the painting from Max Liebermann in eighteen-eighty-nine."

Eli's puzzled expression eased and he smiled a little. "Those were my mother's parents. My grandparents."

Mary shot an enlightened glance across the long table to Hollis. "That makes sense, then."

"If so, then the Liebermann must have hung in your house." Hollis pulled out a color copy of the Max Liebermann painting. "Did you have a painting that looked like this?"

"Yes. Yes we did." Eli looked up at Hollis. "In our drawing room, in the same place he hung *Rachel* when it was finished."

"Do you know when your mother and father received the painting from her parents?" Hollis asked.

Eli shook his head. "I cannot remember when it wasn't there."

Hollis addressed Mary. "Well, that's good enough for me, if it's good enough for you?"

"Absolutely."

"Now what?" Samuel asked.

"You have two choices. You can keep the painting as it is and enjoy it for its sentimental value," Hollis explained. "Or you can have the overpainting removed and restore the original Liebermann."

"That's why you said make two copies." Gerhardt wagged a finger at her. "You are clever."

"How much is the Liebermann worth?" Samuel asked.

Eli glared at his son. "You would consider destroying my father's work?"

Samuel scowled. "That depends on the value of the Liebermann. Obviously."

"After researching the artist and his other paintings which have been sold at auction…" Mary retrieved another sheet of paper from her folder. "We are thinking at least one-point-seven-five million. Maybe as high as two-point-five."

Shocked silence met her announcement.

Even Hollis was stunned. "Really?"

Mary grinned at her. "Really."

"I had no idea…" She looked at the occupants in the room. "And so that's the real reason Benjamin wanted the painting to survive."

All of the man's actions were now falling into their logical position. "He wanted to leave a legacy for his survivors."

"The real kicker is that Max didn't die until nineteen-thirty-five," Mary informed the still silent quartet. "So the painting's value back then was nowhere near what it is now."

Eli pushed himself up from his chair with some effort, eschewing Samuel's help, and walked slowly to the easel. He stopped in front of it, and reached out one finger to stroke his long-dead sister's cheek.

"She was a beautiful girl with such a life ahead of her. *Such* a life." He drew a shaky breath. "Wilhelm would have made her happy, I think. If such a marriage could have been permitted."

The old man grasped the edges of the canvas with arthritic, blue-veined hands and lifted it from the easel. He kissed Rachel's image tenderly. Then he pressed the painting to his chest and closed his eyes.

"You did a wonderful thing, Rachel. I hope you can see this." Eli sighed heavily. "You could not save our parents or yourself, but you saved your family."

His voice held the reverence of prayer. Hollis wiped the tear that ran down her cheek.

"You saved us first with your uncomplaining patience as our father painted you." An odd smile sculpted the old man's features. "And you saved us secondly by loving an Aryan boy."

Hollis was in full-blown cry mode now. She reached for the ever-present box of tissues and yanked two out. She blew her nose as quietly as she could, unwilling to interrupt Eli's prayer.

"Yes, I agree. That is the right thing."

Hollis glanced at Samuel, then Gerhardt and Amelia. Who was Eli talking to?

Maybe the man has undiagnosed Alzheimer's.

Or schizophrenia. That was a possibility.

Eli opened his eyes and turned to her suddenly, ending her musings. "We will make the two copies."

Hollis sniffed and nodded. "Ms. Oberman will take care of that right away."

"Good." Eli carefully placed the painting back on the easel. "And then we will sell Max's painting once it's restored."

"Let's make copies of the original Liebermann first, Dad," Samuel suggested. "We might as well enjoy it too, seeing as how it was in the family for well over a hundred years."

Eli shuffled back to his chair. "Samuel, you are wise for such a young man."

"Young? Mid-sixties?" Samuel laughed. "I guess age *is* relative."

Eli waved a hand as if to wipe away his son's words. "And once the painting is sold, Ms. McKenna, half the money will go to Mr. Kunst."

"What?" Amelia's first spoken word that day jarred the air in the room. "We're getting money?"

Gerhardt was obviously struck speechless. The normally garrulous German simply stared at Eli.

Though Hollis was thrilled, she needed to be certain the old man meant what he said. "Are you sure? Do you want a day to think about it?"

Eli looked at her the way a parent looks at a child who is clueless. "Rachel insists. It was her idea, and I deeply respect it."

After her experiences with Sveyn, Hollis was the last person to argue with anyone claiming to communicate with a dead person.

"Thank you, Eli." Gerhardt's voice was thick with emotion. "You are an honorable man."

Eli made a face. "Me? I would keep the money. But Rachel promises me misery if I do."

As Gerhardt's glance shifted uneasily to Hollis, Eli burst into a delighted cackle.

"I'm kidding. I'm kidding!" Eli grabbed Samuel's forearm as if he made the joke. "She would never threaten her little brother."

Ӂ

Once Eli's decision and subsequent plan of action were committed to paper and signed by both parties, Gerhardt and Amelia left. Hollis had texted Sveyn that they were finished, and he just walked into the room.

"Hang on, I want to ask Eli and Samuel a question," Hollis said to him. "Then I'll tell you all about everything in the car."

"All right." Sveyn lowered himself into a seat to wait for her.

"Mr. Meyer, Samuel, can I ask you something personal?"

Samuel straightened the shoulders on the coat he had helped his father into. "Sure."

"You're from Tomah and I recently learned that my birthparents are from Sparta."

Eli smiled softly at her. "We are neighbors, young lady."

"Yes." Hollis returned the smile. "I was wondering if there was any chance either of you might know my grandmother." Hollis pointed at Samuel. "She would be about your age."

"Maybe." Samuel shrugged. "What was her name?"

"Karen—she married Howard Mueller, but I don't know her maiden name."

Eli looked like he saw a ghost. "Howard and Karen Mueller in Sparta are your grandparents?"

"Yes. Their daughter Kathleen got pregnant when she was fifteen," Hollis explained. "My parents were their best friends, and they couldn't have kids so they asked to adopt me. After Kathleen had the baby, they took me and moved to Milwaukee."

"I always wondered…"

Eli looked like he was about to collapse. Hollis shoved a chair toward him and a very pale Samuel lowered him into it.

"Should I call nine-one-one, Dad?"

Eli wagged his head. "No. I'll be fine."

Samuel squatted in front of his father. "Do you want me to tell her?"

"Yes," Eli breathed.

Now Hollis felt like *she* was seeing a ghost. "Tell me what?"

Samuel stayed by his father and looked up at her. "Karen is my older sister."

Chapter Thirty

Sveyn snapped to attention. "You are Karen Mueller's brother? And this is your father?"

Hollis sat still, her shock and disbelief evident.

Sveyn shifted his attention to the elderly man. "That means you, Mr. Meyer, are Hollis's great-grandfather?"

Eli regarded him as blankly as Hollis did. "Yes. If what she said is true, I am."

"Who has red hair?" Hollis demanded.

If Eli thought the question strange, he did not let on. "Karen. And I did, at one time."

"Did you know Aleksander Hansen?" she pressed.

Samuel's brow furrowed with concentration. "I think he might be the boyfriend Karen brought one Fourth of July… But if I'm right, she broke up with him that fall."

"He is Hollis's father," Sveyn interjected.

"Really?" Samuel pinched the bridge of his nose. "He was a couple years older, I think."

"Yes. Three."

Eli straightened in his chair. "I do remember a time when Kathleen disappeared for months. I asked Karen where she was and she said Kathleen was acting as nanny for one of Howard's cousins in Minnesota."

Hollis looked at Sveyn. Judging by her expression, the reality of what just happened was beginning to sink in.

"Oh my God, Sveyn. This man, Eli Meyer, is my great-grandfather…"

"So it would appear."

"And the man who painted that—" Hollis pointed at the painting of Rachel. "Is my great-*great*-grandfather."

"This is an unexpected turn, is it not?" He smiled. "But a very happy one, I think."

"You are a daughter of Israel, Ms. McKenna," Eli murmured.

Hollis looked confused. "That's a surprise, considering Kathleen was confirmed in the Lutheran Church. Did Karen still practice her faith?"

"No," Samuel said sadly. "She converted when she married Howard."

Hollis looked at the girl in the painting. "Rachel is my great-aunt, then."

"Yes."

"I never imagined something like this would happen." Fresh tears rolled down Hollis's cheeks, but this time they were tears of joy. "So I guess I'll have Mary make me a copy of the painting too."

ӝ

In the car on the way from the museum in downtown Milwaukee to the north-side Italian restaurant where Hollis and Sveyn were meeting her parents for an early supper, Hollis gave Sveyn the details about ownership of the painting.

"What made you ask about Karen?" he asked.

"I don't know," she admitted. "But after being in Sparta with that feeling of a small town, where everybody knows everybody, that kind of thing, I just threw it out there."

"It is good that you did." Sveyn smiled "Now you have all of your answers."

"I can't wait to tell Mom and Dad about Eli." Hollis turned the blinker on and moved into the left turn lane. "And after dinner I just want to go back, take a hot bath, get my pajamas on, and relax."

"What time is our flight to Phoenix tomorrow?"

"Noon." Hollis made the turn into the parking lot. "We should probably be at the airport by ten-thirty."

She parked the car and they climbed out. The wintry afternoon was gray but bracing. Sveyn drew a long breath, the chilled air filling his lungs in a way that made him homesick.

"I do miss snow," he admitted.

"We have snow in Arizona. I'll drive you up there."

Sveyn was growing tired of Hollis acting the chauffeur where he was concerned. "I need to learn to drive."

She smiled up at him and waited for him to open the door for her. "And now that you have a birth certificate, you can get your permit and begin."

Sveyn followed Hollis into the restaurant. She stopped at a little podium near the door.

"Is there a table for Ian?" she asked.

The hostess smiled and gathered up an armful of menus. "Yes. Follow me, please."

Hollis's gaze moved around the restaurant. "I don't see them. Do you?"

"No."

"They're in here." The hostess opened a French-style door to a darkened room.

Sveyn followed Hollis inside the mysterious space, his senses on high alert.

"SURPRISE!"

The shouts startled him and the sudden lights blinded him.

Sveyn acted on his warrior's instinct. With a roar of warning, he grabbed Hollis and pulled her behind him, placing his crouched body between her and danger.

For a moment, no one moved.

The crowd in the room stared at him in stunned silence.

It only took Sveyn a moment to realize there was no actual danger present.

He straightened, embarrassed and feeling very much out of his century.

Hollis stepped out from behind him. "Well, we certainly are surprised. Obviously."

Brianne hurried forward in an attempt to distract everyone from the unexpected awkwardness. "We couldn't let you leave tomorrow without celebrating your birthdays and letting everyone meet Sveyn."

"No. I get it. Thanks, Mom." Hollis turned around and gave Sveyn an apologetic smile. "So this is Sveyn, my birthday twin and fiancé."

"Hey, you're Eric! From the *Match Point* commercials!" someone shouted.

Ӝ

Hollis understood her parents' desire to celebrate her birthday because they had been apart at Christmas. And it warmed her heart that they wanted to introduce her fiancé to their friends here.

And of course they had no idea of what today's meeting about the painting had revealed.

That would have to wait until after the party.

So much for a relaxing evening.

Sveyn held up well, she noticed. He was willing to accept that his actions, which were so out of place in this place and time, were amusing to the gathering. But being recognized as 'Eric' from *Match Point* was something neither one of them had anticipated.

Again, he held up well—posing for pictures and signing his autograph with an unwavering smile.

The one question that she was repeatedly asked and had no answer for was, "Have you set a date?"

"No, but we will when we get back to Phoenix." Hollis always added, "It will be a very small wedding, since both of Sveyn's parents are gone and I don't want to bankrupt my parents' retirement account just for a party."

Then she excused herself to get a refill on her Merlot. Or to check in with her mom. Or dad. Or Sveyn. Anything to change the subject.

She sidled up to her mother. "Do we have an end time to this shindig?"

Brianne's expression fell. "Aren't you having fun?"

"Of course, I am. And so is Sveyn." The Viking really did seem to be enjoying the attention. "But something extraordinary happened today at the meeting that I want to tell you and Dad about when we're alone."

"We only have the room until eight." Her mom glanced around at the happy group. "I know you want to leave for the airport by nine-thirty tomorrow morning and I didn't want to keep you too late."

"Thanks, Mom. I love you." Hollis kissed her cheek. "This was really sweet of you."

Ӝ

Hollis shut the car door and heaved a sigh. "Sorry about that. I had no idea she was serious when she mentioned a party."

Sveyn leaned over and kissed her. That definitely lifted her mood and she encouraged him to kiss her again.

"Do not apologize." He nuzzled her hair. "I had a fine time."

Hollis laughed. "I bet you did, Mr. Celebrity."

Sveyn chuckled. "I had no idea."

"Me neither." Hollis started the car. "Now I just want to get home, get comfy, and tell mom and dad about Eli Meyer."

"I have a question for you," Sveyn said once they were on the way. "Did people ask you about a date for our wedding?"

"All night. Why?"

Sveyn turned in his seat. "When are we getting married?"

"Now that you have your documentation, we can get the license." She glanced at him, his features chiseled by blue streetlights. "What are your thoughts?"

He tucked her hair behind her ear. "I would marry you tonight, Hollis. I see no reason to wait longer than circumstances require us to."

"So, *where* do you want to get married?"

"What do you mean?"

"In a church, outside in a park, in a hot air balloon…" She glanced at him again. "All we need are two witnesses and someone to perform the ceremony."

The Viking looked surprised. "We can get married in a balloon?"

"Yep. It's our decision."

"I suppose it depends on who you want to be there," he observed. "George and Stevie had hundreds of witnesses, but a much smaller reception afterwards."

Hollis laughed. "I don't want to get married on a stage."

"Nor do I."

"Who do *you* want to be there?"

Sveyn leaned back in the seat. "George is my only friend, so I would have him stand up for me. Other than that, the guests would be your friends and family."

"Let's elope, then." Hollis felt guilty about cutting her parents out, but she didn't want to wait anymore. Sveyn proved to be the same man with a body as he had been without one, only much sexier.

She had to confess, watching other women fawn over him added to her urgency. Not that she thought for a moment that she would lose him after all they had gone through to find each other, but speaking the vows and putting a ring on his finger might dissuade the more overt propositions coming his way.

Sveyn grinned. "Is there an Arizona version of Gretna Green?"

"Yep. It's called Las Vegas, Nevada."

"Really?"

Hollis nodded. "Really. We could drive there the day after

we get back."

Sveyn was quiet for several minutes before he responded. "I want something more respectful than running away. When I pledge my troth to you, I do not wish to appear flippant."

Hollis heart melted a little. "So you want to plan something, but soon?"

"The sooner the better."

Hollis smiled. "We'll start as soon as we get home."

"Speaking of home, you told your father you have enough money to buy a house." Sveyn faced her again. "I think we should look for one. Your condo is not the right place for us."

That suggestion was as terrifying as it was exhilarating. "Okay, but let's get married first. Then we'll find a realtor to begin the search."

Hollis pulled into her parents' driveway and parked. "It's time to repack and relax."

Ӝ

Ian, Brianne, Hollis, and Sveyn sat around the kitchen table nibbling leftovers from the dinner.

"How can I possibly be hungry?" Hollis groaned.

Sveyn pointed a garlicky breadstick at her. "Talking to people and avoiding their questions kept you from eating too heartily."

"What questions were you avoiding?" Ian asked.

"Wedding date, mostly."

Sveyn saw the warning look Hollis threw his way and so he changed the subject. "Tell your mother and father what you discovered today."

Hollis set down her steaming cup of hot chocolate. "You two are not going to believe this. If I hadn't been there, I wouldn't believe it."

Brianne used a fork to pick at the salad. "Did it have to do with the dispute over the painting?"

"Not really." Hollis told her parents how that situation

played out, ending with Eli Meyer's decision to split the money from the sale of the Max Liebermann painting.

"After Mary has the high-quality copies made, of course. The museum will keep the painting in their custody during the whole process so nothing happens to it."

"That's a good idea." Ian wagged his head. "Can you imagine? Such a valuable piece tucked away and forgotten in a dusty pile in someone's hoard."

Sveyn flashed a crooked smile. After seeing Ezra's meticulous care of his collection, Sveyn doubted the man forgot about anything he owned.

"And if the *Ghost Myths, Inc.* guys hadn't filmed me in the Collections Storeroom," Hollis continued, "none of us would know what was underneath."

Brianne yawned. "Sorry. So what else did you discover?"

Hollis looked at her mother with a puckish expression. "Do you know Karen Mueller's maiden name?"

"Sure. It's Meyer…" Brianne's eyes widened. "No!"

"Yep." Hollis's gaze bounced from her mother to her father and back again. "Her family was in Tomah, right?"

Ian leaned closer to his daughter. "Are you saying that this Eli Meyer is related to Karen?"

Hollis grabbed her father's hand across the table. "Eli Meyer is Karen Meyer Mueller's *father*."

Brianne was obviously stunned. "Kathleen's grandfather?"

Hollis nodded. "Yep. And *my* red-headed great-grandfather."

Chapter Thirty-One

Tuesday
February 16

Their tearful good-byes accomplished, Hollis and Sveyn walked into the General Mitchell International Airport terminal for their flight back to Phoenix. Hollis decided not to tell her parents that she and Sveyn were going to marry in a planned elopement because she didn't want them to spend the money on a last-minute flight.

"I'll tell them they can plan a reception for us the next time we visit," she told Sveyn. "That way they can do what they want without any pressure."

Sveyn was not convinced that was the best plan, but Hollis was a Hansen, and Hansens were generally stubborn. "As long as we are married soon, I will be satisfied."

When the plane took off they were served assorted warmed nuts in their first class seats. Hollis selected a red wine and Sveyn a dark beer.

The big jet climbed into the clouds, making the whitewashed Wisconsin landscape invisible. Sveyn felt a tug of sadness; walking through the crunching snow, feeling the chill on his skin, and the bracing cold of the air that filled his lungs was so much like his home that he did not want to leave

He had felt none of that since he was stabbed in ten-seventy and it was the only thing he knew before then.

Sveyn knew the Phoenix summers were brutally hot and he wondered what that was going to be like. Maybe once Hollis took him to the mountains and he was able to get the lay of Arizona's high country, he might suggest a cabin of some sort where they could escape the heat when they were not working.

"What are you thinking about?"

Sveyn smiled at his love. "Snow."

"I'll find you some, don't worry." Hollis popped a huge cashew in her mouth. "Maybe we'll go to the mountains this weekend."

Good. "What are you thinking about?"

Hollis held the stem of her wine glass with one hand and the other hand fell into her lap. "How much my life has changed in the last week."

Sveyn understood her overwhelmed reaction. "You came ready to ask about your adoption."

"And I'm leaving having found my birthfather, one great-grandfather soldier whom you manifested to, and a great-great-grandfather killed in the Holocaust camps in Germany." Hollis blew a sigh and twirled the wineglass on her tray. "There is so much history packed into those men's lives."

That was certainly true. "Do you want to know more about the soldier?"

Hollis looked at him, her blue eyes wide. "Yes. Tell me everything."

Sveyn settled in his ample seat. "Tor Hansen went to the American army's Camp Hale in Colorado to train American soldiers in Nordic skiing."

"Why?"

"So they could ski the Alps and attack Hitler's troops from

behind." Sveyn grinned. "You know we invented skiing, right? We taught the Swiss."

Hollis rolled her eyes. "Stick to the story. How many soldiers are we talking about?"

"Three regiments."

"So did they attack?"

Sveyn nodded. "They did. The Germans were taken by surprise and the Americans secured the ridge above their camp for the next day's battle."

"When was this?"

"February of nineteen-forty-five."

Hollis's expression grew sad. "That's where Tor died."

Images of those battles were burned into Sveyn's memory. Blood on snow is a stark contrast, and there was an abundance of blood that day—both German and American. He hadn't been with Tor for long and all he could do was warn the man when danger approached. That saved Tor the first night, but there was nothing Sveyn could do for him the next day.

"It was a very hard battle, Hollis. And the Americans did win." Sveyn took a sip of his beer, his throat was suddenly dry. "In the end, the Mountain Division served for just four months, but they had very high casualties."

Hollis dabbed her eyes with the tiny paper napkin which accompanied her wine. "At least you were there with him."

Sveyn's brows pulled together. "I am not certain that an apparition was a comfort."

She seemed to realize that the idea was odd. "Okay, maybe not to him, but it is to me. What about my great-grandmother? Did you see her?"

"Briefly. She was his translator."

Hollis looked surprised. "He didn't speak English, then."

"He spoke fairly well by the time I got to him. And they were already married."

"But he never saw his son, Thor. Aleksander's father."

"No." Sveyn smiled. "And then I manifested to you and everything changed."

Hollis sipped her wine in silence for a while before she asked her next question. "Did Tor have brothers or sisters?"

"I don't know about sisters," Sveyn answered truthfully. "But we can look on that ancestry site when we get back."

Hollis set her empty glass back on the tray. "But he had brothers?"

"I know of three, because he got letters from them. One was in Bergen, one was in Telemark, and one was in a labor camp in Kirkenes."

Hollis looked shocked. "A labor camp? In Norway?"

"Norway was occupied by the Germans, Hollis. The people resisted where they could, but they were a strong presence nonetheless."

Their smiling flight attendant appeared holding the open bottle of Bordeaux. "Would you like more wine?"

"Yes, please." Hollis handed the woman her glass. When it was filled, the attendant moved on. "I want to know more about that, especially now that I know I'm related to them."

Sveyn gave her a wry smile. "I expect they have interesting stories as well."

Wednesday
February 17

The weather in Phoenix was normal for February, which meant the days were sunny and generally warm, but the nights were forty degrees cooler.

"Air-conditioning in the day and a heater at night," Hollis said as she switched her car's thermostat from cold to hot. "It's kinda crazy."

"I don't need either," Sveyn said. "So don't adjust it for me."

"I'm not." She considered the Viking, looking good in his security guard's uniform. "It's going to be a long day for me after being gone a week. Are you sure you want to come with me now? Our visitors don't arrive until six."

"I am very sure." Sveyn leaned over and kissed her. His

mouth tasted like the strawberry jam he piled on his toast for breakfast. "I do not wish to spend the day away from you."

Hollis smiled. "Your choice."

And I'm so *glad you made it.*

Stevie was back from her honeymoon, tanned and giddy. "Cancun was great. I think I gained five pounds."

Hollis considered the petite blonde. "If so, I don't know where you put it."

"Hollis, I thought I heard your voice." Miranda strode into the staff lounge. "How was your trip?"

"Absolutely incredible. Do you guys have a few minutes to hear about it?"

"We sure do." Stevie claimed a chair at the only table in the room. "Spill."

Hollis pulled out another chair just as Sveyn walked into the lounge. "I'm going to tell them about our trip. Do you want to join us?" she asked.

"No, thank you. I was there." He winked at her. She blushed. "I have been asked to watch some tapes from the security cameras. It seems there is a young man who has visited recently and has been acting suspicious."

Miranda perked up. "I saw your commercial, Sveyn."

"Me, too!" Stevie grinned. "Looking good."

Miranda looked suddenly shy. "So good, I decided to give *Match Point* a try."

Hollis looked at Miranda, astounded by her confession. "You did? Did you find anybody?"

"I had trouble logging on. I'll try again tonight."

"Huh." Hollis waved Sveyn away. "Go do your job, then. I'll see you at lunch."

Then she sank into her chair. "Where do I start?"

Ӝ

Sveyn's phone vibrated in his pocket. The caller was from the Robert Ford agency. He paused the video and swiped the answer icon.

"Hello?"

"Sveyn—how are you doing?" Rochelle's voice held a tinge of doubt.

That was odd. "I am very well, thank you. Is something amiss?"

"Amiss? I love the way you talk." Rochelle's relieved laugh sounded tinny through the phone's speakers. "The answer is yes. And no."

Sveyn hated it when people talked in riddles. "Please begin with what is amiss."

"They are actually both the same thing."

Sveyn refused to speak, forcing Rochelle to tell him.

"Your commercial for *Match Point* was shown all over the country last weekend."

Sveyn nodded, though she could not see him. "I saw it."

"*We-ell…*" Rochelle succeeded in saying the word in two syllables. "So many people logged on to their site that they crashed the server."

That sounded bad. "Was anyone hurt?"

Rochelle laughed again. "You're so funny."

Sveyn rubbed his forehead, trying to figure out what he said that was funny. "How is this good news?"

"It's good because now they want to sign you to an exclusive contract." Rochelle's tone clearly indicated the he should be mightily impressed.

Except he wasn't. Yet. "What does an exclusive contract mean?"

"It means they want you to work for them and only them," Rochelle explained. "You can't take any modeling or commercial jobs for anyone else."

"But I need to make money," Sveyn said. "I am getting married."

"Honey, you made ten-thousand dollars in the last three days and crashed a server in the process. Trust me, you'll make bank."

Ten-thousand dollars?

Ten-thousand dollars?

"I do not know what to say…"

"Say yes. And I'll negotiate the rest."

Sveyn hesitated. "Yes?"

"Great! We get eighteen percent remember, so the more compensation I can get for you, the more money I make."

She has a good point.

"What do I do now?"

"Stay healthy and gorgeous. I'll be in touch."

Ӂ

Hollis started her story with her blood type discovery and the realization that she was adopted. Then she moved through confronting her parents, their trip to Sparta, meeting her birthfather, and her connection to the painting Ezra had in his hoard.

"So my birthmother is Eli Meyer's granddaughter." Hollis chuckled. "How's *that* for a small world?"

Miranda and Stevie remained unmoving, staring at her like she just claimed that she painted the Max Liebermann herself.

Hollis leaned forward. "Do either of you have anything to say?"

"I don't even…" Miranda's voice trailed off.

"You're really sure about all of this, right?" Stevie probed. "Not just jumping to conclusions."

"Samuel Meyer *told* me Karen is his sister—I didn't ask. And besides, Eli knew about Kathleen's disappearing act. I didn't tell him."

"Wow…" Miranda breathed. "This is a great story."

"Don't—"

"Wait 'til I tell Mr. Benton."

"—tell Benton." Too late. *Dammit*. "Do you have to?"

Miranda shot her an empathetic gaze. "It's truly a great story, Hollis. So many moving parts coming together. We have to tell it."

"Oh, fine," she growled.

Maybe the media won't care.

Right. And I did *paint the Max Liebermann.*

"So you're a Hansen? Like Sveyn?" Stevie giggled. "Are you related?"

Hollis's expression must have made her answer clear.

"You are?" The blonde's eyes rounded. "How?"

"Sveyn told me that he only manifested to direct descendants of his father, but I was so sure he was wrong about me."

"Until you realized you were adopted." Miranda leaned on the table. "How closely are you related?"

Hollis laughed. "Not too closely. His father and I are separated by nine-hundred-and-fifty years and thirty-eight generations."

Miranda sat back. "Yeah, that's probably legal then."

Hollis paused, then said softly, "His manifestation right before me was to my great-grandfather during World War Two."

"That's… amazing?" Stevie said. "Unbelievable? Cool?"

"All of those. And tragic." Hollis sighed. "He was killed in a battle in Italy and never saw his son."

"Oh…" Miranda made a sad little moue. "That is tragic."

"But Sveyn can tell you about him," Stevie offered. "Not many people have living eye witnesses to their past."

"True." Hollis stood. "I better get to work. I can only imagine what's waiting for me, plus we have a group coming in tonight."

Stevie and Miranda stood as well. "Who's coming?"

"The first lady who came is coming back. She was frustrated because one of her clients could see Sveyn, but she couldn't."

"We all can see Sveyn, now." Miranda snickered. "Maybe he can dress up in a drop cloth and make her night."

Chapter Thirty-Two

Hollis stretched and looked at the clock. Five more minutes and the museum would be closed. One hour later, her patchouli-scented medium would arrive. A couple hours after that she should be relaxing on the couch with Sveyn and a glass of wine.

Her phone vibrated.

"Hello, Viking. Ready to grab a bite before the séance?"

"Hollis, we have a problem."

"What?"

"There is a young man who refuses to leave the Kensington wing. He is demanding that someone open the case where the Blessing is."

"I'm on my way."

Hollis stuck her head into Miranda's office. "We have a situation in the new wing. You might want to come with me."

Ӝ

Sveyn faced the twenty-something culprit. "She is coming with the key."

The man rocked nervously from side to side. "Good."

If Sveyn was asked to judge, he'd say the man was in the midst of some sort of health crisis. His skin sagged on his cheeks and there was a film of sweat across his brow. His clothes hung loosely on a frame that must have been more robust at some point.

In the gap between his coat and his chest was a holstered gun.

"If you do not mind, would you tell me what you want with the *velsignelse av gudene?*"

The rocking stopped. "The what?"

Sveyn folded his arms over his chest. "That's the Nordic name for the icon—the Blessing of the Gods."

"You say that like you know."

"Norsk was my first language."

The man pointed at the case. "It keeps you from dying if you have it. I need that."

Though he believed it himself at one time, Sveyn flashed an incredulous look. "You don't truly believe the stories, do you?"

The man's face twisted. "If it's not true, then why's the case bulletproof and double locked?"

"It is for show." Hollis appeared in Sveyn's peripheral vision. He turned toward her. "Here she is now."

Hollis stopped where she was. "Can someone explain to me what's going on?"

"I need the icon. I don't want to die."

"No one wants to die." Hollis took a step closer. "What's your name?"

He glared at her. "Why do you care?"

"Because it's more polite than saying *hey you.*" Hollis took another step. "My name is Hollis, and that's Sveyn."

A nervous glance bounced from Hollis to Sveyn and back.

"Keith."

"Nice to meet you, Keith." Hollis gave him a shaky smile. "Are you ill?"

The rocking started up again. “Cancer. In my blood.”

“Bone marrow transplant?”

“Didn’t work.”

Hollis looked empathetic. “Chemo?”

He shook his head.

Sveyn wasn’t sure if that meant he had not tried this chemo thing, or if it did not work either.

Doesn’t matter.

“So you think this metal and wooden object will make you immortal?” Hollis looked and sounded skeptical.

Sveyn stepped forward.

“Get back, man!” Keith opened his jacket to show the gun Sveyn already knew was there.

Hollis gasped. She did not.

Sveyn put his hands up. “I will stay here.”

“Why do you have a gun, Keith?” Hollis’s voice was strained. “I hope you aren’t going to shoot yourself.”

Keith looked momentarily flummoxed by that suggestion. “No! I brought it in case I need it.”

Hollis looked relieved. “Well that’s good.”

Keith blinked. “What?”

“She’s glad you do not plan to shoot yourself.” Sveyn smiled approvingly. “And I assume you do not plan to shoot anyone else, either.”

“I don’t want to. Unless you make me.”

Sveyn shook his head. “I am not going to do that, Keith.”

Keith turned his attention back to Hollis. “Did you bring the key?”

“Yes, it’s right here.” Hollis held up the key on its chain. “But I’m afraid you are going to be disappointed.”

Keith frowned. “Why?”

Hollis took another step closer.

Sveyn glared at her. *Keep your distance.*

“Because the icon has lost its powers.”

“You’re lying,” he growled.

Hollis winced. “I’m sorry, but I’m not. We had some priests in here and they exorcised it.”

"I was there, Keith," Sveyn added. "The thing screamed like nothing I have ever heard in my life, and then it went silent."

"I'm telling you this because it's not too late for you to change your mind," Hollis offered. "The charges will be minimal at this point."

Keith was rocking again. "No. No—you want it for yourself!" He pulled the gun from its holster but pointed it downward. "Unlock the case."

Hollis glanced at Sveyn. He saw the fear in her eyes.

"Keith," he said. "I am here to protect Hollis. Please do not do anything foolish."

"If she gives me the icon, I'll leave. No one gets hurt."

Hollis stepped around the icon's case. She punched in the code, got an error beep, and then tried it again. "Sorry. My hands are shaking."

The electric lock finally *snicked* its acceptance of the code. Hollis slid the key into the manual lock and turned it.

Sveyn had been shifting his weight from leg to leg, inching forward in increments. Thus far, Keith had not noticed. His attention was focused on the icon.

Though initially leery, Sveyn's discomfort around the Blessing disappeared when he heard the screams and saw the priests' arms relax. The pieces stopped trying to reunite; the icon was no longer a danger.

Hollis opened the case and stepped back.

Keith set his gun on the opened acrylic top.

Sveyn evaluated his best moves while Keith reached inside the case and grasped the two halves of the icon.

"How do they fit together? Tell me!"

Sveyn took another small step, his palms out in semi-surrender. "She has never connected them, Keith."

The man's gaze jumped to his. "Have you?"

"Yes," he lied. "Do you want me to show you?"

"And take them from me? I don't think so."

"All right, then. I will walk you through it." Sveyn used his hands as he talked. "Turn them so they face each other like this. Yes. Now slide those grooves into each other.

While Keith concentrated on Sveyn's instructions, Sveyn edged closer. He risked giving Hollis a *back up* nod.

She did so.

Keith's head popped up. "Where are you going?"

"Nowhere." She crossed her arms. "I just wanted a better view."

Sveyn kept talking and Keith kept manipulating the Blessing's two halves. After one last push, the pieces locked together.

No one breathed.

Keith looked at Sveyn. "When does it start working?"

Sveyn shook his head. "It cannot work, Keith. Hollis told you. It died."

The younger man panicked. "It has to work! It's my only chance!"

Sveyn grabbed the gun.

The icon clattered to the marble floor and Keith launched himself at Sveyn.

Sveyn turned away from him and was knocked to the floor. Keith was on top of him, berserk with rage and pummeling him mercilessly. Sveyn rolled, using his superior size to put himself on top of Keith.

The gun discharged.

Hollis screamed.

Blood splattered.

Half a dozen uniformed police officers rushed into the room.

Sveyn waited for the pain. There wasn't any.

Keith was howling and writhing beneath him. Sveyn was manually lifted from the younger man by a pair of officers.

"Were you hit?" one demanded.

Sveyn looked down at his body. "I do not believe so."

Another officer was pressing his hands against Keith's torso. Blood oozed around the pressure. "Paramedics here yet?"

An officer asked that question into his walkie-talkie. Sveyn looked for Hollis. She was talking frantically to another officer. Until her stark gaze met his.

Before he could think about it, Sveyn had her safely wrapped in his arms.

Ӝ

Keith was rushed to the hospital under police guard. Statements were taken from Sveyn and Hollis, and the fingerprints on the gun's trigger were compared to Sveyn's. Even to the naked eye they didn't match.

The Patchouli Medium was rescheduled and sent away with apologies and promises of a partial refund, and now Hollis, Sveyn, and Miranda sat on the floor in the Kensington wing, still in shock.

The Blessing still lay where it fell.

"This is the second time my life has been put in danger by that damned thing," Hollis grumbled. "I wish we never found it."

"Something must be done about it." Sveyn looked at Miranda. "We have to destroy it."

"We can't do that—it belongs to the museum," Miranda objected.

"He's right, Miranda." Hollis lifted her eyes to her boss's. "As long as it's here, and under double locks, people will believe the legend and go to extreme lengths to get hold of it."

Miranda's gaze slid to where the icon lay. "I suppose we could take it off display."

"That's not good enough," Sveyn stated. "If people know it is here, they will come for it."

Hollis climbed to her feet and walked toward the Blessing. She bent over and picked it up, wondering if the thing really was dead.

She felt nothing. She saw nothing. The icon was cold in her hand.

Thank God for that.

Hollis walked back to the pair still sitting on the floor. "Now is our chance, Miranda. We can say that the icon was destroyed in the scuffle."

Miranda looked like a woman caught between a hard place and an even harder director. "I'm not sure."

"Benton loves a good media opportunity," Hollis reminded her. "Let's write up something dramatic and present it to him."

Miranda chewed her lips.

Sveyn leaned forward to catch the curator's attention. "I am speaking the truth. We must tell the world that this icon was damaged beyond repair."

He looked at Hollis. "And then we burn it."

"I concur." Hollis handed the Blessing to Sveyn. "And I think it really is dead."

The Viking turned the steel-and-wood blessing over in his large hands. "I agree. The evilness has fled, along with its power."

"Hold on." Miranda put her hands up. "Are you saying that it did have power at one point?"

"Yes," Hollis and Sveyn answered in tandem.

"But the Exor-Clergy guys got the demons out," Hollis continued. There wasn't a better explanation than that.

She looked at her watch. "We can get this on the ten o'clock news if we hurry."

Miranda stood. "I have to call Benton first."

"Okay." Hollis watched Sveyn regain his feet. "We'll go to my office and start writing the script."

ӜK

"Police were called to the Arizona History and Cultural Center this evening when an alleged thief held a museum employee and security guard at gun-point, demanding to take possession of one of the items on display.

"The item in question, the Blessing of the Gods, is said to make its owner immortal. The Blessing's myth has garnered nationwide attention and as a result the icon has been kept in a bulletproof case with a double lock."

Hollis looked up from her computer screen. "After the newscaster reads that, they'll cut to me."

She pretended to hold a microphone. "When the security

guard was able to take possession of the gun, the perpetrator threw the icon across the room. Unfortunately, the Blessing, which is carbon dated at several thousand years old, was irreparably damaged in the process and can no longer be on display."

Hollis looked up at Sveyn. "Good?"

He nodded. "Good."

"Then we go back to the newscaster," Hollis turned back to her computer. "The would-be thief was injured in the confrontation and escorted to the hospital by police, where he will be placed under arrest on several charges related to the incident."

Miranda walked into Hollis's office. "I heard the last part."

"What do you think?"

Miranda expression was somber. "You can change 'injured' to 'mortally wounded.' Keith died enroute to the hospital."

Chapter Thirty-Three

"Another life ruined." Sveyn looked intently at Hollis. What he had to say to her needed to be said privately. "We must go home now."

"Hold on—we said the icon was irreparably damaged," Miranda pointed out. "Right now, it looks fine. I can't show that to Benton."

Sveyn nodded. "Set it aflame."

"How will we explain that?" Hollis asked.

"We will not. We will say the wood crumbled away from the steel and turned black." Sveyn looked at the sprinklers in the ceiling. "We will do this in the parking lot."

Before they could do so, Miranda took a video of Hollis talking about the icon's damage. Then she emailed the script and the video to Benton's favorite news station and followed up with a phone call.

"Well, they're happy," Miranda said when the call was finished. "They'll show it tomorrow if they can't get it on tonight."

Sveyn nodded. "Good."

That accomplished, the still-reluctant women followed Sveyn to the employee lot, which was empty but for Hollis and Miranda's cars.

"Are you sure about this, Sveyn?" Hollis asked.

He looked down at her. "Do you have a better suggestion?"

"No," she admitted.

"Let's just get it over with." Miranda set down her bucket of water. "I want to get home and see what they put on the news."

Sveyn laid the icon on the blacktop and Hollis struck the match.

The ancient wood burned hot and fast.

Miranda poured water over the flames when enough of the wood was consumed. "That should do it."

Sveyn used his foot to knock the wood from the steel. Hollis wrapped the pieces in a towel and handed it to Miranda.

"Good luck with this."

Miranda accepted the bundle with a sigh. "Right."

Sveyn turned to Hollis. "Shall we go?"

Ӝ

"We are getting married this weekend in Las Vegas," Sveyn declared once they were back in Hollis's condo. "After what happened tonight, I will not brook any delays."

A thrill of anticipation snaked through Hollis's gut. She was one-hundred-percent on board with that suggestion; in many ways and for many reasons.

"We have to make reservations now, then." She reached for her laptop. "Vegas gets busy on weekends."

Sveyn pushed the laptop closed. "I will do this."

"But you—"

He rested his hand on the laptop. "I will do this."

"—have never been to—"

"Hollis." Sveyn leaned close. "I. Will. Do. This."

Hollis sat back in her chair, skeptical. "All by yourself?"

Sveyn's lips quirked. "I will ask for help, but not from you. I want to give you a good wedding, even in the American Gretna Green."

She folded her arms. "So what am I supposed to do?"

"Tell me who you want to be at the wedding."

"Stevie and Miranda." Hollis shrugged. "They are the only real friends I have here."

Sveyn nodded. "I will invite them."

Hollis lifted one disbelieving brow. "Is that it?"

Sveyn held out his hand. She laid her palm against his. He pulled her to stand and led her in a slow twirl. Then he leaned down and murmured in her ear.

"You will need a dress."

Thursday
February 18

Stevie followed Hollis into the wedding dress consignment shop. "This is so exciting. I hope we can find you one that fits."

Hollis smiled politely, her eyes already moving over the racks. Was she insane to agree to a formal wedding with just seventy-two hours' notice?

Probably.

"Yeah. We sure don't have any time for alterations." Hollis stepped up to the customer service desk. "I made an appointment this morning. Hollis McKenna."

The middle-aged woman smiled up at her. "Yes, I'm the one you spoke with." She said something into the speaker hanging from her earpiece. "Maddy will be right with you."

"Whoever said shopping for wedding dresses was loads of fun just wanted everyone else to be as miserable as she was," Hollis grumbled.

"Oh, stop." Stevie made a face and tugged at a gown hanging on the closest rack. "Do you like this one?"

Hollis shook her head. "It doesn't hit me."

Hollis always thought she wanted a ball-gown-style dress with a dropped waist that highlighted her curves. But now she found herself drawn to simpler lines.

"I know it's winter, but I think I want strapless."

Maddy appeared, smiling brightly, and settled Hollis into a dressing room. She proved to be very efficient as she and Stevie brought dresses to her. After trying several on, they finally found her a strapless dress that fit.

Maddy led Hollis into the mirrored center space. "What do you think?"

Blah.

"I don't know…"

"Put your hair up," Stevie suggested.

Hollis grabbed her abundant red curls and held them in a clump on top of her head.

"You have a beautiful tattoo!" Maddy exclaimed.

"Thank you."

Maddy turned to Stevie. "Will you help her out of this dress? I'll be right back."

Hollis and Stevie exchanged puzzled looks.

"I didn't really like this one anyway," Hollis confessed as she stepped out of the gown.

Maddy stuck her head through the curtains. "I want you to close your eyes."

"Me?" Hollis frowned. "Why?"

"Because I don't want you to judge this dress before you have it on." Maddy looked to Stevie for support. "Just trust me on this."

Stevie had clearly jumped to Maddy's side, dress unseen. "There's no harm in trying, Hollis."

Hollis sighed and closed her eyes, and submitted to being clad in what felt like a well-fitting gown.

"Keep your eyes closed." Someone grasped her hand and led her back to the mirrored area.

"Okay," Maddy said. "Step up."

Hollis stood on the tiny platform while the dress was adjusted around her feet. "You can open your eyes now."

Ӂ

Sveyn and George walked into the huge membership warehouse and straight to the jewelry kiosk.

"These guys don't have the widest selection," George admitted. "But the prices are unmatched for the quality."

Sveyn peered into the case, nearly blinded by sparkle. "I like that one."

George leaned over the case. "That's three-thousand-dollars. Are you sure?"

"I made ten thousand dollars last weekend, and *Match Point* wants me to sign an exclusive contract." Sveyn shrugged. "I believe I can pay for this."

George blew a low whistle. "I guess you can. Let me get somebody to help us."

The red-vested salesman came to the case with a key to unlock it. "Which one?"

"That one."

The man laid the ring in Sveyn's palm. "That's a nice one."

Sveyn examined the workmanship closely. It was flawless as far as he could tell. Much finer than anything he had seen in any of his manifestations.

"That's a half-carat princess-cut diamond in the center," the salesman said. "The total weight is one-point-five carats, counting the smaller stones."

Sveyn nodded. The ring looked like Hollis to him. "I will take this one."

George laughed. "That was easy! Leaves us plenty of time for the tuxedo fitting."

Sveyn grinned and patted his belly. "And lunch. I saw food here.

George clapped his hand on Sveyn's shoulder. "Best hot dogs in town."

Ӂ

The reflection in the mirror took Hollis by surprise. "Is this dress blue?"

"Ice blue, so a lot of brides pass it by. But it's a copy of a Vera Wang."

"Hollis…" Stevie's eyes brimmed with tears. "It's stunning on you."

Hollis had to admit it was. The way the dress conformed to her body was amazing.

"Here's the best part." Maddy handed Hollis a large hand mirror. "Turn around."

Hollis did and looked at the back of the dress. The back was cutout and framed her tree-of-life tattoo perfectly.

"The other dresses you were looking at covered it halfway, and that looked weird." Maddy beamed at her. "But this makes it a feature."

The realization that she was actually marrying Sveyn hit her like a smaller version of the hammer that nearly killed her. Only this impact was bringing her fully to life.

I'm buying a wedding dress.

My wedding dress.

Hollis burst into happy tears. "I'll take it."

ӜК

"What about the ring?" Stevie asked over lunch.

Hollis kept her expression non-committal. "I have an idea for that, but it's a secret."

"You can tell me, can't you?"

"I'm not sure I can pull it off, so no. Not yet."

Stevie looked hurt. "What if you can't? Don't you need a plan B?"

"That actually might be a good idea," Hollis admitted. "Okay, I'll go to one jewelry store. But only after we buy your maid-of-honor dress."

Hollis and Stevie made it back to the museum at mid-afternoon, a miracle considering how picky Stevie was about her dress. She finally settled on a burgundy cocktail dress with a halter neckline that echoed the neckline on Hollis's wedding gown—which Hollis would pick up from the shop on their way to Vegas, after it was refreshed and pressed.

"I need to meet with Miranda about the flowers," she told Stevie. "Can you make sure the Blessing's case has been removed from the floor, and start planning the display for the Viking sunstone in its place?"

"Sure." Stevie hung her dress on the back of her office door.

Hollis walked to Miranda's office and knocked on the open door. Miranda was on the phone, but waved Hollis inside. Hollis closed the door behind her and dropped into the chair facing the curator's desk.

"Okay. Great. Bye." Miranda hung up the phone. "Did you get a dress?"

"I did. But first I want to hear what Benton said about the icon."

Miranda clenched her fists. "He wasn't happy, I can tell you that. But he was pleased with how we handled it, in terms of the publicity."

"Good. Did he ask about it being burnt?"

"Didn't give him the chance. I took the offense and said that once the wood was exposed to air it oxidized." Miranda flashed a crooked smile. "Then I jumped into how we were going to capitalize on the sunstone and got him all excited about that."

Hollis felt the weight of that damned thing lift from her life. "Thank you."

"No worries. Now tell me about the dress."

Hollis described her dress and Stevie's. "So I'm thinking my bouquet could be white with touches of burgundy, and Stevie's could be ice blue with touches of burgundy."

Miranda made notes. "Good."

"Do you know where we're staying?"

"Some resort a block off the strip that George's brother recommended." Miranda looked up from her pad and made a face. "Doesn't his brother run a tattoo parlor?"

Hollis laughed. "Yeah. A big one. The guy's loaded."

"Hmm. Hope he has good taste." Miranda tapped the eraser of her pencil against her cheek. "Is there anything else we need to do before we leave tomorrow?"

"There is one thing, actually. Something I need your help with." Hollis lifted her brows and caught her lower lip in her teeth.

Miranda laid her pencil down. "What is it?"

"It has to do with one of the items in Ezra's hoard, and who has provenance."

Miranda straightened. "Not another painting, I hope."

Hollis shook her head. "No, nothing like that. But it is a piece that can be attributed to someone who is currently living."

Chapter Thirty-Four

Friday
February 19

After the Friday work day ended, George drove a custom rental van to Las Vegas with Stevie, Hollis, Sveyn, and Miranda in tow.

"It's actually faster than flying when you add in check-in times, baggage claim, and the hassle of rental car pick-up and drop-off by the airport," he explained to Sveyn. "Not to mention, we have everyone's suits and dresses to contend with."

"And now we get to party on the way!" Stevie passed around a tray of cheeses. "I have margaritas, wine, and beer in the van's mini-fridge for us, and colas for the driver."

"Sorry, George." Miranda lifted her glass in a toast. "Remind me to buy your dinner."

George laughed. "I'll take it."

Sveyn stretched out his legs and leaned back in his swiveling chair. "I never imagined traveling like this. I like it."

The Viking's gaze landed on Hollis and sizzled with promise. Her cheeks warmed, as did parts much lower.

As they crested a hill, the lights of Las Vegas were laid out below them. The beam from the top of the Luxor was clearly visible, shooting straight into the clear winter sky.

Sveyn moved to the front seat, his eyes fixed on the multicolored scene. "I have never seen anything like this."

"It's one-of-a-kind, that's for sure." George grinned. "Just wait 'til we get to the Strip."

Sveyn looked back at Hollis. "It's beautiful."

Hollis laughed. "As George said, wait 'til we get to the strip."

George opted to take the longer route which allowed the van to drive down South Las Vegas Boulevard. Though tightly clogged with traffic and pedestrians, the slow pace gave Sveyn and Hollis—who was crouched in the front of the vehicle between the two men's seats—ample opportunity to gawk at the lights and the architecture.

"This is crazy!" Hollis looked up at Sveyn. "Have you ever seen anything like this?"

"Never." He wagged his head, eyes still focused on the scene. "And if someone asked me to explain this, I would not know how."

The resort was one block off the Strip and it was gorgeous; apparently George's brother had excellent taste. And even though they arrived at eleven that night, the bellmen were right on top of things.

Before George checked them into their rooms he handed out a schedule for the next day. "The reservation at the chapel is for one o'clock tomorrow. After that we'll have a celebratory lunch before Miranda has to get to the airport."

Hollis scanned the document. "Mani-pedis for the ladies at nine-thirty, then hair at eleven." She looked at Stevie. "This is great."

George handed out key cards. "Sveyn and I are bachelors tonight. You three ladies are in a champagne suite. Tomorrow night Sveyn and Hollis get the suite, so Hollis keep that key.

Stevie and I will stay with my brother."

"You have everything worked out so well, George," Hollis complimented. "Thank you."

George tipped his head toward Sveyn. "Thank your fiancé. He made all the decisions. I just presented options."

ӁК

So far, Sveyn was well pleased with the accommodations and the schedule. Everything he asked George about was taken care of. As they waited for the elevator, rented tuxedo bag slung over his shoulder, Sveyn thanked George again for his help.

"Without you, I would not have been able to become part of this new world."

George blushed. "And without your unique existence and situation, my life would not be half as interesting."

"Thank you, as well, for helping me with the payments." Sveyn hated to ask George to loan him money, but until he was paid he was a pauper. "Again, none of this would be possible otherwise."

George clapped him on the shoulder. "I'm glad I'm in a position to do it."

The men disembarked the elevator on the twenty-fourth floor and walked down the hallway until they reached the door labeled twenty-four-eleven. George swiped the key card and opened the door. He let Sveyn enter first.

The wall opposite the door was completely made of glass. Sveyn walked into the dark room and crossed to the window, dropping his suit and satchel on one of the beds. The view was astounding.

George stepped up next to him. "What do you think?"

"I am amazed."

"The suite you have tomorrow night is another eight floors up. You should be able to see over those buildings there."

"Gretna Green for America." Sveyn laughed. "My life is unusual."

"To say the least!" George switched on a light. "Let's get settled. Are you hungry?"

ӜК

Hollis snuggled into the king-sized bed that tonight she shared with Stevie, and tried not to think about sleeping here tomorrow night with Sveyn.

She didn't succeed.

"Are you thinking about tomorrow?" Stevie whispered.

"What else?" Hollis rolled onto her back. "I wonder what it will be like."

"Sex?" Stevie sounded surprised. "Haven't you guys already…"

"No." *At least not in the three-dimensional realm.* "He's had a difficult time with his body re-adjusting to various sensations."

"Will he be able to… you know?"

"The equipment seems to be in working order."

Stevie sighed. "That's good."

"Yeah." Hollis rolled back to her side and closed her eyes. Maybe if she pretended to sleep, reality would catch up.

I wonder what Sveyn is thinking about.

ӜК

"So you put the quarter in here," George dropped the coin in the slot. "Then you pull this handle."

Sveyn watched as the images flashed, until each one stopped. "They do not match."

"No. So if you want to try again, you have to feed it another quarter."

Sveyn shook his head. "I do not wish to throw money away."

"Keep that mindset." George walked toward a bank of felt-topped tables. "Here's where they play poker."

Sveyn watched the action which moved rapidly. He saw stacks of tokens move between the man passing out the cards, and the men hoping to get the right numbers. "There must be a strategy."

"There is." George backed away from the table. "But the best is to count cards and that's illegal."

Sveyn scoffed. "How can it be illegal to think?"

"Don't ask me." George led him to a set of large tables with spinning centers. "This is roulette. The strategy here is to bet with the odds. Like, choosing red, which gives you a fifty-percent chance of being right. Of course, that choice pays the least amount."

Sveyn did a slow turn. All around him were bright lights, ringing bells, women in tiny outfits serving drinks, and people pouring money into the machines.

"This is a sad place," he observed.

"I agree with you when it comes to gambling." George pointed to a sign advertising a group of blue men. "But the shows are incredible."

"Thank you for explaining this." Sveyn's belly rumbled and he grinned at George. "Can we go to the buffet now?"

Saturday
February 20

"I could get pampered like this every day." Miranda held out her champagne glass for a refill. One of the salon workers hurried over with the bottle of chilled bubbly.

Hollis wiggled her toes in the hot water. "I don't remember the last time I had a pedicure."

"Or a manicure," Stevie pointed out. "The whole time you worked on Ezra's hoard there was no point."

"True." Hollis waved away the champagne refill. She wanted to be clear-headed for the ceremony.

"Have you seen the ring Sveyn bought?" Stevie asked.

"No. He wouldn't let me. Did George say anything about it?"

Stevie held up her hand and considered the nail color. "Just that it's gorgeous."

Miranda turned and gave Hollis a conspiratorial smile. "Does he know about the ring you're giving him?"

A surge of warm excitement filled her chest. "Nope."

"What does it look like?" Stevie asked.

"Like him," was Hollis's mysterious answer.

Stevie's brow puckered. "What does that mean?"

Hollis laughed. "You'll see."

Ӝ

Hollis stood in the hotel suite while Miranda and Stevie bustled around her, patting and prodding.

"You look absolutely gorgeous in that dress," Miranda declared. "That blue does amazing things to your eyes."

Stevie pinned up a curl that had strayed from the carefully constructed salon coif. "This is perfect, Hollis. You still look like you, but a glamorous version."

Hollis regarded herself in the mirror. "I hope Sveyn likes it."

"How could he not? You're spectacular." Miranda picked up the box of bouquets. "Shall we?"

The women took the elevator down to the twenty-fourth floor and found room twenty-four-eleven. Stevie knocked on the door. George answered.

"Ready?" she asked her husband.

"We are." George stepped to the side and Hollis got her first look at her husband-to-be.

She forgot to breathe.

Standing six-and-a-half feet tall, clean shaven, with his hair tied back to highlight his cheekbones and jawline, Sveyn looked every bit the part of Desirable Male Model.

And he's mine.

Stevie and Miranda stepped aside so that Sveyn could see her.

His eyes moved over her from her sparkling tiara to her open-toed heels. "*Å min gud…*"

"Is that a good thing?" Stevie whispered.

Hollis smiled. "Very."

Sveyn walked toward her. "You are always beautiful, Hollis. But today you have taken the light from the sun and the stars from the sky. I am humbled in your presence."

"I wish men today talked like that," Miranda murmured.

Stevie sighed. "Me, too."

Sveyn held out his hands and Hollis laid her palms in his. "Will you have me, Hollis?"

Hollis nodded. "Will you have me?"

"I waited nearly a millennium for you." Sveyn leaned down and spoke in her ear. "You are well worth it."

Ӝ

A stretch limo carried the wedding party to a sweet little chapel, also off the Strip. After the appropriate forms were filled out and signatures witnessed, Miranda gave Hollis her bouquet. Then Hollis stepped next to Sveyn and took hold of his arm.

She smiled up at him and he thought his heart might burst. "Last chance to back out, Viking."

"This Viking's word is his bond, Hollis," he replied. "I will never leave you."

Hollis squeezed his arm. "Then let's do this."

The group of five walked to the front of the chapel and arrayed themselves in front of the altar. Sveyn was surprised to see people in the pews.

"Who are they?"

Hollis looked around. "George's brother said that locals come here to watch weddings for entertainment."

"Or to act as witnesses for the unprepared," George added.

"Unprepared?" Sveyn asked.

"Gretna Green, remember?" Hollis answered. "Spur of the moment decisions."

She is serious.

At least the Gretna Green-bound Londoners had an eight

hour carriage ride to consider their actions before following through on their impulses.

A man in a priest-like suit came out a door behind the altar and stood in front of them. "Are we ready?"

The ceremony was short, considering there were no scripture readings, music, or prayers—unlike the Regency wedding that united Stevie and George just a fortnight past. The vows, however, were almost identical.

When they got to the rings, Sveyn pulled the diamond-crusted ring from the pocket he had been obsessively touching since leaving the hotel.

Hollis looked up at him, her eyes wide with wonder.

"Do you like it?" he asked.

"I *love* it." She looked at her hand, then back up at him. "It's the most beautiful ring I've ever seen."

"Do you have a ring for him?" the officiant asked.

Hollis's expression shifted so suddenly that Sveyn thought something was amiss. She nodded and turned to Miranda, who placed something in Hollis's hand.

Hollis smiled. "Give me your hand."

He did.

"With this ring, I thee wed."

What she did next nearly buckled Sveyn's knees. His vision blurred. He felt the warm, heavy weight of the ancient Nordic ring from Ezra's hoard.

My father's ring.

"I told Miranda the story of the ring and convinced her you have provenance over it," Hollis explained, still holding his hand. "After all, it does belong to you as your father's son."

Sveyn wiped his wet eyes. "I do not know how to thank you."

Hollis's eyes crinkled at the corners. "Finish marrying me."

Chapter Thirty-five

Sveyn was nervous. So nervous, in fact, that he ate far less than he normally would at the buffet luncheon the wedding party enjoyed after the ceremony that made Hollis his wife.

"'Til death do us part has a whole new meaning for me now," he whispered in her ear after sealing their vows with a passionate kiss. "But perhaps even death shall not part us after all."

Hollis had gazed up into his eyes, hers misty with tears. "If our love could overcome what it has, I wouldn't be surprised."

"Are you all right?" she asked him now.

Sveyn looked at Hollis. "Not as hungry as I thought, is all."

Her lips pressed into an impish smile. "If you get hungry later we can order room service. After."

After.

The bugs crawling through his gut stepped up their activity.

Imagining making love to Hollis involved his mind, not his body. Now that he had his body back, he was still adjusting to its strengths and limitations. At least his morning erections were no longer painful. That was helpful.

Though there were only five of them in the group, Sveyn swore they drank at least ten toasts. The interesting combination of champagne and orange juice went down easily. Too easily. He was feeling a little woozy, though that could also be his nerves.

"I better get going," Miranda said sadly. "I don't want to miss my flight."

"That's our cue as well." George stood and held the chair for Stevie. "Sveyn, Hollis, call me tomorrow when you're ready to head back to Phoenix."

Sveyn stood and shook George's hand. "Thank you for everything."

"My pleasure." George smiled down at the still-seated Hollis. "Congratulations. I couldn't be happier for you."

ӜК

Hollis was nervous.

Why did she feel like a virgin about to have her first experience? That was stupid.

Though Sveyn was only her second lover ever, he was the one she would keep forever. She knew from his imaginings in her dreams that he was tender and capable. Besides that, she had been sleeping beside his naked body for over a month now. No part of him was unfamiliar.

And he'd seen her naked as well.

Even before he got his body back.

Sveyn held her hand tightly as they silently rode the elevator to the thirty-second floor. His smile was a little stiff, she noticed. Was he nervous, too?

Hollis let her husband—*husband!*—swipe the key and open the suite's heavy door.

He grinned at her. "Shall I carry you over the threshold?"

That made Hollis laugh. "No, not here. Wait until we get home."

"Fair enough." He turned sideways to make room for her to walk past him.

The door closed behind her.

The time had come at last.

Ӝ

Sveyn took off the jacket of his tuxedo and hung it over a chair. The cloudy Las Vegas afternoon made the huge room feel cozier, and allowed the multitude of lights to be visible in the late afternoon. He walked to the floor-to-ceiling, wall-to-wall window and gazed out at the city below. While the view from the twenty-fourth floor was impressive, this one topped even that.

"It's something, isn't it?"

Hollis had removed her tiara and high-heeled shoes, but her hair was still pinned up.

Sveyn wanted to pull the pins out until her red curls tumbled over her shoulders.

Maybe I will.

"I saw photographs of this place," he said. "But none of them could capture the size of the display."

"I agree." She smiled softly. "And even though I'm not thrilled with what this all stands for, I still love the lights and colors."

Sveyn unbuttoned his vest, deciding to attack the situation head-on. "How shall we proceed?"

Hollis gave him an odd look. "I don't know. This is my first wedding night. Or afternoon."

"What do you wish to do right now?"

She stared out at the scene below. "I think a shower would be a good way to start."

Pleasant possibilities flooded Sveyn's mind. "How big is the shower?"

Hollis grabbed his hand. "Come see."

ӝ

The shower was huge and had two shower heads. When angled correctly, their streams met in the middle.

Though once she unbuttoned the halter top she could step out of her wedding gown fairly easily, Hollis asked Sveyn to unfasten the rest of the back. He did so without rushing and she loved the feel of his knuckles against her skin.

When he finished, she turned around and unbuttoned his shirt.

"I think the best thing to do is to take this slowly." She felt her face warming. "You are only the second man I've ever been with, and I'm a little out of practice."

Sveyn huffed a laugh. "I believe I have you soundly beaten in that aspect."

Hollis rested her hands on Sveyn's solid chest. "Well, your imagination is up to speed."

He bent down and kissed her, his lips lingering but not going deep.

When the kiss ended, Hollis opened her heavy-lidded eyes. "Keep that up, and you can have your way with me, Viking."

Then she turned around. Still holding her gown up with one hand, Hollis turned the water on.

ӝ

My wife is beautiful.

Sveyn smiled as he removed the rest of his clothes. Hollis stood under one of the streams in the shower, her hair still pinned up.

Perfect.

Sveyn joined her. He adjusted the angle and the temperature of the water until it sluiced over his frame in hot, soothing sheets.

Hollis looked down at his half-hard member, a reaction to both the pleasurable water and the anticipation of what lay ahead. Then she reached for the soap.

Sveyn groaned as Hollis's slippery hands moved over his body. His skin was still becoming accustomed to touch and so many things felt more intense than he remembered. Normally, that was not a good thing.

Today, it was.

When she finished, Sveyn commandeered the fragrant bar. He mimicked her actions, washing every inch of her.

Every inch.

Hollis closed her eyes and grabbed his arms when his soapy fingers moved through her intimate folds. "Ohhh…"

Sveyn felt her arousal. After a long moment he withdrew his hand and rinsed the soap away. Then he reached for a towel.

Ӂ

The white towel was thick, soft, and luxurious. Hollis turned off the water and let Sveyn pat the wetness from her skin. When she tried to do the same for him, he stopped her.

"Go to the bed. I will join you."

That was the sexiest thing anyone ever said to her. Hollis wrapped the towel around her and obeyed.

She pulled back the high-thread-count white cotton covers and dropped the towel on the carpet. She climbed onto the mattress and sat on her knees, watching her gorgeous husband dry off.

His eyes met hers as he set the towel on the bathroom counter. Smiling softly, he walked to the bed.

"Let me take your hair down."

Hollis nodded.

Sveyn knelt beside her on the mattress and undid her hair, pin by pin. Her curls drooped over her shoulders in stages, until all of her hair was freed from constraint.

Sveyn combed her damp locks with his fingers. "My god, but you are beautiful."

"So are you…"

With his fingers still embedded in her hair, he pulled her head to his and kissed her. He leaned her to the side as his tongue explored her mouth, shifting his weight and hers until they laid side-by-side. The heat of his eagerness pressed hard against her hip.

Hollis pulled away from his mouth and opened her eyes. Her breath came in short, rapid bursts. "Make me yours," she begged. "And then you'll be mine."

Ӝ

The intensity of sensation when Sveyn entered her made him light-headed. He held still, pressed deeply inside her, and suspended above her on his arms with his knees between her thighs.

He gasped and closed his eyes. Heat from her core suffused his groin with fluttering electricity.

Do not finish too quickly.

Hollis ran her fingers through his hair and he opened his eyes. "Take your time or finish in a blink. It's only the first of a lifetime of making love," she whispered.

Hollis understood his hesitation. She knew what re-entering his body had been like for him, at least as much as anyone could. That knowledge anchored him.

He began moving slowly. "I want to take you with me."

There were no words Sveyn could think of to describe how completely consumed he was by making physical love to his bride. His imaginings had been varied and powerful, but they were only imaginings.

This was very, very real.

Hollis let out a little cry and twisted under him.

Sveyn pushed himself so deeply into her that his body was indistinguishable from hers. Then his core exploded.

Ӝ

Hollis held her panting husband tightly. His culmination was loud and bed-shaking. While hers was less overt, she doubted it was less intense. Even now her thighs still quivered.

Several minutes passed, their only conversation being shared sighs. Eventually, Sveyn lifted his heavy body from hers.

"*Å min gud…*"

Hollis agreed. "I love you so much, I can't even say."

He peered at her, his pupils wide in his deep blue eyes. "And I love you, wife."

Wife.

Hollis had never been happier.

Ӝ

Their supper was delivered to the suite as the sun disappeared and the Strip's neon lights fully took over. Hollis and Sveyn were wrapped in the comfy robes that came with the room and sat close beside each other at the suite's dining table.

Hollis sipped her Merlot and set the glass on the table. "I'm really going to hate to leave tomorrow."

Sveyn looked like a man whose contentment could not be greater. "I agree. I wish we could stay here forever."

"Let's come back every year for our anniversary."

"Consider that done." He reached out his fork and stabbed the last bit of his steak. He placed it in his mouth and closed his eyes while he chewed it.

"We didn't talk about birth control," Hollis ventured.

Sveyn opened his eyes. "Why would we want to prevent a child?"

Hollis started to list reasons—until she realized she didn't have any. "I guess we wouldn't. Are you ready to be a father?"

Sveyn grinned. "I have been waiting for nearly a thousand years."

Hollis laughed. "I suppose you have."

Sveyn leaned closer. "Why do you mention this? Do you feel like something might already be begun?"

"No. I don't even think that's possible to know." Hollis quirked her brow. "Is it?"

Sveyn shrugged. "I have heard women say yes. But not often."

Hollis's phone rang. "Ugh."

"You do not have to answer it," Sveyn reminded her.

Hollis looked at the screen. "I don't recognize the number." She set the phone back down. "If it's important, they'll leave a message."

Sveyn slid a warm hand through the gap in her terrycloth robe. His sultry smile sent a shiver over her skin. "Let's save dessert for later, shall we?"

Sunday
February 21

Hollis and Sveyn waited in the lobby for George and Stevie to collect them. Last night's clouds turned into a chilly rain, which gusted toward them every time the resort's doors opened automatically.

Their wedding attire was packed in black plastic garment bags which hung over Sveyn's shoulder. Hollis's overnight bag was at her feet, and Sveyn's at his. He kept shooting her knowing smiles that made her heartbeat stutter.

"Stop looking at me like that," she chastised.

"Like what?" he asked looking happily guilty.

Hollis punched his arm. "You know."

Sveyn laughed. "I cannot help myself. I am completely captivated by my wife and have no control over how I look at her."

The rented custom van appeared under the protective cover of the resort's entry. "There they are."

Hollis hefted her bag and braved the damp wind. George ran around the front of the van and opened the sliding side door. Hollis climbed in with Sveyn right behind her. George slid the door closed and ran back around to the driver's door.

Sveyn hung the garment bags behind his seat while Hollis pushed both suitcases behind hers. When she settled in her chair, Stevie was beaming at her.

"What?" Hollis asked.

"Nothing." Stevie giggled. "I'm just so happy for you."

"Ready?" George adjusted the rearview mirror.

"No," Hollis replied honestly. "But we have no choice. We have to go back to real life."

Sveyn chuckled. "Sadly, this is true."

Once they were underway, Hollis pulled up the voicemail that she ignored last night.

And this morning.

"Hello, Hollis. My name is Kathleen Mueller Corbin. I was told you were looking for me." The woman hesitated before adding, "I'm your birthmother."

Chapter Thirty-Six

One Year Later

Hollis took another deep breath and concentrated on pushing her son out of her body. Thirteen hours after hard labor began the boy was proving as stubborn as his Norse father.

Once Sveyn was convinced that twenty-first century fathers really were active in the delivery room, he reluctantly agreed to take the hospital's birthing classes and be at her side. He was amazed at the effect of the epidural, which took away the pains of Hollis's labor, and he even managed a short nap on the hospital room's couch.

Hollis's labor began earlier in the afternoon, but she didn't say anything to Sveyn until she was sure this wasn't another round of false contractions. She stood in the kitchen of their two-story Paradise Valley home watching her husband trim the bushes around their backyard pool for a while, before climbing the stairs and making one last check on the blue-and-yellow nursery. Hollis rubbed her contracting belly and smiled.

Ian Aleksander Hansen, are you ready for this?

The nurse braced Hollis's leg. "Okay, push."

Hollis drew a deep breath and concentrated with all her might. *Go.*

"You are doing well, Hollis," Sveyn spoke in her ear. "I can see his hair."

Go go go go.

"His head's almost out!" the nurse said.

Hollis exerted more effort than she thought she was capable of—until she felt a sudden shift in pressure.

"Okay! Hold up!"

Hollis opened her eyes. She couldn't see anything in the mirror because the doctor and the nurses were in the way.

"His head is out, Hollis…" Sveyn stared in awe. "There's his face…"

"Don't push, let me guide him out," the doctor instructed.

Hollis felt the baby slide out of her.

Sveyn gasped. "He's so big!"

One nurse laughed. "I'm guessing nine pounds."

Hollis stared at her son, lying on her chest, blinking and squinting. Then the boy let out a wail.

"Hey, buddy," she said softly, resting her hand on his sturdy little back. "Welcome to the world."

Ӝ

Sveyn walked into the waiting room on legs that felt as solid as pickled herring to announce the birth of his nine-pound four-ounce son to the assembled crowd. He was completely astounded by the entire experience and still in somewhat of a daze.

Hollis's dad Ian stood up first. "Is he here?"

Sveyn grinned. "Yes. And he's huge."

A beaming Brianne clasped her hands together. "I'm a grandmother!"

George helped Stevie to stand and laid his hand over her swelling belly. "Now you can tell *me* all about an experience, for a change!"

Miranda, newly engaged to a widower with two children whom she met on *Match Point*, grabbed her fiancé's hand. "Isn't this exciting? I'm an honorary auntie."

Sveyn watched the beloved group of friends and family members now chatting excited about the birth of his son. He looked down at his father's ring. A centuries-old ring that would someday be passed to baby Ian.

Like this ring, my life's path took an unusual route, getting lost for a long time.

But now the ring had finally come back to where it belonged. Sveyn smiled and said a silent and sincere prayer of thanks.

I am where I belong as well.

THE HANSEN FAMILY TREE

Sveyn Hansen* (b. 1036 ~ Arendal, Norway)

***

Rydar Hansen (b. 1324 ~ Arendal, Norway)
Grier MacInnes (b. 1328 ~ Durness, Scotland)

Eryndal Bell Hansen (b. 1327 ~ Bedford, England)
Andrew Drummond (b. 1325 ~ Falkirk, Scotland)

***

Jakob Petter Hansen (b. 1485 ~ Arendal, Norway)
Avery Galaviz de Mendoza (b. 1483 ~ Madrid, Spain)

***

Brander Hansen (b. 1689 ~ Arendal, Norway)
Regin Kildahl (b. 1693 ~ Hamar, Norway)

***

Martin Hansen (b. 1721 ~ Arendal, Norway)
Dagne Sivertsen (b. 1725 ~ Ljan, Norway)

Reidar Hansen (b. 1750 ~ Boston, Massachusetts)
Kristen Sven (b. 1754 ~ Philadelphia, Pennsylvania)

Nicolas Hansen (b. 1787 ~ Cheltenham, Missouri Territory)
Siobhan Sydney Bell (b. 1789 ~ Shelbyville, Kentucky)

Stefan Hansen (b. 1813 ~ Cheltenham, Missouri)
Kirsten Hansen (b. 1820 ~ Cheltenham, Missouri)
Leif Fredericksen Hansen (b. 1809 ~ Christiania, Norway)

***

*Hollis McKenna Hansen (b. Sparta, Wisconsin)

Kris Tualla is a dynamic, award-winning, and internationally published author of historical romance and suspense. She started in 2006 with nothing but a nugget of a character in mind, and has created a dynasty with The Hansen Series, and its spin-off, The Discreet Gentleman Series. Find out more at: www.KrisTualla.com

Kris is an active PAN member of Romance Writers of America, the Historical Novel Society, and Sisters in Crime, and was invited to be a guest instructor at the Piper Writing Center at Arizona State University. An enthusiastic speaker and teacher, Kris co-created ***The Dreams Convention***—combining Arizona's only romance reader event: ArizonaDreaminEvent.com and its author-focused companions: BuildintheDream.com and Realizing Your Dreams.

"In the Historical Romance genre, there have been countless kilted warrior stories told. I say it's time for a new breed of heroes. Come along with me and find out why: ***Norway IS the new Scotland!****"*

53898565R00178

Made in the USA
Charleston, SC
22 March 2016